SCHOOL OF DEATHS

THE SCYTHE WIELDER'S SECRET: BOOK ONE

Christopher Mannino

MuseItUp Publishing

School of Deaths © 2015 by Christopher Mannino

MuseItUp Publishing
14878 James, Pierrefonds, Quebec, Canada, H9H 1P5

Cover Art © 2014 by Celairen
Layout and Book Production by Lea Schizas
Print ISBN: 978-1-77127-683-2
eBook ISBN: 978-1-77127-524-8

To Rachel, my eternal muse.

School of Deaths

Christopher Mannino

MuseItYA, division of

MuseItUp Publishing

www.museituppublishing.com

CHAPTER ONE

The Girl Who Looked like Death

She wanted to scream but no sound came. She wanted to run, but her legs wouldn't move. The hooded man grinned.

Suzie's heart pounded as she opened her eyes. Laughter echoed in the back of her head. The terrible laughter she heard every night. She wiped the sweat from her face, pushing aside the sheets. Sunlight spilled into her room from between frilly curtains. Mom would be knocking on the door to wake her soon.

She turned to one side as the dream started to fade. Every night the same nightmare. Every night she heard the laughter. The hooded man with a scythe. The feeling of complete terror.

What did it mean?

Above her clock radio, a worn teddy bear stared at her with its single eye. She pulled the bear to her chest and clutched it with her bony fingers.

Suzie Sarnio. The hooded man had written her name down. He always wrote it right before the laughter began. The man looked like Death. But why would Death have a stammer?

"Suzie," said Mom, knocking on the door. "Come on, you'll be late for school."

"I'm coming."

Suzie changed, staring at the mirror in her pink-wallpapered room. Each rib stuck out from her chest; she counted all twenty-four. The skin on her face stretched tightly over her skeletal face, and dark patches surrounded each of her gray eyes. As much as she tried to comb it, her long black hair tangled into stringy knots. Her arms hung from her shoulders like twigs, and her legs looked too weak to hold her up. In the past few months, she had lost nearly half of her weight. She glanced at an old picture, taken last year, on the first day of seventh grade. A chubby, pigtailed girl with freckles smiled back at her from the photo. Her braces gleamed in the sun, only a month before their removal. Suzie sighed. She opened the door, looking for a moment at her room. She didn't want to start another year of school. Slowly, she turned around.

"Hey, squirt, watch out," said Joe.

"Sorry." Joe was a pest and a bully, but he was her big brother, and Suzie supposed she loved him.

"Get your skinny butt out of the way already. We've got a run before school."

"Today's the first day—"

"After last year, coach says we have to practice early."

Suzie stepped aside, watching the bulky frame of her brother lumber downstairs.

"Later." He winked at Suzie. "Have fun at school." He ran out the front door, slamming it behind him, while Suzie went to the kitchen and sat down.

"I've made you a special breakfast," said her mother, carrying a plate and a glass of orange juice.

"Let me guess, something big."

"I've made three eggs, two slices of sausage, four pieces of toast, two slices of bacon, a bowl of oatmeal with raisins, and a doughnut."

"Mom, I keep telling you, I eat as much as I can."

"You're skin and bones, literally. Your father and I are worried sick. You have another appointment with Dr. Fox after school today. Did you take your pills this morning?"

"No, Mom, but I will."

Suzie gave up arguing. Her parents, friends, and doctors were wrong. She didn't *want* to lose weight. Everyone kept talking about anorexia, about eating disorders. The strange thing was Suzie ate more than she ever had before. She ate twice as much as any of her friends, hardly exercised, and certainly never—what was the word the doctor had used—oh right, purged. Gross. No, the way Suzie ate, she figured she should be fat. Only she wasn't.

Suzie managed to eat most of the massive breakfast. Her stomach ached, but maybe a little would stay this time. She wiped her mouth, rubbing her fingers across the bones of her face. Doubtful.

"Are you ready for school?"

"Yes, Mom."

"Go brush your teeth, and I'll be in the car. Don't forget, we're picking you up at one for your appointment with Dr. Fox."

"Yeah, I know."

"Today's your first day of eighth grade. Isn't that exciting?"

Suzie didn't answer. What would her friends say? She'd spent the summer avoiding them, dropping out of camp and swim club. She was embarrassed. She honestly didn't want to lose weight, and didn't have an eating disorder, but she appeared skeletal.

She brushed her teeth in silence, dragging her feet. She put on her backpack and got in the car.

"Honey, you're nervous, but you'll be fine. Tell people you've been sick, and—"

"I'm *not* sick, Mom. If I was sick, the doctors would cure me. If I had an eating problem, they'd work with me. I eat more than ever, and I hardly exercise anymore. This doesn't make any sense." Suzie wiped a tear from her eye.

"Are you sure this isn't because of Bumper?"

Bumper. The family beagle for ten years. He had died three months ago, about the time Suzie had started losing weight. Mom believed the two were connected. Dr. Fox agreed. Sure, Suzie missed Bumper, but that wasn't the problem.

"No, Mom, I was sad for a little while, but I never changed what I eat. If anything, I eat more now."

"Susan, you'll be all right. I promise. Your father and I will continue to get the finest doctors, until we figure out what's wrong with you. Remember what Dr. Fox said last time? For now, the best thing is to go to school and be around other kids."

She sighed. Mom still didn't understand, and if Mom and Dad didn't relate, her classmates would be even worse. They pulled up in front of school, and she gave her mom a quick peck on the cheek.

"Don't forget. One o'clock." Mom smiled, trying to hide the strain in her eyes.

"Okay, Mom."

"Suzie, my gawd, you look like death."

Crystal hadn't changed. The smiling redhead with large blue glasses and the ever-present smell of cherry bubblegum was her best friend. She was grateful Crystal had spent the summer away. "Did you have a nice summer? How was Colorado?"

"My summer was great. Colorado's cold. Geesh, what happened to you, Suzie?"

"I've been sick," said Suzie. Not a complete lie, obviously something was wrong with her, but she didn't know what.

"Sick?" Her voice lowered to a whisper. "You look like you're dying."

"I'll be fine."

"Crystaaal. Suzieee," shouted a voice from across the parking lot.

"Oh gawd, it's Monica," said Crystal. "Let's go inside quick."

Suzie and her friend started to walk away, but the tall, lanky girl with small eyes caught up to them. Monica. She wasn't too bad, if you ignored her whiny voice and her inane stories.

"Hiii guys," said Monica. "I missed youuu this summer. Did you lose weight? The funniest thing happened the other day…"

Suzie realized the worst of the day was over. She got teasing looks from the kids and concerned frowns from the teachers, but like Monica, most people were too wrapped up in their own little world to pay any attention to her. Even Crystal eventually stopped asking questions.

"Tell me again, do you like the way you look?"

"I'm sorry, what?" she asked.

Suzie snapped to attention. The day had blurred by, and she was sitting in Dr. Fox's office, wearing a hospital gown.

"Suzie, I asked if you like the way you look?"

Suzie was cold and annoyed. The office smelled of bleach, and the fluorescent light overhead hummed like a dying fly. Dr. Fox glanced up from her notes and smiled a dry, lifeless smile she probably practiced in front of a mirror.

"No, Doctor." She repeated the same answers she had given last time, and the time before. "I despise the way I look. I'm a damned skeleton. You can see every bone. I love to eat, I don't purge, I hardly exercise, and I actually feel fine."

"Yes, that's the strangest part," interrupted Dr. Fox. "Every test seems to indicate that you're at the peak of health. No lanugo, no joint issues, no skin problems, and your stomach and the rest of you are actually functioning fine. I've almost completely ruled out anorexia, but your weight is still drastically low. It's like your calories are vanishing into some other dimension." She laughed. "My husband wishes that would happen with me."

"May I get dressed now?"

"Susan, I will get to the bottom of this. I have called a specialist in from the West Coast, from San Francisco. He might be able to shed some light on this condition. Your mother and I set up the appointment for next Thursday."

"May I please get dressed now?"

"Yes, yes. I'm sorry I can't do anything else for you." Dr Fox sighed.

None of them knows what's wrong. To them I'm just another puzzle to solve. She dressed and gave Mom a smirk, turning up her lips on one side to show she was unhappy. Mom smiled and shrugged.

"We'll figure out what's wrong, honey," Mom said. They lied; no one knew.

* * * *

The next day was even worse. Now that the kids were starting to settle back into school, they had more time to notice her.

"Suzieee," squealed Monica, her breath reeking of garlic and orange soda. "You're skinnier than a skeleeeton. It's weeeird."

"Gawd Monica," said Crystal. "Leave her alone already."

Suzie rolled her eyes and sat at her desk.

"Susan Sarnio," called Ms. Warwood, glancing up from a seating chart. "Would you come here for a moment?"

"Oooh." The few who didn't speak aloud were certainly thinking it. The whole class watched. Suzie's face reddened as she got up and walked to the teacher.

"Yes, Ms. Warwood?"

"Susan, are you all right? When I took roll yesterday, I noticed you appeared tired."

The whispers behind her grew louder. Couldn't she have waited until after class? And on the second day of school.

"I'm fine," said Suzie. "I've been ill lately."

"Yes, well, tell me if there's any way I can help. Have a seat, dear."

This was going to be a terrible year. Suzie didn't even raise her head when the teacher started talking about books or maps or whatever. She sat at her desk, staring at her hands. Each bone poked through her tightly stretched skin. She counted nineteen bones in each hand, not counting her wrists. Disgusting.

Finally, the bell rang for lunch. Mom had packed four sandwiches, three apples, two cans of soda, six bags of potato chips, and two candy bars. Overcompensating again, despite the doctor's orders to feed her normally. Suzie ate one sandwich and an apple, putting the rest back in her bag. She sat in a corner, not talking to anyone, not even Crystal. She didn't have the heart.

After lunch, she had math, her least favorite subject. She walked up the stairwell and trudged into class. She sat down and felt a soft squish. A boy behind her started laughing. Suzie got up slowly, eyeing the gum he'd placed in her chair.

She didn't even tell the teacher. She stood; tearing the wad off her pants, then threw it on the floor and sank back into her seat, hiding her head in her hands. Everything went dark.

"Are you all right?" Suzie sat up slowly. Mr. Thompson, her math teacher, was standing over her, worried. "Do you need to go the nurse?"

Suzie got up. Somehow, she had landed on the floor. She must have passed out. That was new; now the doctors would have even more to worry about.

"Paul, why don't you help Ms....?"

"Suzie. I'm Suzie Sarnio."

"Right. Paul, take Suzie to the nurse's office, please. The rest of you, back to page thirteen."

Suzie got her bag and followed Paul to the nurse's. She had always liked Nurse Cherwell. She had rosy cheeks and always reminded Suzie of a massive gingerbread cookie. Her office smelled like peppermint.

"Oh deary, deary, dear. What's the matter with you, sweetheart?" Nurse Cherwell had a voice like gumdrops. Suzie had only been to the nurse's office a few times before. Last year, they'd called her to tell her about Bumper. It had seemed surreal at the time, the year was winding down, and everything was going well. Then she found out her dog had died, and they told her in an office resembling a gingerbread house.

"I fainted in class. Maybe I should go home." Suzie didn't need to go home, but why stay any longer at school? The kids were making fun of her, and she wasn't in the mood for gingerbread.

"Deary, my deary, sweet poor dumpling, oh my. I guess we'll have to call your mommy and get you straight to beddy-bye, now won't we, deary dear?" Nurse Cherwell smiled a huge smile full of marshmallow-white teeth and reached down to pinch Suzie's cheek.

Mom arrived soon after. She spoke to the nurse and gave Suzie a frown.

"Did you eat the lunch I packed for you, Susan?"

"Mom, I ate what I could. You packed a dozen lunches in my bag, and I'm your only kid in middle school."

"You have to take care of yourself, honey. It's only the second day of school." Mom sighed.

For the first time, Suzie sensed how stressed her mother was. Mom wanted to understand what was wrong, but was helpless. She wiped a tear away, trying to hide it, but Suzie had seen. She reached up and gave Mom an enormous hug, wrapping her skeletal arms around her mother's waist.

"Come on, Mom, let's go home."

* * * *

"You okay, squirt?" Joe bounded through her bedroom door. He smelled of sweat and dirt.

"I'm okay," said Suzie. She sat up in her bed, putting her book aside. "They teased me a lot today."

"You? My sister? I'll beat 'em up." He slapped her on the back playfully, making Suzie slump forward. He leaned closer to her and peered in her eyes. His cinnamon gum stank.

"Tell me honestly." He lowered his voice to whisper. "What's going on? You've been losing weight since Bumper died. Mom and Dad are freaking out."

"I'm not trying to scare them, Joe. I'm sure I look anorexic or something, but I keep eating and eating and nothing changes. It must be some disease the doctors haven't heard about, they're bringing in a specialist and everything."

"Suzie?" Joe sat next to her and wrapped his big, muscular arms around her wiry frame. "You'll be okay?"

"I will be, yeah."

"Susan," called Mom from downstairs. A moment later, her head appeared in the doorway. Joe released Suzie and stood.

"How are you feeling honey?" asked Mom.

"I'm fine."

"Why don't you both come down for dinner?"

"Okay, Mom," they said in unison. Joe turned to Suzie and smiled. They headed downstairs and sat down.

"Your father had an urgent call, and won't be home until late," said Mom, carrying a steaming dish of delicious-smelling rosemary chicken and potatoes to the table. The doorbell rang.

"I hope it's not the Mormons again," muttered Mom, rising.

"I'll get it," said Joe. Whenever Dad wasn't home, Joe tended to act like the man of the house. Suzie wasn't sure if he was annoying or endearing, or perhaps a little of both. Mom sat down, and Joe opened the door.

"Can I help you?"

A hunchbacked man in a black robe, carrying an immense scythe, stood in the doorway. Something shiny hung around his neck.

"Er, um. H-h-hello. I-i-i-s Su-su-su-Susan here?"

Joe laughed. "Halloween's not for over a month, man. Why don't you come back then?" He started to close the door, but the strange man lowered his scythe, propping it open.

"What are you doing?" yelled Joe.

"P-p-please. I n-n-need to ta-talk to Susan," he stammered.

Suzie gasped, remembering where she had seen the strange man. He was the one who opened the door looking out in the strange dream she kept having.

Mom touched the blade of the scythe and drew her hand back in surprise.

"That thing's real," she said. "Get out. Get out of my house!"

"P-p-p-please," he started again.

"Wait, Mom," Suzie said, rising. Joe, Mom, and the strange man turned to her. "I want to talk to him." Was it the man from her dream?

"Susan, sit down," said Mom, her voice trembling.

"No, it's okay," said Suzie. She walked to the door. The man seemed scared, even a little confused. He was probably her father's age, but was nothing like Dad. His face was chubby, unshaven, and pockmarked, and his blond hair was uncombed. A golden chain with a charm hung from his neck. He raised his scythe and nodded. Joe held the door, ready to slam it, but Suzie stood in the entrance.

"Who are you?" she asked.

"My n-n-n-name is K-k-k-Cronk. C-Cronk Averill."

"C-Cronk Averill?" laughed Joe. "Is this guy for real?"

"I've c-c-c-come to t-t-t-take you b-b-b-back."

"Take me back where?" asked Suzie.

"You are a D-d-d-d…"

"What?"

"A Death," said Cronk. Joe reached for Suzie, but before he touched her, Cronk grabbed Suzie's arm. His speed surprised her. She yelled, but he raised his scythe and lowered it, cutting the air. Suddenly, the house, Joe, Mom, and the entire world vanished. Colors and smells, noises and strange sensations, flowed past Suzie in a blur.

She opened her eyes. She was standing in a field. Cronk stood in front of her, frowning.

"What did you do?" she demanded. "Where are we?" She looked up. It was sunny. But there were two suns.

CHAPTER TWO

In-Between

Suzie pinched herself. When she didn't wake up, she pinched harder. She squinted at the sky again, shielding her eyes.

One of the stars resembled the real sun. Never mind it was night a moment before, at least the sun was familiar. The other sun was farther to her right, and dim enough to gaze at without squinting too hard, though it was still bright. The massive star was about three times the size of the sun, *her sun*, and was red. An open field of dead grass stretched around them, littered with pillars of crumbling stone. In the distance, a massive building rose from the plain.

"Mr. Averill," she started.

"C-c-c-call me Cronk."

"Cronk," she said. "Where the hell are we?" She pinched herself again. Her thigh stung from the constant pinches. The air smelled bitter, like smoke and bad fish. The dead grass crumpled beneath her feet, as she started to rock back and forth. A breeze blew across her face, chilling her.

"I'm s-s-s-sorry, b-but I h-had to bring you."

"Where are we?" she repeated. This wasn't a dream. She didn't want to believe it, but everything she sensed told her this was real.

"In-between," answered Cronk. "Th-th-th-this way." He started walking toward the strange building.

"No," said Suzie, folding her arms across her chest. "You kidnapped me. You bring me home right now."

"I c-c-c-can't," stammered Cronk.

11

"Well you'd b-b-b-better," she mocked.

"C-c-c-come with me, he'll ex-ex-explain."

"Who will?" she demanded. "Explain what? Where are we anyway? If you don't take me back, you're going to be in big trouble."

She broke off as Cronk walked away. Suzie glanced around. Staying wouldn't do any good. She followed him across the plain.

They walked the rest of the way in silence. The place was far *too* quiet. There were no cars, no birds; even the faint hum of insects was missing. The wind blew across the dead grass without making any noise. The only sound was the crunch of their feet and their own anxious breaths. Cronk, she noticed, still seemed nervous. Maybe she was his first kidnapping job. But where were they?

They came to a large iron door, covered in a strange writing like runes. The silver doorknobs were shaped like skulls. Cronk tapped with his scythe and the door swung open without a sound.

"Enter, enter," called a deep voice from within. "I've been waiting."

Suzie's knees trembled in fear. Everything sunk in at once. She had been kidnapped, and was alone in some strange otherworld. Her kidnapper dressed like Death, and doorknobs were skulls. Her heart pounded against her chest.

Her *chest*. Suzie peered down. Something was different. She turned her back to Cronk and lifted up her shirt. She couldn't see her ribcage. She looked at her arms next. They were thick, covered with flesh. She wasn't fat, but certainly wasn't thin and bony. *What was going on?*

"Please come in, Cronk," called the low voice. "Bring our new arrival."

Cronk tapped her on the arm. She fixed her clothes and turned around. Cronk watched her with a worried expression, as if he wanted to say something but couldn't. He walked into the corridor. Suzie followed. She glanced behind her as the massive door swung shut.

The air was warmer. The faint smell of rotten eggs lingered around her, mixed with something else, like the slight smell of strawberries. The floor and walls were marble, like a fancy mausoleum. The corridor was well-lit, yet Suzie couldn't see any visible sources of light. Cronk walked to the end of the corridor, turning into a small chamber.

"Come in, come in," said the voice again. Suzie walked into the room. Strewn papers covered the floor, and hundreds of loose sheets swamped a massive desk. On the floor near the desk a four foot hourglass stood, slowly draining pitch-black sand.

"Hello, Cronk," said the voice behind the immense sheets of papers. "Who have you brought me now?"

"You should m-m-m-meet this one," said Cronk.

"Yes, yes, of course, of course." The low voice sounded friendly, but perhaps that was only Suzie's wish. She watched the papers rustle. Something moved behind them.

A man appeared from behind the stack, if he could be called a man. His features were human, yet strangely goat-like. He had two large horns, and walked upright, but hunched over. His fingers were clenched together, like hooves, and his wide eyes were bright yellow and snakelike. His mouth gaped open, showing two massive rabbit-like buck teeth. Suzie suppressed a chuckle at his odd appearance.

"My gods," he said. "A girl."

Behind the strange man, working in the corner, stood a boy in a cloak. The cloak covered his face, but he turned and she glimpsed bright green eyes.

"Yes," said Cronk. "Her c-c-c-contract." He pulled out a sheet of paper similar to the thousands lying around the room. The goat-like man took the paper and scrutinized it, pouring over every word.

"This is impossible," said the man.

"What's going on," Suzie asked.

"That's a good question," goat-man said, "but never mind, you're here. I suppose we must..." He paused, again staring at her with his wide yellow eyes. He shivered, like a dog shaking after a rain and placed Suzie's contract on the table.

"Susan Elizabeth Sarnio," he read. "Age: thirteen. Home: Damascus, Maryland. Parents, brother, yes, yes. Cronk, a word please." Cronk shuffled through the messy office and lowered his head. The goat-man whispered something and Cronk nodded, leaving the room. The goat-man turned to Suzie.

"Forgive me, I haven't introduced myself." He extended a hand which Suzie shook. "I am Athanasius, the Gate-Keeper."

"I'm Suzie," she said. "Please, I want to go home. What's going on? Where am I?"

"You are in the Gatehouse of the In-Between. This is the world between the World of the Living and the World of the Dead. Plamen." He turned to the green eyed boy in the corner. "Bring my seal."

Suzie pinched herself again, but Athanasius kept talking.

"I'm sure this is hard to believe. I've sent Cronk to get someone who may help you understand. Tell me, in your world did you suddenly lose a great deal of weight?"

"Yes. How did you—"

"Your soul was fading to the World of the Dead. The flesh follows. I'm afraid if you went home now, you would soon die."

"What?"

Athanasius tapped the piece of paper. The boy handed him a small object and retreated into the corner. When he walked away, he gazed at Suzie again, his eyes flashing green.

"This is a contract," said Athanasius. "If you sign it, you will need to complete at least one full year as a Death. After your contract is fulfilled you may return, and will have no memory of this place."

"What do you mean, a Death?"

"A Death," he replied, "brings souls that have died from the World of the Living to the World of the Dead. You've probably seen pictures of hooded skeletons with scythes."

"Yes, at Halloween. They're not real."

"Oh, but they are. The images, like most myths, have a foundation in truth. The Deaths wear robes, which is their uniform. The scythe, which will be explained to you in greater detail later, allows transport. As for the skeletons, well, you yourself witnessed what was happening to you. If a Death stays too long away from the Land of the Dead, they lose their soul and flesh. The bones are always the last to go."

"I don't want to be a skeleton." She glanced at the corner, but the boy had gone.

"No, of course not, don't be silly. Still, you must understand there are no more…" He paused and studied her again. "I suppose I should tell you this now."

"What?"

"Deaths are chosen from the Living, and serve in the Land of the Dead. Everyone serves at least one year, though the vast majority serve until they fade."

"Fade?"

"When a Death has served for about a hundred years, he passes permanently into the Land of Death. In a way, they die. although that term is used differently. To *fade* is a good thing. You live on in the Land of the Dead. If you are killed as a Death, you *cease*."

"What do you mean?"

"I mean you stop existing, and no one remembers you. You are wiped from memory, from the universe, but I'm off topic. I was trying to tell you something important."

"I'm sorry, go on." It was easiest to listen. Maybe he'd let her go home if she heard him out.

"Well, there are no new Deaths born. Names are selected, it's usually an error-free process, never been a problem before now."

"Yes, and now?"

"There are no female Deaths." Athanasius raised his hoof-like hands in exasperation.

"What do you mean?"

"Once, *once*, a million years ago, long before I was born, there was one. A female Death named Lovethar." He shuddered. "She was a terrible witch, a horrible beast who tried to sell the Deaths to the Dragons." He paused, and whispered. "Never again."

"You want me to be a Death for a year, but I'm—"

"You're a girl," he said. "This has not happened for a million years and was never supposed to happen again."

Suzie laughed. "This is absurd," she said. "You want me to be a Death? Like the Grim Reaper? Kill people and bring them to—"

"Kill people? Certainly not. Deaths do not kill, only transport. The details will be made clearer in class, of course."

"Class?" Suzie laughed again. "What, is there a school for Deaths?"

"Like any job, you need to be trained. Even if you're only here for a year, though chances are you'll be here far longer."

"You said if I sign the contract, I only need to be here, be a Death, for one year." Suzie surveyed the room again, her eyes lingering on Athanasius's goat face. This was too vivid, too real. The pinches did nothing. Was it possible?

"True, however you will take a final test at the end of the year. Less than a tenth of Deaths actually pass. Those who do not pass, remain Deaths."

"You mean if I fail, I'll be a Death forever?"

"Until you fade or are killed, yes," said Athanasius. "I suppose I should tell you, many believe in another way of returning. Nearly every Death who fails has tried at some point or another. Yet no Death has ever returned to the Living World after failing the test."

"What if I want to go back now?"

"It's not that simple. Yes, you're free to return now, but if you do, your soul will continue to fade into the Land of the Dead. You will die within the month."

"And my family? My mom and dad? What about my brother or my friends?" Suzie thought of Mom and Dad, of Joe, of Crystal and Monica, even of Nurse Cherwell and Dr. Fox. "I can't vanish for a year."

"They will be worried. This will be difficult for your family if you do go back after a year. The few, and I do stress *extremely* few, who have returned often find their absence hard to explain, since they have no memory from the year. Yet it has been done."

"This is impossible." Suzie's mind spun. This had to be a dream, or some sort of trick. Maybe her illness had spread to her mind. Even Dr. Fox hadn't been certain what was happening.

"Plamen," said Athanasius. "Show them in." The green-eyed boy emerged from the corner and walked to the door behind her, opening it. Cronk came back into the room with something behind him. The beagle barked, leaping at Suzie. She recognized him at once, though it couldn't be.

"Bumper?" she asked, astonished.

"He lives in the Land of the Dead," said Athanasius. "We can bring more souls to convince you; most find the reality of this position difficult to accept."

Bumper appeared young and healthy. The limp in his leg was gone, but something different stared from his eyes. He had a dull, glassy look as if part of him was somewhere else, far away. Still, he was definitely her dog. She'd known him for ten years; they'd grown up together. He licked her face and she petted him.

This was real. Bumper was real. Somehow, everything here was real. The Deaths, the world, the possibility of going home in a year, the danger she'd be trapped here, the possibility of dying if she went home now. She sat, petting Bumper for what felt like hours.

The world turned, whatever world it was. The In-Between, with two suns, dead grass, and the smell of eggs and strawberries. The Death with a stutter and the Gate-Keeper who looked like a goat. It was ludicrous, but real. She wanted Mom and Dad, wanted desperately to go home, yet there was only one way home.

"If I go home now, I will definitely die?" Suzie said.

"I'm sorry," said Athanasius. "An old rule, to encourage more Deaths. You can only return when your contract has been fulfilled. I'm afraid there is no other way."

"I will sign," she said. "But I'll pass your stupid test. I'll spend one year as a Death, and I *will* go home."

"That's all we ask," said Athanasius. He picked up a large quill pen and dipped it in ink, before passing the parchment to her.

Cronk took Bumper outside again. Suzie didn't turn to say goodbye. She fought back tears when she took the pen.

"It will be quite difficult for you," said Athanasius. "This won't be easy. You will be the only one in the entire world."

"The only girl?" Suzie blinked but a tear still fell.

"Yes," said Athanasius. "They will mock and scorn you. Many will say you will not complete the year. I fear for you, Susan."

"I was sick. I understand what it's like to be different, and I'm not afraid." She put the pen on the paper and scrawled her name.

Athanasius took the contract from her and stamped the parchment with wax. He added it to the piles on his desk.

"I admire your courage," he said, peering at her with his snakelike yellow eyes. "I have seen many who were terrified or who denied this place to the end. Hundreds came here only to return home." He sighed. "Hundreds who died a needless, ignorant death."

"I don't want to die."

"Nor should you, my dear. No one should wish death before their time. Though death comes to us in the end, it must not be sought out in haste. Wait and fade gently, that's my motto." His expression softened. "Don't listen to an old man, Susan, I'm foolish I suppose."

"My friends call me Suzie."

"Do they indeed? May I call you that?"

Suzie hesitated, but she needed every friend she could find. She nodded.

He laughed. "Well, Suzie, things aren't that bad. Don't believe the terrible stories. Being a Death is pleasant, and you may like your classes." He rose and turned away.

"I have something I'd like to give you. Where is...? Ah, yes." He opened a cupboard and started rummaging through drawers. "A sign of friendship that may come in handy." He pulled out a small cake and placed it in a red pouch.

"This is food from the In-Between. More potent than the food they eat in the World of Deaths. The cake will bring you strength. Eat it sparingly, and only when your courage fails you. You'll learn how they respond to a girl. My guess is it won't be pretty. You will need to be strong."

"Thank you, Athanasius," she said, taking the pouch. It seemed to shrink when she touched it, and slipped easily into her pocket. Athanasius winked.

Cronk entered and held out his hand, beckoning Suzie to follow.

"Until we meet again," said Athanasius.

"Thank you again," she said, her voice stiff. "Goodbye."

"You're welcome, Suzie, and good luck."

She glanced at the desk, where a massive pile of contracts sat in a heap. She wasn't sure which one was hers. She wiped a tear away again, following Cronk out the door.

CHAPTER THREE

The World of Deaths

"Hol-hold on," said Cronk.

Suzie held on to his robe as he raised the massive scythe. He swung down and the world blurred. Colors, sounds, and smells assaulted Suzie at once. The ground was gone and even Cronk's black robe seemed to fade in and out of focus. A moment later the ground appeared.

Night blanketed the World of Deaths. The ground was soft, and she stepped on fresh grass. Her eyes took a few moments to adjust. The air was moist but cool, and had a pleasant smell of strawberries. The rotten smells were gone. Above her, stars shone in a dazzling display, far clearer than she had ever noticed at home. Large trees stood some distance off: the edge of a forest. A cluster of fireflies buzzed like fairies near the trees.

"This is the World of the Dead?" she asked. Cronk nodded.

"Can't be," she continued. "This seems like home, even nicer than home, in fact. And it smells like strawberries."

"This is the La-La-La-land of Deaths," said Cronk. "A ni-ni-ni-nice place."

"But where are the skulls and fires and stuff?"

"Wou-would you ra-rather have those?"

"No, of course not."

"Come on," said Cronk. He led her away from the forest and down a hill. They were on a path, leading away from a small stone on the spot where they had first appeared. The moon above shone bright, and though nighttime, she could see.

Cronk led her beside something shimmering. The reflection of the moon glistened on the water, probably a pond or small lake. Cronk held out a finger, pointing.

She leaned over and let out a gasp. A girl stared back at her: her reflection, yet, unlike the one she had seen at home for months. The girl staring back was fleshy but not plump. Her features were pretty. Her usually stringy black hair looked thick and smooth, hanging like silk around her lightly freckled cheeks. Her cheeks were full; the skin didn't cling to her skull. Even her gray eyes seemed to shine. The skeletal girl she had come to expect in the mirror was gone.

"Is that me?"

"Yes, your tr-tr-tr-true self. This is your home now."

She gazed again. She wasn't her old self, she looked better than she ever had. She smiled, but glanced up. The smile faded as she remembered.

"I'm only here for a year. Then this nightmare will be over."

Cronk shrugged. "Few p-p-pass the test. Too ha-ha-hard."

"What's on the test? What makes it hard?"

Cronk shook his head. He either didn't know or wouldn't tell her.

"You can't tell me?"

Again, he shook his head. He motioned her to follow and they walked along the shore, climbing a rise, moving away from the water. They reached a flight of marble steps and Suzie followed. Small lights stood on either side of the steps. They lit up when Cronk walked near them, and turned off behind Suzie. She peered closer, bending down, and realized they were flowers. Each flower glowed brighter the closer she got; the lit ones shined like hot flame. Cronk coughed and she kept moving.

They climbed higher and higher. From the top of the steps, a vast plain opened, stretching beneath them. A path was lit with flowers, and many men in black robes walked beneath two enormous mountains. Or were they towers? The two pillars stretched for miles into the sky, like enormous stalagmites: great columns of twisted, gnarled rock pocked by thousands of tiny lights. They stood taller than any skyscraper Suzie had dreamt of, yet were far too narrow to be mountains. The pinnacles of the rocky towers were lit as well; two of the brighter stars she had seen earlier were actually those tips.

Between the well-lit towers stretched an elaborate maze of long, rocky mounds. A strange, fiery white light filled the area, with occasional darker squares amid the mounds. Around the entire complex, a ring of arches glowed. Cronk started walking down the hill, toward the arches.

"The C-C-C-College," he said, gesturing with a hand.

"College?"

"The C-C-College of Deaths."

Suzie didn't ask more, but looked around in apprehension and wonder. She climbed down step after step, until they got to the plain. The air still smelled of strawberries: not a fake strawberry smell like when her mom made sandwiches with jelly, but the delicious smell of fresh-picked strawberries in spring. They were Suzie's favorite fruit. Her mouth watered and her heart calmed.

Cronk led her down the lit path toward the glowing arches. As they approached, Suzie realized the arches were blades: pairs of oversized scythe blades, like Cronk's. The steel on each blade glowed, and each pair formed an arch. The arches stretched over twenty feet high, but seemed tiny compared to the strange stony formations beyond, which in turn were dwarfed by the gargantuan towers. Cronk stopped before the arches.

"Only D-D-Deaths can p-p-pass," he said. He walked under two of the glowing blades. Suzie wondered if they were sharp.

He raised a hand, beckoning her forward.

"But you said only Deaths can pass," said Suzie.

He nodded and waved her forward again. She took a deep breath and walked through the arches. Nothing happened. Cronk smiled and continued walking.

Suzie wondered why Cronk had told her that. Was she actually a Death now? Was that what she had signed?

They continued into the complex, and she passed more men in black robes. Some were her father's age, like Cronk, while others seemed ancient.

"Billy, get a load of that." She turned and a group of robed boys, no older than herself, stared and pointed. Others looked as well, until every figure around them gawked at her.

"Keep wa-wa-walking," said Cronk. Suzie turned her face down, but felt the cold stares of a hundred boys and men.

"It's a girl," somebody shouted. "I don't believe it."

Everyone seemed to talk at once. Suzie glanced up. The area was packed, and more men and boys were pouring in from every direction. They stood on their tiptoes to try and watch her.

Cronk pulled her to the side, and they entered a doorway in one of the stone mounds. He ushered her through a hall and to another door, where he knocked.

"Come in," said a gravelly voice.

Cronk opened the door and Suzie stepped in. She glanced behind her at two robed boys peeking from behind a corner. Cronk closed the door.

"Hello," said the gravel-voiced man. He extended a hand, which Suzie shook.

"I am Hann," he said. "A teacher here. You are Susan Sarnio?"

"Yes," she said. "Please, Mr. Hann, what am I supposed to do here?"

He laughed. "You are supposed to go to school, to train as a new Death. Surely the old goat told you that? He may be a 'Mental, but it's his job."

"You mean Athanasius?"

"Yes, that's right," replied Hann. He smirked. Was he mocking her?

"He said I have to be a Death for at least one full year. This is where I train?"

"This is the College of Deaths, Susan. This will be your home for the next year, and probably much longer."

"I'm not staying."

"Of course, of course, everyone says that, and yet everyone stays. Funny how things work out."

Something about him bothered her: something mocking, almost predatory. He smiled down at her. Hann wore a black robe like the other men. The hood was pulled back, revealing a thin face with short hair. He had a dark goatee and dark, piercing eyes.

"I will not be here more than a year," she said.

"Perhaps, but I guarantee the year won't be easy. No, not easy for you."

"Because I'm a girl."

He shrugged. "We have not had a female Death in a million years. The College is built for men and boys. You saw how they looked at you."

Suzie let out a long sigh. This was real. The nightmare wasn't ending anytime soon. She had to survive in this terrible place for a year. She had no one to help her; she was completely alone in their world. Tears formed in her eyes.

"Wait a moment." Hann put his hand on her shoulder. "Don't cry."

"You'll b-b-be okay," stammered Cronk.

Suzie wiped the tears away. Hann frowned but Cronk smiled, trying to reassure her.

Cronk pointed to her pocket. She nodded, but didn't pull out the cake. She forced herself to grin, squinting to hold back tears. She wouldn't show weakness here.

"I should be g-g-g-going," said Cronk. "You b-b-be okay?"

"I'll be fine," her voice surprised her, she sounded full of conviction.

"Nothing to worry about, Cronk," said Hann. "Why don't you go fetch the next one, always a busy job, busy indeed."

Cronk gave her a final pat on the shoulder. Suzie did not turn to say goodbye. He walked out of the room and shut the door behind him.

"I'm ready," said Suzie. "What do I need to do?"

Hann smiled. "You have the right attitude, Susan. Maybe you'll do better than I feared."

"I have to get through the year. Just one year."

"Yes. We'll see in time." He opened a drawer and pulled out a file. "At any rate, you're only thirteen now. This shouldn't be too different from school. You'll take three primary classes: Theory, History, and

Applications. You also get to choose one other class, an elective of your choice."

"What are my choices?"

"Music, Literature, Gymnastics, or Art."

"Art," said Suzie. It didn't sound too bad, classes like school back home, even art. She had always enjoyed painting, though she was never good. But was this a school? It stretched like a maze of rocks, huddled under two oversized stalagmites. Where were the classes?

"All right." Hann made a few marks on her file. He glanced up and gave her a form.

"Here is your schedule. Classes begin Monday at precisely nine. Time is rigid here, you'll notice hourglasses everywhere. I'd learn to read them. Meals are noted on the schedule, and are served in the Lower Hall. You'll be at the Junior College until you are eighteen. Yes, yes," he said holding up a hand to stop her protests, "you don't plan to be here that long. But if you are, you'll move to the Senior College, where Deaths become fully licensed."

"Deaths need to be licensed?"

"Of course, this is a profession." Hann seemed offended. "Yes, each Death eventually needs licensing. Those are the ones who work alone. As a Junior Death, you'll be in a group and won't start for some time, all under your teacher's guidance. I'm getting ahead of myself; you'll learn the details in your classes."

"Where will I live? There are no other girls."

"It has been arranged. You will have your own room, but will have to share a dwelling with two other Junior Deaths."

"With boys? The ones who were staring at me?"

"Yes, I'm afraid we don't have enough space for you to have your own house. Keep the schedule, and make sure you're on time. Today is Friday. You have the weekend to get acclimated. Ask one of the boys in your house to show you around."

"What if they refuse?" asked Suzie.

"If you absolutely need help," said Hann with a sigh, "come back here and ask. Helping young Deaths is my job. And take this." He pulled out another sheet of paper.

"A map of the Colleges, both Junior and Senior." He circled a few things, before handing it to her. "I've circled this office, your house, the Halls, and your four classrooms. Couldn't be easier. You'll be in my Applications class."

Suzie stared at Hann. Had she misjudged him? He seemed to be helping her, yet his smile still seemed mocking.

"I'll show you to your room now."

CHAPTER FOUR

The College

When they left Hann's office, most of the men outside were gone. She wondered if Cronk had told them to leave, or if they'd gotten tired of waiting to stare at her. A few black-robed Deaths watched from behind a corner.

Hann led her through a long corridor of weathered stone. In front of her, one of the enormous rocky towers shot into the sky like the gnarled finger of a stone giant. Hundreds of the flowers flickered like fireflies on the tower's outer walls, while windows glowed with light from within.

They came to a wall with a picture of an eagle holding two scythes in its claws. Its red eyes seemed to watch her as she approached. Suzie glanced at the map again.

"Here," said Hann, pointing to a small mound marked "Eagle Dormitory Two" on her map.

Hann opened an iron door and led her through a well-lit hallway. He stopped at a blue door with a large number VI painted in white.

"This will be your home for the next year," he said. "Eagle Two, room six. When you fail your test. *If* you fail, I mean," he added, noting Suzie's frown. "This will become your home until you leave the Junior College."

He reached into his cloak and pulled out two narrow keys, one silver and one gold, which he handed to her.

"Gold opens the front door, and the silver is for your room." Hann knocked. The door clicked and opened.

A shy-looking boy of about twelve peered out. He wore a colored T-shirt, shorts, sneakers, and a pair of wire glasses. He coughed and blinked at Suzie.

"Jason," said Hann. "This is Susan Sarnio, she'll be living in the blue room. You got the notice earlier, I hope?"

"Yeah," said Jason.

"You and Billy will need to show Susan around this weekend. Remember, *you* two are being held accountable." He raised his voice. "Especially you, Billy."

"Gotcha," said a voice behind Jason. Hann frowned.

Jason coughed, wiped his nose on his sleeve, and shuffled his feet, looking down. A second boy hovered behind him, a taller, older boy with sandy-blond hair, freckles, and piercing blue eyes. He smirked and turned away.

"Here," said Hann, turning back to Suzie. "This is where I leave you. What you need is in your room. Your housemates, Jason and Billy, will help you this weekend. Remember the schedule and use the map. If you need anything else, come and ask me. Otherwise I will see you in class."

Hann closed the door and she heard his footsteps echoing down the hall. She surveyed her new home, which was homey enough. Large lamps stood in each corner; she wondered if they had real light bulbs or more of those weird flowers. A lumpy brown couch sat in front of a window, next to a short table. A bookshelf in the corner had a few books she didn't recognize. The room smelled like potato chips, and was quite warm, a change from the cool strawberry-smelling air outside. After walking through the strange College, she'd expected the Deaths to live in stone caves.

"Jason, don't stare at her, show her the room," said the taller boy.

Jason wiped his nose with his sleeve and walked past the couch, his eyes fixed on the tan, crumb-covered carpet. Suzie followed him inside. The living room ended at a small hallway, with three doors, each a different color.

Jason opened the blue door and gestured, before ducking behind the taller boy. Suzie went inside. Her room was cozy with a bed, closet, and bathroom. The walls, curtains, and carpet were shades of blue. She breathed an inward sigh of relief at the bathroom; at least she wouldn't have to share that. On the bed lay a pile of clothes, a towel, and some books. Two long black robes lay next to the books.

"You've caused a lot of trouble," said a voice behind her.

"I didn't want to be here," she replied. She turned. The tall boy stood in the doorway eyeing her with a mix of disdain and something else. Curiosity?

Suzie and the boy watched each other in silence. He was lanky but cute in a way. His eyes were brilliantly blue, like shining sapphires. The side of his lip curled up in a smirk, but deepened into a broad smile.

"I'm Billy," he said. "I'm in the green room. The yellow one is Jason's."

"I'm Suzie."

"Never been a girl here."

"I've heard."

"It's not bad here. I'll show you around, if you like."

"Have you been here long?"

He shrugged. "This is my second year. Jason arrived a week ago; he's a first-year like you."

"Didn't you want to go home? I thought we only had to be here a year."

He hesitated. "I failed the test. Everyone here past first year has failed. But life here isn't too bad. You get used to it."

"What is the test?"

"Ha, can't tell you that even if I wanted to. The test is different for everyone. But you'll find out eventually."

"Will I pass? I want to go home, Billy."

His faced darkened, and his expression grew serious. "We'll find out. Please don't ask more, or worry every day. Honestly, you have too many other things to worry about, especially being a *girl*. I would focus on getting through the year."

"Right," murmured Suzie. She wasn't sure what to make of Billy. Jason seemed afraid of him, never looking at him, but never looking at her either. He hovered in the living room, not watching them, but paying attention to every word they said. Billy was a different story. He was a kid like her, but had been here a year. He had failed the test. Yet he wasn't depressed. He lived in the world of Deaths, but still smiled and seemed happy. Suzie wouldn't stay, but maybe he could help show her around.

"You still in there Suzie?" asked Billy.

"Sorry, just thinking."

"It's your first day in this world. It's tough for anyone, and I'm sure it's even harder for you. Why don't you get some sleep? I'll knock on your door tomorrow morning if you sleep too late. I'm showing Jason around and can take you around too."

"Thanks," she said.

"Get some sleep. I'll see you tomorrow morning." Billy went into his room. Jason sniffled and hurried to the yellow room, peering out the door. Suzie watched for a moment then closed her door.

She walked to the bathroom. A shower, sink, toilet, and mirror. An unwrapped toothbrush, toothpaste, and soap. This was definitely not a cave.

She walked back to the bedroom. The black robes each had a yellow patch on their front shaped like a skull. She put them away without trying them on. The other clothes were casual, jeans and shirts, socks, panties, and bras. A long purple dress hung in the closet. How had they known what sizes to get? Where had they found girls' clothes? She moved the clothes to her drawers.

Three books sat on the bed. The first book was large and had a black cover, which said *Methods* in large elaborate letters. Suzie put the heavy book on a table in the corner. The second book was even heavier. Its title was *Michael Darkblade's Theories on Deaths*.

The third and final book was *A History of Deaths for Beginners*. Suzie sat on the soft bed and flipped through the pages. Pictures of black robed men holding scythes stared lifelessly out at her from between the lines of text. She turned to the index and searched for Lovethar. She found the page.

Lovethar was a hideous and terrifying monster. Her face was sunken in and her eyeballs jutted out. Her hair flew out in every direction as she held her scythe in front of her. It was a drawing, not a photo, but the image was gruesome. She reminded Suzie of pictures of Medusa with her wild snake-hair and furious expression.

LOVETHAR. Born? - Died year 275 (997,990 BCE). Lovethar was the first and only female Death. She became a fully licensed Death in year 260 and continued as a Death for ten years. In year 270 she made a pact with the Dragons, directly starting the Great War. She personally destroyed the Temple of Others, causing over one hundred endings. She was tried and found guilty of crimes against Deaths following the War and expulsion of the Dragons. She was ended in 275, on what is now Widow's Mount. The Lovethar Protocol passed in 276 decreed that no other female would become a Death. See also: GREAT WAR, Lovethar the Witch, Lovethar the Terrible.

Suzie closed the book. Why was she here? If no female could become a Death, what had gone wrong? Lovethar's entry in the history book read like a dictionary definition. Yet Athanasius had mentioned her with fear. Suzie picked up the book and put it with the others. The bed was now clear and she lay down, staring at the blue of the ceiling.

As she lay, her strength faded. She was alone again. Alone in the world, this strange and hostile world of Death.

Alone.

Tears came quickly and did not stop. She cried and cried, not caring if the boys heard her. She wanted to go home, wanted to hug her mom. Mom and Dad and Joe. What would they be doing now? How worried were they? She pictured Dad pacing back and forth, fingering his moustache, trying to remain calm, while Mom screamed at the police. Joe would be silent, unsure of what to do. Would he even miss her?

Her teachers had been worried about her health. Now she was gone. Not just gone, but vanished, missing. Gingerbread Nurse would pout and Dr. Fox wouldn't learn the reason for her weight loss.

Crystal, her best friend, would wonder. Monica, Julie, Freddie, that annoying kid with the sniffles, sort of like Jason. She stopped short.

Jason was here. Here. Here was where she was. Simple, yet terrifying. This was the Land of Death. The Land of Deaths. Everyone here was a Death. Jason wasn't an annoying kid in her Science class, he was a Death. She was a Death too. She would be a Death for a year. She might be a Death forever.

Suzie cried until her eyes hurt and her throat stung. She stopped. She didn't feel better, but she'd run out of tears. She was too tired to cry anymore. She rose and washed her face, staring in the mirror.

Her eyes were red and she looked frightful, a bit like the terrible picture of Lovethar. Her hair hung out at angles, and she began to comb it. She was better than this. She was thirteen, not some little girl. This was terrible and hard, but she could do it. She had to. She would.

For the first time since arriving in the world of Deaths, she smiled. She'd show them. They *expected* her to fail, the only girl in a million years. She'd teach these boys something. And in a year, she'd leave.

Suzie heard a grumbling and glanced down. She needed food. She took out the bag with the cake, and hid it carefully in one of her drawers. She'd have to be careful with that. She looked at the door to her room and turned the doorknob.

Jason's door was open a crack. She heard a scampering noise when she opened her door. He had probably been listening to her cry. She walked into the kitchen. The two lamps in the corners lit. She peered at one; a small white flower glowed in its center. Suzie walked to the refrigerator and pulled out a banana.

"Hey," said Jason as she peeled the fruit. He stared at the floor and she kept eating. She finished the banana and pulled out an apple. At least they had fruit here.

"I cried when I first got here too." Jason's voice was scarcely louder than a whisper and he still didn't look up. "It must be super-hard being a girl."

"What do you want?" Suzie didn't mean to sound cold, but she was tired and hungry. Jason was a Death. He might look like a sniffling little boy, but he was one of them.

"I had a backpack when they took me. They grabbed me right at recess. If you want this, it's yours." He held out a chocolate bar. Suzie put down the apple and looked at him.

"I'm sorry I snapped at you," she said.

For the first time since meeting him, Jason looked up. His eyes were wide and watery. He straightened his glasses and turned away. He put the chocolate bar on the counter.

"I'm scared too," he whispered. "Being here, I mean, in this place."

Suzie nodded. "Thanks for the chocolate, Jason."

"Good night." He started toward his room.

"Wait a second," she said. Jason stopped and Suzie walked to him. "We'll get through this. It's only a year."

"Maybe."

"We will." She wasn't sure she believed herself, but opened her arms and gave Jason an awkward hug. He stiffened and then started to relax, but did not open his arms. She sensed he wanted to cry.

"Good night," she said.

He hurried into his room and closed the door. Suzie threw out the apple core and took the candy into her room. She closed the door and peeked in the drawers. They had even left her a long pink nightgown. She wondered where everything was from, but guessed they had stolen it from somewhere in the real world, the *living* world.

She finished getting ready, lay down, and closed her eyes. Billy was supposed to show them around over the weekend, and on Monday, school would begin. Though depressed, she was also curious. What would school be like for a Death? How do you train a Death?

Suzie smiled again. She'd always imagined Death being one guy: a fairy tale skeleton who takes souls to Hell or something. Yet here she was, one of many in an entire world.

A world of Deaths.

CHAPTER FIVE

Fire by the Lake

Suzie's dreams were strange. A man in a purple robe laughed when Cronk stumbled out a door. The dream shifted. Screams echoed in the darkness beneath the flapping of enormous leather wings. A pair of red eyes glowed in the distance, and whispered voices hung in the air. Someone called out to her, a beautiful woman dressed in white with long flowing hair. Men in black robes surrounded the woman, waving scythes and yelling. The woman opened her eyes. Suzie stared at her own face.

"You awake?" Billy's voice called through the door. "C'mon, time to get up."

Suzie muttered something, and Billy must've heard because the knocking stopped. She crawled out of bed and opened the curtains. The window looked over a large grass courtyard. An enormous tower stretched to the sky, looming over one side of the lawn: a mass of twisted, writhing stone. The sky was light and blue.

She showered and dressed in some of her new clothes. They fit perfectly. She looked at herself in the mirror and smiled. She looked good, better than she ever had. Her face was fleshy and her body hinted at curves. The skeletal girl was a distant memory, she was pretty again.

Suzie walked into the kitchen and sat at the table. Jason stared at his breakfast, while Billy gave her a big grin.

"Morning Suzie, are you doing a little better today?"

"Yes, thank you."

"I made you some eggs and toast, for your first morning here. I'll show you two around when you've eaten."

"Thank you, Billy." She took the breakfast and started eating. "This is delicious."

"Where are you from?"

"I'm from Damascus, Maryland, in the United States."

"Yeah," said Billy. "We're both from the States. I'm from Connecticut, and Jason's from Virginia."

Jason nodded but didn't look up.

"He's shy," said Billy. "You'll both open up sooner or later. It's not too bad here." Suzie caught his eye and he looked away.

"It'll be harder for you," he added. "The older Deaths will never accept you. This is a male world."

They finished their meal and prepared to leave. Suzie slipped Athanasius's cake into a pocket. Billy led her and Jason out of the door, through the hallway, and out into the courtyard.

"I'll start by taking you up the Tower. West Tower is open to students, it's mostly classrooms. East Tower is for staff only."

"Okay," she said.

Clouds shone in shades of gold and yellow, scattered above the maze of stony mounds forming the College. Across the lawn, sunlight fell onto the colored rocks below. *The sun.* Not some weird double sun, and not anything else either. The sun from home. The World of Deaths seemed a little less cold. The air still smelled like strawberries.

"Billy?" she asked as they crossed the courtyard.

"Yeah?"

"Why do I keep smelling strawberries?"

"That's how it always smells, you get used to it after a while."

They arrived at West Tower, which stretched past the mounds, over one hundred fifty feet wide. Rising overhead for thousands of feet, if not miles, the Tower soared into the clouds. Up close, it looked even more like a stalagmite. Rocks of every color twisted and writhed up its stony surface, broken only by windows. Billy opened the large wooden door, which creaked with a low groan. Inside, they walked through a marble hallway. Doors extended in either direction. At the end of the hall, they reached a gated elevator.

"The old Deaths brag about the elevators." Billy laughed. "Just installed fifty years ago," he said in a mocking old voice. "I can't imagine trying to go up the stairs."

They climbed into the small elevator and closed the gates. Billy pushed a button and the floor creaked and shook, before starting to rise. They rose for about ten minutes before they reached the top.

"Let's take a look," said Billy. Jason clung to the side of the elevator looking uneasy. Suzie patted him gently on the arm and he followed them out.

The gate swung open and Suzie found herself in a well-lit open room. The ceiling was a dome, painted with a vivid fresco. Large Dragons, green and black, with glowing red eyes were painted on the left. On the right, Deaths wielded scythes. A character who must be Lovethar stood near the center, robed but with her hood down, pointing her scythe at the Deaths. Flames surrounded her.

"The Great War," said Billy, following her gaze. "You'll learn about it in History class."

Below the dome, enormous glass windows stretched on every side, giving the impression the walls were glass, although stone supports stood between each enormous panel.

Jason looked around and sighed when he saw the windows. Suzie guessed he was glad not to be outside at this height.

Billy walked to one of the windows and pointed out. The College spread out beneath them in a labyrinth of trenches, rocky mounds, and small green patches. East Tower faced them, filling much of the sky. Contorted stone sides narrowed as they rose; small rocky points jutted into the clouds along much of its twisted walls. Beyond, blue ocean shimmered.

"The Council is directly opposite us," said Billy. "I've never been, but they say the Headmaster's office is at the top of East Tower, right below the Council of Twelve. I've heard they use telescopes to watch over everything, probably watching us right now. The Council certainly has plenty of spies."

"The Council?"

"They're in charge of the world. The Council of Twelve, twelve old Deaths, one of whom is Headmaster Sindril. Lord Coran, who's sort of like the president here, gets the credit and makes the speeches, and he breaks any tie vote in the Council. He's separate; it's the Council who're supposed to be the real power. If you ever meet a Death with a purple robe, be careful."

"A purple robe?" Something tugged at the back of Suzie's mind, but she couldn't remember.

She looked back at the College. In the distance, she glimpsed the Ring of Scythes she had walked through. She walked along the windows, gazing beyond the Ring to a field and a hill with steps. That must be the way Cronk had taken her. A pond stood behind the hill, which looked tiny from here. Open fields led to a forest that stretched unbroken for miles. At the end of her vision, on the horizon, a line of pale blue shimmered.

"The sea," said Billy. "You'll see better from down here, facing northeast." He led her back around the room.

"The Junior College is to the left, and the Senior College is to the right. They do overlap."

"What's that?" Suzie pointed to the center of the campus. A small building stood out, unlike the rest. A cube of solid black, like a die dropped by a giant into the middle of the College, sat amid the canyon-like rock.

"The Examination Chamber, where you'll take the test. Everyone takes it the end of their first year. Don't worry now," he warned, "just get through the year first."

He led her farther around the room. They turned. The sea ended, and the distant lands grew hilly. A few small clumps of buildings were outside the Ring, beneath tall craggy peaks. A range of mountains covered in snow and draped in low clouds stood to the west.

"They're beautiful," said Suzie.

"Yes," said Billy, "but forbidden. That's where the Dragons live. The 'Mentals are somewhere in the forests to the north. Don't ask, they'll explain in class."

In front of the mountains but beyond the Ring, trees and tiny villages spotted the hilly land. A lake glistened in the sunlight, and a river snaked away, winding toward the sea to her left.

"Silver Lake is one of my favorite spots to go, and it's not far from the College. We can head down if you want."

"I'd like that." An isolated hill stood behind the lake, and a small island sat near the middle of the water. Something jutted out from one shore, maybe a pier.

Suzie peered down at a mound of stone jutting out right beneath one of the windows, like a gargoyle. She walked around the room again, looking at the mounds of the College, the enormous East Tower, the distant blue of the sea, and the snowy peaks of the Mountains. How could a World of Deaths be this beautiful?

Billy was talking to Jason in the center of the room. Suzie looked at the domed ceiling again. Lovethar smiled back at her, taunting. The only other female Death had been a terrible witch.

"You ready to head down?" asked Billy.

"Yes."

The elevator lowered, and Jason clung to the walls, looking like he wanted to puke. His face twisted into a silent scream. Suzie put an arm around him and he clutched it close to him.

They reached the bottom. Four boys, young Deaths, walked through the hall. As Suzie came out of the elevator the four fell silent and stared at her.

"Let her be," said Billy.

"You with her, Bill?" said a boy with an English accent.

"She's housed with me, yes, Connor. I'm showing them around."

"Your funeral, mate. C'mon guys, let's leave the girls to play."

The four burst into laughter. Billy brushed past them. Suzie and Jason hurried, though, while Suzie tried not to look at the boys. *Was this going to happen every day?*

They emerged in the courtyard again. Another group of boys looked up briefly but ignored them.

"I don't understand," said Suzie, her voice low. "Almost everyone stares at me, but some don't. You and Jason aren't being mean either."

"Those kids are first years," said Billy. "They don't even realize anything's weird about you. As for me, I remember how difficult the adjustment was, living here. No one should make this harder for you."

"Thank you, Billy," she said, smiling.

"I like you too," said Jason, looking up. She turned to him, and he looked down again.

"Let's skip lunch in the Hall for now," said Billy. "I'll take you guys to Weston, the nearest village. We can buy some lunch and head to Silver Lake."

Billy led them away from the Tower. As they walked through courtyards and corridors, Suzie noted the reactions of the men and boys they passed. The oldest Deaths gaped in horror, and the older boys stared. The youngest boys ignored her; many of them seemed terrified themselves. The College was full of men and boys of every size and ethnicity: from tall, white-bearded men in robes, to young, acne-covered boys in jeans. One teenager with a Yankees cap threw an apple core over her head, and Billy chased him away.

They reached the ring of massive scythes and walked under the blades. A cobblestoned street led away from the College toward a cluster of houses. In the distance, snow-covered mountains held up the sky, craggy peaks blanketed in trees, shadows, and cloud.

They walked along the road. Suzie continued to receive stares but she ignored them. She could get used to this. They stared, but nothing else. She looked at a tall hill standing apart from the others, behind the villages. Billy followed her look.

"Widow's Peak," he said. "On the shore of Silver Lake."

Widow's Peak, she remembered reading. Where Lovethar was burned. She had been here less than a day, but kept encountering the strange woman, the only other female Death.

Weston was a cluster of houses and small shops centered on an open square and a fountain. Suzie and Jason sat on a marble bench circling the gently rising fountain water. Cool drops splashed onto her cheek. A slight strawberry-scented breeze blew through the pleasant air. Billy went to a store on the corner to buy them food.

"I want to go home," said Jason.

"Me too," said Suzie. "But this isn't such a terrible place. It's pretty here, and besides we're only here for a year."

"Maybe."

Suzie put her arm around Jason, but he didn't respond. Billy walked out of the store holding two bags. He smiled.

"You guys will need some money, if you ever want to go off the College campus."

"How do we get money?" asked Suzie.

"Same way you get money anywhere," he said. "You work. Regular work as a Death isn't paid unless you're licensed, which takes years. I work in an office, help out with paperwork. You don't need money on campus; it adds up. C'mon, I bought us a picnic. We can eat at the lake."

She got up, eager to visit Silver Lake. The more time she spent in this world, the better she felt. Sure, people stared, but she'd only be here a year. Besides, it was beautiful here.

Jason trudged behind while Billy led her away from Weston. Suzie looked at some of the houses. Who lived here? What was a family like, if there were no women? A world of men was such a strange idea.

The cobblestones ended, sinking into a narrow dirt lane. The lane twisted to the right. Mountains looked down from the horizon, and the ground swelled into small hills. Trees grew on either side of the path, strange trees with old, gnarled trunks and bright, yellow-green leaves with tiny red berries. A pair of birds with blue-tinged feathers watched her from a tree, chirping.

They climbed another hill, emerging onto a clearing. In front of them, Silver Lake glistened in the sunlight. Widow's Peak, the lone hill, stood off to her right. Scattered clouds covered the sky, while the sun shone above, casting its reflection onto the lake.

The path veered farther to the right, toward Widow's Peak, but Billy led them onto the grass. They sat near the shore of the lake, and Billy opened the bags.

"I have gorgers, fruit, some cookies, and a few bottles of water."

"What's a gorger?" asked Suzie.

"Typical Death food," replied Billy. "First time I had one, I thought they were magic. Here, try." He unwrapped a nondescript sandwich and handed it to her. "Before you eat, imagine your favorite food."

"What?"

"Trust me," said Billy. "What's your favorite food, or at least something you love to eat."

"Chocolate. Though, right now I feel like a cheese pizza."

"Well, pick one. If you want the pizza, get a clear idea of pizza in your head. Visualize everything from the cheese to the crust."

"Okay."

"You got that image? You can practically taste that pizza?"

"Yes"

"Now take a bite of the gorger."

Suzie took a bite, and her mouth filled with the taste of hot cheese dripping off a Tony's Pizza, her favorite pizza parlor.

Suzie took a few more bites and looked at Billy. "This tastes like pizza. I don't understand." She turned to Jason who was clearly enjoying his.

"Mine's a ham and cheese sandwich," said Jason.

"A gorger takes whatever taste you want. My teachers insist it's not magic, but they won't explain further."

Billy took off his shoes and socks, walked over to the edge of the lake, and dipped his feet in the water, while chewing on his own gorger. "Right now I'm eating a bacon cheeseburger. I try to have different tastes each time. We'll get these a lot on campus."

He finished his gorger and tossed an apple to Suzie, who caught it.

"You don't catch like a girl," said Billy.

"Not funny."

"I'm teasing." He lay back on the grass.

Suzie finished her lunch and lay down on the grass, watching clouds drift overhead. A strawberry-scented breeze blew gently across her face. Billy rolled onto his side, watching her. She looked at Jason; he sat looking out at the lake.

"Well, what do you want to do next?" asked Billy.

"Let's go to Widow's Peak," she replied.

"All right. I've never actually climbed up."

They continued to Widow's Peak. Its slopes rose from the fields, falling straight into the lake. Overgrown grasses and clover blanketed the sides of the large hill, which had no path.

"We're here," said Billy. "Doesn't look like it's worth going up. No one comes here, I guess."

"I want to go up," said Suzie. She pictured the wild-haired Lovethar in flames. What had actually happened to her? Why had she betrayed the Deaths?

"It's only grass," said Suzie. "I'm going to climb up. You guys can stay here."

"You sure?" asked Billy.

"I'll climb where those rocks jut out. Should be easy enough. I'm curious."

"Be careful," said Billy.

Suzie walked up the hill, which was steeper than she had realized. She stumbled but caught herself and didn't look down. She climbed over rocks and through grass until she reached the summit.

Silver Lake glistened beneath her. Turning, she saw the stony towers of the College in the distance. A structure stood on the peak of the hill, an old building. She walked up to it.

A marble staircase rose for a few feet; its top had fallen into a heap of ruins. Weeds poked through the stairs, which appeared thousands of years old or older. On the other side of the staircase, the remnants of a stone tower lay on its side, with broken walls. The entire site seemed ancient.

Suzie climbed up the stairs and leaned over the tower. A window faced skyward, covered in dirt and cobwebs. A flock of birds fluttered out of a tree whose roots grew right through the ancient stairs.

"What is this place?" she whispered.

Suzie remembered Lovethar, burned on the top of Widow's Peak, burned where she now stood.

Flames.

The vision startled her. What had happened?

Bright red flames. Burning, burning, burning.

Images of fire poured into Suzie's head. Her skin burned and charred, she felt the heat. She screamed, waving at the air.

Red flames, searing, scorching. Red eyes, burning with red heat. Eyes filled with rage.

Suzie fell into the tower, and the wall collapsed beneath her. She crashed through dust, landing hard. As she tumbled through stone and dirt, a pair of glowing red eyes surrounded by flames watched her.

The red eyes cooled, changing to green.

Beneath the green eyes, the faint outline of a flame-lit smile flickered.

She blacked out.

CHAPTER SIX

Echoes and Expectations

"Suzie? Suzie, are you all right?"

She opened her eyes. Billy stood over her, his face full of concern. She was in a ruin; broken stones lay all around. Her body throbbed with pain, and something sharp was digging into her back.

"What happened?"

Billy shrugged. Jason's head popped up behind his, also worried. Suzie sat down again, groaning in pain.

"Slow down," said Billy, "you're stunned. We came up when you screamed. You must have fallen into this old ruin."

"My side hurts," said Suzie, "but I'm okay. What is this?"

"I have no idea. I've never been up here. Were you trying to climb the ruin or something?"

"No, there was—" Suzie stopped herself.

"What?"

"I had this weird experience."

"What?"

"It was weird." Suzie didn't want to say any more. She was the only female Death; she didn't want them to think she was also crazy. Were visions normal in this strange world? Somehow, she guessed they weren't.

"What did you see? What happened?"

The pain continued, but was bearable. Billy held her in his arms, helping her stand. Suzie blushed.

"What happened?" repeated Billy.

"A bird," she lied. "A big, strange bird flew at me."

"A bird made you scream and fall into this?" Billy eyed her skeptically. "And that was weird?"

"The bird flew right at me, and scared me. Anyway, what is this place?"

"Looks like an old tower," said Billy.

"With weird pictures on the wall," said Jason.

Suzie stood up, wincing at the pain in her back. Billy helped her walk over to Jason. He pointed to a carving on one wall, which was broken but showed a bat-like wing.

"I think they're Dragons," said Jason. "There are some more pictures over here."

"We should get out of here," said Billy.

"Look at this picture of a woman," added Jason.

Suzie nodded, wincing again. "Billy?"

"Yes?"

"In my pocket. Aghh." She grimaced. "Can you get my pouch?" She hurt too much to move.

Billy leaned her against a wall and looked at her. She nodded, but blushed when he reached into her pocket and pulled out the small bag. He handed the cake to her.

She bit into Athanasius's cake. Instantly, her pain flowed away and her muscles relaxed. She put the cake back in the pouch.

"The woman," she asked Jason, while studying the images of Dragons. "Where did you see her?"

"Here." He pointed.

Suzie looked at a section of the crumbling wall. A woman with long hair and a fair face looked out from the stone. The carving was beautiful, and more detailed than the crude Dragons. A group of Deaths stood to one side of the woman, carrying away a bundle. The woman's mouth was open and her arm outstretched. Was she supposed to be Lovethar? This picture looked nothing like the wild-haired witch burning in fire. However, there were no other women in this world.

Until now.

"Let's go," she said.

They climbed out of the ruined tower

"I wonder what that place was?" asked Jason, taking another glance back at the pictures.

"Don't know," said Billy, "but we should probably keep this to ourselves. The Dragons are the enemies of the Deaths. I've only seen one once, from a distance. There are rumors of them on the borders from time to time. The senior Deaths go out and fight. One of my teachers came back missing an arm, nothing left but a charred stump. I tell you those things are evil."

"Lovethar was supposed to be connected to the Dragons, and my history book said she was burned up here," said Suzie. They climbed down Widow's Peak as they talked, working their way to the bottom of the hill.

"You studied before you slept?" asked Billy. "I'm impressed. School hasn't even started yet."

"I was curious. She was the only female Death...until me."

"Hope you have a better legacy than she did," muttered Billy.

"I'll be gone in a year. I wondered what she was like."

"Right, well, be careful about what you do. I was worried. If you die in this place, you cease, you're done."

"They mentioned that before," said Suzie. "I don't understand."

"We don't know what happens after people die," said Billy. "Whatever happens, we bring them to their fate. We're ferrymen in a sense, escorting souls. However, if a Death dies unnaturally they cease, they end. Every memory of them vanishes, and it's like they never existed. Imagine your parents and everyone you loved suddenly forgetting that you were ever born. It's scary."

Jason shuddered.

"I don't want to die here," said Suzie. "I'll do whatever I need to, to get through the year, and then I'm going home."

They reached the bottom of the hill. For a split second, Suzie thought she glimpsed movement behind a tree across the path. She stared but saw nothing.

They continued back through Weston and then walked back through the Ring of Scythes.

"I'll show you around campus a bit. We can do dinner back at the house," said Billy.

He led them through the stone maze, by mounds and windows, over courtyards, and under rocky bridges. Reactions to Suzie continued to be mixed. Younger boys ignored her, while many older ones stared. A skinny Death with black hair smiled at her, but another, noticing the smile, punched the black-haired boy in the side.

"It'll take some time," said Billy, "but some are trying to be friendly."

"Trying," she murmured.

They turned a corner, and Suzie cringed. The Examination Room. Standing in a large open courtyard of white stone, the solid black cube looked ominous.

"I can't say where you guys will have your actual lessons," said Billy, hurrying them into the next corridor. "You'll probably be with other first years for some classes and in mixed age groups for others."

"I have a map back at the…" She paused. "Back at home." The last word caught in her throat. Her courage started to fail again, and a shot of pain coursed through her back where she'd fallen.

"Are you all right?" asked Jason.

"I should lie down for a bit, I'm still sore from the fall."

"I'll take you home," he said. "We can relax until dinner."

The rest of the day seemed to fly. The three returned to Eagle Two, and Suzie lay in her bed. She kept going over the incident on the top of Widow's Peak in her mind. She heard Billy and Jason fixing dinner, but couldn't stop picturing the flames and the eyes. The fire had seemed real, and she glanced at her hands expecting to see burn marks.

Widow's Peak. Where Lovethar had burned. Strange that Suzie, only the second female in this world, should see flames in the same spot.

And what about those eyes? They had changed color when the fire died. Or had they? She wasn't certain. She only remembered flames and a terrible burning sensation.

She rolled onto her side, gazing out the window. The sun was setting, turning the sky orange and red, with bands of blue and violet. It was strangely beautiful, this World of the Dead.

She remembered the Tower. The pictures seemed related to Lovethar, but something else was happening. They weren't just burning a witch. The Deaths in those carvings had a package, and Lovethar was upset. Perhaps they were bringing Lovethar a package she didn't want. Suzie's head hurt. What did it matter? It was a million years ago and had nothing to do with her.

"Hey, you awake?" Billy asked, knocking on her door.

"Yeah."

"Dinner's ready."

"Great, thank you."

"You look stressed, Suzie. Still getting used to this place? Or still upset from Widow's Peak?"

"A little of both. What's for dinner?"

"Runny eggs and burnt toast." He laughed. "Jason and I, well, we're not exactly the best cooks. I can fix you a tuna sandwich if you'd rather have that."

"No, eggs and toast sounds fine. Thank you, guys."

"What elective did you choose?" asked Jason, starting to eat.

"Art. I liked to paint in school."

"Hey, I'll be in Art too," he replied.

"Not me," said Billy. "I'll be in gym. I've got boskery this year, and competition will be tight."

"Boskery?" asked Suzie and Jason together.

"The big sport here on campus. It's a game with a ball and four teams, the only sport I've heard of where more than two teams play at once. Only, it's not just for fun. Every Death in the Junior College, other than first years, has to play. You try out for teams, and the teams compete. Each Death is monitored, and your performance in boskery determines your placement when you go to Senior College. It's a game with scythes, supposed to show how well you can master a blade. If your team wins, you're guaranteed a great spot by the time you graduate. With thirty-two teams, competition is rough."

"Well, I don't understand what the game is, but good luck," said Suzie, finishing her runny eggs. "And thanks for dinner."

"You'll catch on if you come to a game," replied Billy. "And you're welcome. I'm sorry many of the guys here keep giving you a hard time. It'll probably be even worse on Monday. Once school gets going everyone will have their own work to worry about."

"Well, thank you again, for being considerate. Back home, it seemed like my friends didn't care how people treated me."

"Did you get skinny too?" asked Jason.

"Yes, everyone said I was anorexic."

"Me too," he replied.

"It happens to every Death before they're brought here," said Billy. "My parents," he stopped and looked away. A tear slipped from his eye.

"Billy, I'm sorry."

Billy shook his head, rose, and started to clear the table.

"I haven't thought about them in a while. I've been here over a year. Now they don't even remember I exist."

"Billy, I'm sure they haven't forgotten you."

Billy shrugged. "They say our existence in the human world is erased when we fail the test. If that's true, my parents have no memories I ever existed. Yet, I still wish I could go back. If I saw my parents one more time—"

"Isn't there any other way you can go back home?"

"I go back to that world frequently to reap. But no, if someone I care about dies, they won't send me near them, it's against the rules. I'm not allowed to see anyone ever again. Seems like a long time ago, sometimes."

"You've only been here a year."

"A year in this place ages you, Suzie. This is a tough place." His eyes focused inward, lost in thought.

"I'm going to pass the test," said Jason.

"Me too," said Suzie.

"Well, who will stay and keep me company after you've both gone?" Billy smiled, breaking the tension. "These guys are death to hang with. Right? 'Cause they're Deaths?"

Jason rolled his eyes and Suzie grinned.

"Guys," she said. "We're going to be all right."

* * * *

Suzie awoke the next day to the sound of raindrops. She looked outside and watched steady rain falling from dull, gray clouds.

"We'll stay inside today," said Billy at breakfast. "No reason to go out in the rain."

"What do you do when it rains? With no TV or anything."

"Rain here never lasts too long, but we usually read or talk. I've a few comic books and novels, if you ever want to borrow one. Deaths sneak a good amount from the Living World."

"You mean you've stolen books from people and brought them here?" asked Suzie.

"Me? No," said Billy. "I buy 'em off of others who have. The job again. You two might want to consider working, even if it's only part-time. You'll find a ton of openings around the College or in the villages."

"I just want to get through the year."

"Let me take your plate," said Jason. He seemed less inward today, though he still stared at the floor more than he looked up.

"Thank you, Jason. I'll help clean up too."

"Rain sounds like it's letting up," said Billy. "We can head out in a little while, and go around the campus a bit. Or we can stay here. It's up to you two. I'm supposed to be showing you around."

"You showed us a lot yesterday," said Suzie. "I liked climbing the Tower."

"I'm glad." He broke off as someone knocked at the door. Billy looked at Suzie and Jason but neither moved. He rose.

"Yes?" he asked, opening the door a crack.

"I've seen you around," said a boy's voice. "You're Billy, right?"

"Yeah."

"We had Theory together last year. I'm Frank."

"Yes, I remember now. What do you want?"

"May I come in for a second?"

Billy opened the door, and Frank walked in. Suzie realized he was the same skinny Death who had smiled at her yesterday. He had freckles and dark brown eyes, almost black. He reminded her a little of herself, with dark hair and freckles. His hair was blacker than ink, it almost looked fake. A cluster of pimples on his cheeks and nose combined with the freckles, giving him a mottled appearance. He smiled again, brushing strands of wet hair out of his eyes.

"What do you want?" asked Billy.

"I'm sorry for the guys yesterday," he said. "A lot of them, especially the later years, well they're freaked she's here."

"Yes, and?" said Billy, his expression icy.

"Well." He turned to Suzie. "I wanted to tell you we're not all like that. Some of us admire your bravery. Takes guts just to be here."

"Thank you. I'm Suzie."

"I'm Frank." They shook hands. "Not every Death here will be mean to you. Some of us accept you."

"How'd you find out she lives here?" Billy seemed suspicious. Had he forgotten the smile yesterday?

"I asked Hann. Look, if you want me to go—"

"No," said Suzie. "Sit please, make yourself comfortable."

"Thank you."

"You've met other Deaths who don't mind that I'm here?"

Frank hesitated, sitting awkwardly on the side of the couch. "Yes," he said. "Not too many, and most won't admit right away. Sometimes people like to blend in."

Jason snorted a short laugh.

"You are a normal person, even if you're a girl," said Frank. "Yes, others agree with me."

"And why didn't they come as well?" asked Billy.

"I asked some of my friends to, but like I said, people like to blend in."

"It's fine," said Suzie. Despite Billy's hesitation, she trusted Frank. She sensed something kind and familiar about him. "You're a second-year student like Billy?"

"Yes."

"Do you like being a Death?"

Frank turned to her with a puzzled expression. "Doesn't matter if I like it or not," he said. "I'm here."

"I wondered if you were getting used to this place, or if you still missed home." She sighed. "I miss home."

"This is home now," said Frank. "And being a Death, well, I guess I do enjoy it, at times."

"You ready for term? Starts tomorrow," said Billy.

"I am ready. I don't like summer, gets boring. And we've got boskery this year."

"What team are you hoping for?" Billy's expression changed, and he smiled.

"Dragon Seekers. Angus Wright told me he'd keep an eye on me."

"Francois Martin told me the same. I guess I'll be competing with you at try-outs."

"Frenchie?" asked Frank. "You guys friends?"

"Not friends, not exactly. We worked together in Applications a bit."

"He's an interesting guy," said Frank. He turned to Suzie. "And he's one of the ones I'd avoid. Been saying a lot of things against women, ever since word got out that a girl was here."

"Who's this?" asked Suzie.

"A third year student, and a bully," replied Frank.

"He is a bit tough," said Billy. "I'm not too surprised he's said things about girls."

"Good luck at try-outs," said Frank.

"You too."

"I'd better get going," said Frank. He turned to Susan. "If you ever need anything, I'm in Lion Three, room five."

"Lion Three, room five." she repeated.

"Yes, or send word through Hann or another teacher. They seem creepy, but it's their job to help."

Frank rose and again shook Billy's hand. "See you Thursday," he said.

"Okay."

Frank left and Suzie sat at the table.

"This won't be too bad," said Billy. "Some people will be nice to you. Let's go look around the school a bit. Looks like the rain's stopped."

Suzie spent the rest of the day walking through corridors and peering into classrooms. When Billy brought them by a mound with a picture of a lion holding three scythes, she circled the location on her map, although she didn't see Frank. They went to the Hall, but it was closed.

"They'll open for breakfast tomorrow," said Billy. "The Hall's pretty amazing."

Jason was silent most of the day, and for long periods Suzie, too, found herself growing silent. Her life was radically different now. She was alone in an alien world, the only girl, and tomorrow would be the beginning of school, the beginning of her real trial here.

When they walked back to Eagle Two, Suzie caught a glimpse of East Tower, looming above her with menace, disappearing into the gray clouds. Light flickered in a high window, and she wondered if anyone was watching. She turned to her side as the edge of a black cube emerged from around a corner. The Examination Room. Would she make it through the year?

It would begin tomorrow, when school started. She took a deep breath. She was ready.

CHAPTER SEVEN

The First Day

Suzie awoke early. Peering behind her curtain, she gazed out at the still dark sky. Her first day of school in the College of Deaths. She showered and changed into the nicest outfit left for her, a purple dress with white trim, which fit nicely. She pulled out a small lipstick tube from the back of the dresser. It had been in her pocket when Cronk took her from home, the only makeup she owned. She dabbed a bit on her lips: if she was the only girl in this world, she might as well look feminine.

"Wow, Suzie, you look great," said Billy, when she walked into the kitchen.

"Thanks, Billy."

"Since term is starting, the Hall will be open for meals. That's where everyone goes, at least for breakfast and lunch, and most guys for dinner too. I'll take you in, and then we'll start school. They usually make a few speeches and stuff at the first Hall anyway. Welcome to school, that sort of thing."

"I'm nervous," said Jason, wiping his nose on his shirt. "Classes and stuff. Being a Death."

"It's a living," said Billy.

"Is that a pun?" asked Suzie.

"Maybe," said Billy, smiling.

Suzie returned to her room and got her books, her map, and the pouch with Athanasius's cake.

"Here," said Billy, popping his head in. He tossed her a backpack. "From a job in Mexico last year."

"This looks like a kid's backpack," said Suzie.

"Everybody dies."

She said nothing. The grim morbidity of this world was only now sinking in. It was beautiful, but this was still the World of the Dead. This wasn't any normal school; she was training to be a Death.

"You can wear the dress, you look great," said Billy, "but you'll need a robe over it. First day of school is formal, supposed to wear our robes. Starting tomorrow you only have to wear a robe for Applications, though some guys never take theirs off."

"Okay," she said. She went to the closet and put on one of the large robes. She tucked the hood beneath her long hair and went to the mirror. She still looked pretty, though her dress was completely covered. The sleeves were far too large, hanging down in great flaps. The yellow skull patch glared at her.

"The skull means you aren't certified," said Billy, pulling on his own robe, which also had a yellow skull. "Every kid at school has one. Other than your hair and face, you look like a Death."

"Thanks. I think."

They met Jason, who also wore his robe. "C'mon," said Billy. "We don't want to be late."

They hurried across the campus, passing through mazes of stone. A few other Deaths walked in the same direction.

"Where is everyone?" murmured Billy. "We're not late."

They walked past East Tower and climbed a long flight of stairs. Then they stopped.

Standing in front of the Hall was a mob of at least a hundred Deaths. They shouted and some held signs. One sign read "*No Girls*," another "*The Bitch Is A Witch*" and another said "*Burn Her*." Suzie shuddered, and Billy put a hand on her shoulders.

"What's going on?" he shouted.

"We don't want girls here."

"Send her away. She's not wanted."

The crowd shouted taunts and jeers, one after the other. One Death threw something over their heads and the crowd cheered. Another threw a stone, striking Suzie in the face. She staggered back, her cheek stinging.

"Let us through," said Billy. "She's a student here too."

Jason stood near them but didn't speak; he looked ready to run away.

"Why are you helping her, Billy?" shouted one Death. "You got a girlfriend now?"

The crowd laughed. Several older boys surged forward and tried to grab them. One knocked Jason's books to the ground. He went to pick them up, and Suzie knelt to help him. The crowd surged, pulling Billy away from her. One boy pulled up the bottom of her robe.

"She's got a dress on," the Death laughed. "Girly wants to be pretty."

"Leave them alone," shouted a voice. The Deaths backed off, and Suzie spun around. Billy broke free and returned to her side. Frank and three other older boys stood behind her. Frank turned to the crowd again.

"Leave her alone, I said. You should be ashamed of yourselves." Frank's eyes flashed with anger.

Another stone flew out of the crowd, soaring above his head. He clenched his fist and closed his eyes. The crowd yelled and taunted again. One Death smiled at Suzie then opened his mouth and spat at her.

"Enough," boomed a loud voice. The Deaths fell silent. A dozen men in bright purple robes climbed the stairs behind them. An older man in a white robe followed. The Deaths parted, making a path.

"Get into the Hall," said one of the men. The Deaths started leaving.

"It's the Council of Twelve," whispered Billy as they followed the others into the Hall. "The one in white is Lord Coran. They're in charge of the World. I've never seen all thirteen at once."

Suzie was relieved to find a group of Deaths already in the Hall. Not everyone had protested her entry. Some of the ones from the crowd glared, but others avoided looking at her.

The Hall was long and narrow. Portraits of Deaths in purple robes, each holding a scythe, lined the walls. The walls themselves were earthen, like the walls of a cavern, similar to the mounds they passed when walking through the College. At the far end of the cave-like Hall, two massive scythes hung on the wall, with a painted skull between them. A large hourglass protruded from the rocky wall beneath the scythes. A series of arches and columns supported the ceiling, which held massive bowls filled with the strange, glowing flowers. Several skylights let in shafts of early sunlight, which shone into the Hall at angles. Three enormous tables with benches on either side stretched the length of the hall. A fourth table was raised and perpendicular to the others, beneath the skull and scythes at the end of the Hall. The Council of Twelve and Lord Coran sat at the far table. Billy led Suzie to the corner of one of the long tables, and they sat with Frank and Jason.

Plates and silverware were already laid out. The Deaths sat, and the Hall buzzed with anxious conversation.

"Silence," shouted a voice from the table at the end. One of the purple-robed figures rose.

"The Headmaster," whispered Billy. The Hall silenced.

Headmaster Sindril stood behind the center of the table next to the white-robed Lord Coran. A neatly trimmed black beard, flecked with gray, framed his angular face. His hair was short and slicked back, and he wore a monocle. He smiled.

"Welcome," he said, his deep voice filling the room. "Welcome Deaths, new and old. And a special welcome to Susan Sarnio. Susan, please stand."

Suzie's face turned beet-red. She rose, staring at the table in front of her, aware that the entire Hall was staring at her. Several Deaths muttered.

"Susan is the first female Death in a million years," said Sindril.

"Kill the bitch," shouted a voice from the far side of the Hall. Several others murmured their approval. Suzie sat down.

"Now, now," said Sindril. "I understand many of you are angry about this situation. I myself was surprised to learn she was here. However, Susan is a Death. She is one of us." He paused, letting the words sink in. "This is a historic opportunity, a chance to change this world for the better. Do not sink to hate, but instead rise to the challenge. I ask all of you to treat Suzie with respect, and show her

every courtesy. If anyone does not, if we have any more incidents…"
He glared around the Hall and several Deaths looked away. "There will
be serious consequences."

Billy put a hand on her shoulder. She looked up and forced a
smile.

"Do not let this overshadow our purpose," said Sindril. "You are
here to learn, study, and one day take your places as fully-certified
Deaths. I expect excellence. Please rise."

The entire Hall stood.

"Have a wonderful year, and good luck."

He nodded and they sat again. Suzie glanced at the head table and
watched Sindril help Lord Coran sit. The Headmaster leaned to Coran
and whispered something in his ear, which made Coran smile. The
white-robed old man stared Suzie in the eyes and she quickly looked
away.

Servants came in with large platters of food, placing them on each
table. Suzie noticed one of the servants had large yellow eyes,
reminding her of Athanasius. Another servant pulled his hand away
from the tray, as she stared at what looked like green skin.

The meal passed in a blur. The food smelled good but Suzie hardly
ate. Her stomach clenched in anger and tension. Billy and Frank talked
about boskery. Jason never looked up from his food. Suzie didn't talk,
even when Billy tried to bring her into the conversation.

"It's time," said Billy, glancing at the hourglass over the head
table. Strange-looking servants cleared the plates and the Deaths rose.

"Time for classes," said Frank. "You ready?"

Suzie glanced down at the schedule Hann had given her. What did
it matter? They hated her. Every one of them.

"Hey," said Billy. "Don't let them get to you. Headmaster Sindril
doesn't mess around, and once classes get going, no one will have time
to worry about you."

"I hope you're right."

"What do you have first?" asked Frank.

"I have Theory first, in Room thirty-two."

"That's in West Tower," said Billy, "where we went on Saturday."

"I have Theory first too," said Jason, "in the same room."

"At least I have a friend in my class."

"Can I see your schedule?" asked Billy. "We have Applications together at the end of the day. It's your only mixed-year class. Well, you and Jason should get going. I'm headed the other direction, myself. I'll meet you guys back here for lunch."

"I hope we get into lunch without another scene," said Suzie. "Maybe I'll eat somewhere else."

He leaned in close, whispering in her ear. "Suzie, what happened didn't surprise me. It's a male world, and they're not ready for you. You can't let them get to you. Jason, Frank, and I—we're your friends. You're not alone. Don't forget."

"Thanks, Billy."

"Bill," shouted a voice across the hall. Billy walked away.

Frank nodded, following Billy.

"You ready?" asked Jason.

"Yes."

They left the Hall. When she walked onto the staircase outside, a Death grabbed her arm from behind. He stood behind her, and Suzie couldn't see his face.

"I don't care what Sindril says," he growled. "You're not wanted, bitch."

He let her go, and Suzie stumbled forward. Jason, walking in front of her, hadn't even noticed. She continued, without bothering to turn around.

"Susan, wait a minute," called a low voice. She stood still but didn't turn around. Jason stopped.

"Susan," a voice touched her back.

"Back off," she said, spinning around. She stared at Headmaster Sindril's frowning face. He adjusted his monocle and scratched his beard.

"I'm sorry, Headmaster," she said, blushing. "I didn't—"

"It's all right. I'm sure this is difficult for you. Let me walk you to your first class. You have Theory now?"

"Yes, how did—?"

"Susan, it's my job to oversee the students here. I'm Headmaster of both Colleges, Junior and Senior. But we've never had a student like you."

"You mean a girl."

They walked downstairs, heading toward the enormous West Tower. The sky was bright now, and the sun shone behind them. Scattered clouds lingered around the tower. To her right, in a barren stone courtyard, sat the black cube of the Examination Room.

"Susan, I'm a friend. If you ever need anything, come to my office in East Tower. I want you to feel comfortable here at the College."

"Thank you, sir."

"The year will be hard for you, of course. But if I can help in any way, let me know."

"Again, thank you."

They reached West Tower. Deaths glanced at her, but no one approached, probably fearful of Sindril.

"Your class is on the third floor. We will meet again. Good luck." He held out a hand, which Suzie shook. Sindril turned and walked away.

"What was that about?" said Jason.

"Let's go to class."

They went to the third floor, following a crowd of young Deaths. Most of the boys ignored Suzie. First years, she supposed.

The crowd filed into a long room with a vaulted ceiling. She sat next to Jason at one of the narrow desks and put her books in front of her.

A short, chubby Death with long blond hair walked to the front of the room. He turned and stared directly at Suzie while he spoke.

"Good morning *lady* and gentlemen. Welcome to your first class of the new term, and your first class at the College. I am Dr. James. I will learn your names later this week. Now we will start with work. Please take out your theory books."

Suzie pushed her other books aside, opening the cover of *Michael Darkblade's Theories on Deaths*. A grim-faced skeleton holding a scythe stared from the cover page.

"Michael Darkblade," continued Dr. James, "was my teacher's teacher. His theories are indisputable and will form the basis for this class." He paused and walked to Suzie.

"However, one of his theories seems appropriate to begin with, given our special guest. Please turn to page fifty-four."

Suzie flipped to the page, which was labeled "Sex in the World of Deaths." A number of the boys giggled.

"Silence," said Dr. James. "This is no laughing matter. Do I have a volunteer to read the first section?"

A few hands lifted into the air, including Jason's. Suzie did not raise hers.

"Susan Sarnio," said Dr. James. "Why don't you read for us?"

This was going to be a bad class. Her teacher was singling her out on the first day. Billy had warned her older Deaths were more sexist than the others, but she hadn't expected this from a teacher.

"Well, Susan? You can read, can't you?"

Some of the boys snickered.

"The World of Deaths," she read, "is a male world, and always will be. Females have no place here. Deaths are obtained through contracting living boys. Only one female Death ever lived, the evil witch Lovethar. Females are useless." She trailed off.

"Continue please," said Dr. James.

"Females are useless. They are lazy and spend their time distracting the true Deaths. They are too weak to wield a scythe, and too stupid to use them. A deficiency in arm muscles renders the female body unable to perform the responsibilities of a Death. The Polton Hypothesis, later upheld by Decrion's Law, decrees females will never be allowed in this world."

"Thank you, Susan." Dr. James grinned.

"Sir," she said, rising. "May I say something?"

"No, come to me before class tomorrow if you have a concern."

Suzie sat again, fuming.

The class continued for another hour, as Dr. James continued to point out that females were unwanted. The class ended and Suzie ran into the hall, choking back tears.

"Suzie, are you all right?" asked Jason.

"Are you joking? Our teacher spent the whole class telling us girls are useless."

"He's probably trying to scare you, maybe the rest of the week will get better. I mean we can't focus on girls for every class, and we did half of that chapter in the book today."

"I don't want any more of this. I want to go home."

"It'll be okay," said Jason.

"I have to go," said Suzie.

"We only have a year and then we can leave. What's your next class?"

"No, I have to *go*. To the bathroom. Do I have time to return to Eagle Two?"

Jason shrugged. "Remember what Billy said about being on time."

"I'm not asking Dr. James if there's a bathroom. He's a total jerk."

"He's our teacher, but yes, you're right," said Jason. "What do you have next?"

"History, what about you?"

"I have History too. Are you in Room 17?" He looked at his schedule.

"No, Room 86. We must be in different classes."

"I guess I'll see you at lunch. There's a bathroom down the hall. I can guard the entrance for you."

"Thanks, Jason. I'm glad I have friends like you here."

They walked to the bathroom, which had rows of urinals and three stalls. Jason stood outside the door, and Suzie heard several Deaths asking him why they couldn't come in.

She emerged a few minutes later.

"You can't hog the bathroom," shouted one boy.

"Yeah, get your own," said another.

"Let her go to class," said Jason.

He gave Suzie a smile and walked away. She hurried down the hall and to the staircase, pulling out her map.

* * * *

Suzie was the last one into her History class. The teacher droned on without turning to her, but the class turned their eyes on her while she hurried to a seat in the back. When would the day end?

"To learn your names," continued the old Death in the front of the class. "You, Susan, since you were late, why don't you go first."

"I'm sorry, what was the question?"

The class giggled.

"Your name, Susan. Stand and tell the class your name, and where you lived before coming to the World of the Dead."

"I'm Suzie, Suzie Sarnio. I lived in Damascus, Maryland." She sat quickly.

Each Death rose and did the same. Boys had come from every country around the world, yet somehow she understood them. Did they all speak English? Or was this a world beyond language?

"I'm Luc," said a lanky boy with dark black hair, dark skin, and thick eyebrows. "I'm from Bordeaux, and I'm one of the only Deaths whose brother is here too. I'd like to add that I hate girls."

A few boys turned to Suzie but the teacher didn't seem to notice. He wore thick glasses and slouched over his desk, pressing his nose deep into a stack of papers. He perched on top of a tall stool, and his long white hair fell down past the hood of his robe. Behind him, a shaky hand had written the name "Professor Stevens" on the chalkboard.

The class dragged on but Suzie stopped paying attention. She drifted into her own thoughts, picturing her friends and her mom. She dreamed of women, of wonderful women like her mother. Of comforting women like Gingerbread Nurse Cherwell. Of respected women like her grandmother, or the First Lady. Of her girlfriends at school. There were none here now, no other women in the entire world.

Deaths rose on either side of her and she realized class must be over. She gathered her books. Luc walked behind her and shoved her, making the books fall on the floor. He left the room, laughing. Professor Stevens hadn't even looked up.

She walked with her head down through the corridors and back toward Lower Hall. She didn't want to encounter more Deaths protesting her existence. They didn't want her. Didn't they realize she didn't want to be here either?

The crowds turned right, and she turned left, trying to catch her breath. She tossed her backpack down in an empty courtyard. A sundial stood in the middle of a grassy lawn, surrounded by stone walls with arched windows. High overhead, a screech pierced the sky. An eagle soared down, plucking a mouse from the lawn. It perched on the sundial and devoured the rodent, while staring at Suzie.

Suddenly the walls of the courtyard turned red. The ground seemed to shake beneath her.

Fire. Everywhere burning. Flames.

Two green eyes stared at her from the inferno.

The eagle turned its head, and Suzie heard the distinct sound of a baby crying for its mother.

Flames.

A single word formed her in mind: a plea, an appeal, a name.

Suzie.

Suzie's skin burned for a moment, before the sensation faded. The courtyard faded from red flame to white stone. The eagle finished its meal and flew away. Suzie grasped the side of the stones to steady herself.

"Suzie? Are you okay?" asked Frank.

She turned to him. "I'm fine," she said.

"Billy and I've been looking for you. It's lunch now. What are you doing here?"

"I wanted a breather away from the crowds."

"Are you sure you're all right?" Frank gave her a piercing look. "You seem pale."

"It's been a long day. The kids were rough, and my theory teacher was absolutely horrible to me."

"I'm sorry. Can I give you a hug?"

She nodded and he wrapped his arms around her. She felt hot again, but not from flames or strange visions.

"Come on," he said. "Let's get to the hall and grab some lunch."

"Suzie?" She heard Billy's voice.

"We're here," said Frank, letting her go.

"Hey guys," said Billy. "What are you doing here?"

"We were going to lunch," said Frank.

Billy gave him a puzzled look but the three left the courtyard and returned to the Hall.

"How were your classes, Suzie?" asked Billy.

"My history class was boring; the teacher's didn't even realize class had started. A few jerks in that class too. Theory's even worse. The teacher himself spent the class making me feel like dirt."

"I'm sorry." Billy sighed. "It will get better after this week. Soon everyone will be wrapped up in their work, they won't even pay attention to you. You're new, but they'll get used to having you around."

"Will they?" she asked.

"Look," said Billy, pointing to the top of the staircase leading to the Lower Hall. No Deaths stood to block her way and none stared at her. She climbed the stairs one at a time, afraid of what waited for her in the Hall, but the area seemed normal. If anything here was normal.

Deaths sat around the tables served by bizarre creatures. Billy, Frank, and Suzie sat where they had eaten breakfast.

Jason looked up. "How bad?" he asked.

"The teacher was boring, and one of the kids picked on me, but it wasn't like Theory. I'm hungry."

A servant brought her a plate with a plain-looking sandwich.

"I hope it's not tuna," she said. "That would make this bad day even worse."

She bit into the sandwich. Tuna filled her mouth; not fresh tuna, but tuna that tasted two weeks old.

"Gorgers?" she asked, spitting into a napkin.

"You're learning," said Billy. "Here, you can have the rest of mine, it's a meatball sub."

"They won't bring me a new one?"

"I'm afraid not. It's one of those annoying rules people tend to learn the hard way. I did too, last year." For a second, a desperate, lonely look crossed Billy's face. He turned away, and when he turned back, he smiled again.

Suzie sighed and took the gorger.

"What's with the helpers?" asked Suzie, lowering her voice. "They look, different. Not like Deaths."

"They're 'Mentals," said Billy.

"What's a 'Mental?"

SCHOOL OF DEATHS | 67

"Short for Elementals. They're weird." He whispered, "We're not supposed to talk about them. I'll tell you at home if you want."

"All right."

"What do you have after lunch?"

"Does it matter?"

"Suzie, you can't give in. You have to stay strong. They're trying to get to you because you're different. You need to show them that you're as good as any boy."

"That's easier said than done. It's frustrating."

"It's only one year," said Jason.

"If I pass the stupid test." She looked at Billy. He had failed his test. Would she be able to sit here calmly a year from now? Would she even last that long? And why couldn't they talk about the Elementals?

A servant came in to clear the dishes away. His eyes were dark green and glowed like a fish. His skin shimmered like scales. Were the Elementals part-animal? She remembered Athanasius and his strange goat-like features. While she mused over the connection, a second servant entered, a man with long blond hair. His eyes glowed red, but he seemed normal in every other way. He noticed her attention and quickly turned away. But why? Suzie decided she'd find out later, when Billy talked to her at home.

She looked at her schedule. She had Art next. Maybe that wouldn't be too bad, since she'd picked the elective herself.

The Deaths were rising from the tables and heading out of the Hall.

"I have Art now," she said.

"I'll walk with you," said Jason. "I've got Art too." He smiled.

They left the Hall, heading away from the others. Suzie turned back to watch Billy give her a thumbs up and an encouraging smile. She crossed through a courtyard with a fountain: one of the few displays of water in this desert-like stone maze of the College. She walked under a bridge. A skull sat between two large hourglasses, grinning down at her. All skulls grin, yet this one seemed to mock her. The notion was ridiculous, but it pestered her. She took a deep breath and hurried after Jason.

They entered the classroom. A dozen young Deaths stood behind large blank canvases on tripods. This was a small class, her smallest yet. Jason and Suzie took the last two positions, near the front. The room grew silent, waiting for the teacher.

"Late on the first day?" whispered a boy behind her.

"I got here on time," she said, turning.

"Not you. The teacher. Where is he?"

"I don't know." She paused a moment. "I'm sorry I snapped at you."

They waited five more minutes before the door opened and a Death hurried in, coughing.

"I-I-I-I'm I'm s-s-s-s-sorry for being l-l-l-late," he stammered.

"Cronk?" Suzie asked aloud.

"S-s-s-some of you have already m-m-m-met me," he added, blushing. "This is a n-n-n-new p-p-p-position for me. Wel-wel-wel-welcome to Art."

Suzie noticed several of the boys glancing at others, and one rolled his eyes.

"My n-n-name is C-Cronk. I t-t-trust this will be a g-g-g-good class for—"

"Spit it out," said one boy behind Suzie.

Suzie turned and glared, and one of the boys turned beet red. She smiled; this was going to be a good class.

It was.

Cronk stuttered his way through the introductions, before giving them free time to start a pen drawing. Draw something that made them happy. Suzie glanced around the room; most of the Deaths drew crude stick figures. Jason's picture seemed to be a house, probably his home in the Living World. Suzie turned to her own canvas. She let the pen loose, letting the ink find its own shape. Mom's face emerged first, followed by her father and brother.

"G-g-g-good S-S-S-Suzie," said Cronk, walking up behind her.

"Thank you. I love to draw."

He put a hand on her shoulder and looked her in the eyes.

"Enjoy this c-c-c-class," he said. "You'll n-n-n-need it."

"Thank you, Cronk. Are you all right?"

Cronk wiped a tear from his eye and walked quickly away.

"Jason, is that your house?" she asked.

"Yeah. Your family?" He pointed to her canvas.

"Yes. You're a good artist."

He laughed. "Not nearly as good as you."

"Thanks." Their pictures did seem better than most of the Deaths around her, though she couldn't see everyone's. The class came to an end too soon. This would be the best part of each school day.

When they left the room, she walked up to Cronk. The class was a welcome change from her first two.

"See you tomorrow," she said. He nodded, but she sensed sadness in his face. Did he regret bringing her to the World of Deaths? It was only his job. She glanced at her schedule again. Applications next, her final class.

"Meet you at dinner," said Jason. He had a different Applications class.

She walked to a mound near the twisting mountain of West Tower. The sky had grown cloudy, and a light rain fell on her head as she entered the massive classroom.

She realized at once that this class would be trouble. The room was an enormous stone arena. Forty Deaths stood around the room in their robes. Luc, the boy from History who had teased her, stood off to her right next to a taller boy who looked similar to him.

Frank and Billy came over.

"Welcome to Applications," said Frank.

"You're here too?"

"Applications is always mixed-level and always the end of the day. It's the focus of what we learn here. They'll put you in a group with older kids like us, and we'll practice."

"Practice?" she asked. "Practice what?"

"Reaping souls," said Billy. "Bringing the dead to the Hereafter."

"Oh."

"We are training to be Deaths." He shrugged. "Sounds crazy, but it's actually interesting."

"Quiet down," said a deep voice at the front of the room. The Death who entered the room glowered at the class. Hann scowled, pulling at his thin goatee. His presence seemed to grow into the entire room, extending into every crevice. He wasn't another Death, he actually resembled *Death*, the Grim Reaper Suzie had seen in movies. The distrust Suzie had felt when she first met him returned. He stood menacingly in the front, daring anyone to speak. In his right hand, he held a scythe gleaming in the light of the large room.

"My name is Hann, and I will be your teacher this year. To begin, form groups of three or four. I don't care who's in your group, but at least one member must be an older student. No groups of only first years. Go." He said the last word softly, but it was a powerful command. The students hurried to form groups.

"We lucked out," said Frank. He put a hand on Suzie's shoulder. Billy copied the gesture.

"Is everyone in a group?" called out Hann. No one answered and he continued.

"Good," he said. "This will not be a fun class, or an easy one. Yet this will be your most important class, the only class where you'll learn anything that actually matters. Raise your hand if you are a first year."

Suzie and about two-thirds of the class raised their hands.

"You are the learners. The fresh meat. You must look to the older students for guidance. Second years?"

Frank and Billy, along with several others raised their hands.

"Much to learn. Professor Orell tells me half of you babies still have trouble wielding a scythe. Any third years?"

Only two hands rose. Billy tensed as he glanced at the tall black boy standing in Luc's group with a raised hand. It must be Frenchie.

"Not much help. I wonder how pathetic you two must be to get stuck in this class." Suzie glanced at Frenchie, whose face was tense. He looked ready to hit someone. Luc cringed as his brother grabbed his shoulder, probably trying to control his temper.

Hann laughed. "Well this is what I've been given, but I guarantee this is not where we'll end. I will make Deaths out of all of you. Right, your groups will begin general exercises. I issue training scythes tomorrow, and you have your first skills test a week from today. Any questions?"

The older students gasped.

"Only a week," muttered Billy. "That's impossible."

"Good," continued Hann. "Spread yourself around the room and begin warming up. Second and third years lead your groups in arm exercises. I will come around to each group to get your names. Go."

Everyone spoke at once, darting to different parts of the room.

"Hey Bill," said Frenchie, approaching them. "You got stuck with the little girl? Didn't they have any men left?"

"I chose this group," said Billy.

"You're not going soft on me, are you? Maybe I shouldn't let you on my team for boskery."

Billy went to Frenchie and whispered something in his ear. The tall boy shook his head and laughed.

"Yeah that makes a lot more sense," said Frenchie. "I'm looking forward to try-outs." He walked away.

"What was that?" asked Suzie.

"Don't worry about it," said Billy. He looked embarrassed.

"Let's go to the corner," said Frank, leading her away. Billy followed.

"Wow," said Frank, when they reached a spot away from the others. "I've heard of Hann, but never dreamed he'd live up to the reputation."

"A week before the first scythe test?" said Billy. "You and I will be fine, but these first years? There's no way they'll be ready."

"He probably expects them to fail," said Frank. "Come on, let's stretch our arms."

They began a series of arm exercises and stretches. Some of them were ones Suzie had done in gym class, and she remembered her old teacher, Coach Barker—not his real name, but she always called him that. He'd barked at her and his other students like a dog. Suzie snapped back to the present as Hann walked over.

"Suzie," he said, "how has your first day been going, as a *girl*?"

"I've been a girl all my life," she replied.

Frank and Billy chuckled, but Hann glowered at them.

"This is your first day here. Don't get smart."

Her mind flashed to the protest outside the Hall, Dr. James taunting her, and the vision with the eagle.

"Fine," she said.

"Good. What are your names?" He turned to Frank and Billy.

"Frank Pierce."

"Billy Black."

Hann nodded and turned back to Suzie. He was even fiercer up close. Suzie smelled tuna on his breath and wondered if it was from a gorger.

"You two better keep an eye on Suzie. If she fails, I will hold you accountable. The group passes or the group sinks in my class. Understand?"

"Yes sir," said Billy. Frank nodded.

"Good."

Hann left and they finished exercising. Sticks were passed out to each group, and Billy showed Suzie how to hold hers.

"No, no," he said. "The position of the hands is critical, they have to be perfect."

Suzie kept trying, but by the time class ended she had no idea how they expected her to hold the stick. She hadn't even gotten to the training scythe, and they had a test in a week.

* * * *

Dinner was uneventful, which was a relief. Suzie looked at Billy.

"I want to go home," she said.

"That's where we're headed," he said. "It's been a long day."

"No. I want to go *home*."

"Come on," he said, and led her back to Eagle Two.

CHAPTER EIGHT

Beginners

On Thursday morning, the sun shone through the windows of Lower Hall. Suzie sat at one of the long tables, in the spot she and her friends had used since their first chaotic day. The head table was empty, the Council didn't return after Monday, and she hadn't seen Headmaster Sindril again.

A 'Mental with glowing red eyes brought her a tray.

"More gorgers?"

"Not today, ma'am," said the 'Mental softly. He opened the tray and stepped away.

"Eggs, toast, and bacon?" asked Jason. "This is the first real breakfast they've served. What's going on?"

"Probably wishing everyone good luck," said Frank, digging into a tray of Danishes and sausage.

"It's boskery try-outs after school," added Billy. "Every Death other than first years has to try out, but few get on the teams they hope for."

"You two should come," said Frank, his mouth half full. "Especially with Billy and me trying out."

Suzie put some eggs on her plate. Going to try-outs sounded like an open invitation to repeat the scene from Monday. Frenchie and Luc would be there, and probably plenty of others who hated girls.

"I'll go," said Jason. "You're coming, too, right Suzie?"

She looked at the expectant faces. Don't show fear. Besides, if everyone's preoccupied with the actual boskery try-outs, how bad could they be?

"Yeah, I'll come cheer you guys on. Which'll be tough, since I have no idea what boskery is."

"Me neither," said Jason. "But we'll go. It'll be fun."

"It'll be brutal," said Frank. "It's not a pretty game."

"That's for sure," added Billy.

They finished the meal and Jason walked with her to Theory. Dr. James sat behind his desk, glowering at them as they entered. She sat down, winced, then rose, and pulled a tack from her seat. Luc winked at her.

"We've established the World of Deaths is for males only," said Dr. James. "My superiors," he adjusted his glasses, peering at Suzie, "want us to move on. Open your books to page eighty-three."

Move on. Was he done bullying her?

For two days, Dr. James had singled out Susie, assigning her Theory class extra work on the uselessness of females in the World of Deaths. Luc picked on her every time they had class.

Of course, they couldn't spend the whole year talking about girls, when she was the only one in the entire world. A question struck her.

"Doctor James?" she asked.

"Yes," he snarled.

"Before we move on, are there any female 'Mentals?"

"Of course," he snapped. "Now stop wasting our time. Our lesson today is on metals."

Suzie stopped listening. She was not alone. No female Deaths, but other women, other girls lived in this world. All of the 'Mentals she'd met had been male, but women lived here, too, somewhere.

She was confused. The three races in this world were Deaths, Dragons, and Elementals. The Dragons and Deaths were enemies for some reason. The Elementals, or 'Mentals, seemed nice. The Deaths used them for servants or workers, but didn't socialize with them. Billy hinted that some Deaths might be afraid of the 'Mentals, but he wasn't sure. Frank said he didn't know anything about the 'Mentals, but when she asked, his eyes glazed as if trying to block an unpleasant memory. She wondered if something had happened he didn't want to talk about.

"Are you listening Susan?"

"Yes sir."

"What are scythe blades made of?" The corner of Dr. James's lip curled up in a sneer.

"Mortamant, sir."

His sneer deepened into a malicious scowl. "Yes. Yes, that is correct. Mortamant is a special metal that can slice through dimensions. A metal said to be alive. You've seen it, on the scythes that brought you here, or on the Ring surrounding the College. Pure mortamant is only used in scythes, and is the most precious commodity we have. This is impure mortamant, the way it is mined." He pulled a block of silver from his desk and passed it around the class. "Take a moment to hold it in your hands when you're able. Even the impure mortamant is no ordinary metal."

Suzie took the block. It looked heavy, but felt lighter than a feather. Tingling in her hand, the metal pulsed with unseen electricity. Or magic. She moved the block around her palm. Was the metal watching her? No, don't be ridiculous. But as she passed it to Jason, she sensed that the mortamant knew it was leaving her hand.

After Theory, Jason turned to her.

"That was a lot better than usual," he said. "And you talked about mortamant. When'd you learn that?"

"Billy told me in Applications. Still, you're right, the class went better. Maybe it'll be okay now that we're done talking about girls."

"I hope that's true. Good luck in History."

She nodded and trudged down the hall. She glanced to her right. A large pink sign outside the bathroom announced it as a "Girl's Bathroom." Another one had been labeled near the Hall. Sindril must still be watching out for her. She wondered if he had told Dr. James to move on with the class. Someone, probably Luc and his brother Frenchie, had scratched out the word "Girl's" and written "Bitch's." Lovely.

She walked into History to find Professor Stevens dozing. He sat cross-legged on top of his desk, with his eyes closed, and his mouth open. She coughed as she walked by his desk, but he didn't move.

The other students filed in and waited.

"Guess History's a bore, right teach?" asked Luc in a loud voice.

"Wrong," said Professor Stevens. He opened one eye and yawned.

"Sorry, you looked like you were sleeping."

"I was," said Professor Stevens. "Now open your books to page thirty-five. And you are?"

"Luc."

"Luc, why don't you read first?"

Luc read about the Dragons and the Great War. Dragons, she learned, had once ferried the souls of the dead to the Hereafter. The War changed that.

She went to lunch feeling better than she had since arriving in the World of Deaths.

"What's gotten into you?" asked Billy, as he noticed her smiling.

"Having a pretty good day for once."

"Good," said Frank, "are you ready for Applications?"

"I guess." She looked at her gorger and focused on a hot cheese pizza. The gorger warmed in her hands.

At the end of each day, Applications class arrived with the swing of a scythe. Suzie couldn't master it. She'd practiced on the training scythes, and everything seemed fine, but both Frank and Billy continued to tell her she was doing it wrong. Hann rarely helped anyone in the class; the groups were left on their own. On Wednesday, Suzie had glanced at Luc's group. His brother Frenchie was screaming at him. She wasn't the only one having trouble.

"You ready for try-outs?" Frank asked Billy.

"I hope Curtis isn't around," he replied. "That guy is huge."

"Frenchie'll be hard enough. They make you battle for the try-outs, no matter what your position."

"I'm not surprised."

"Any idea what they're talking about," Suzie said to Jason.

"Nope," he replied.

"Jason, I like what you started in Art yesterday. The colors are amazing."

"It's my first time with oils," he said. "But Cronk lets us do pretty much whatever we want."

"It's my favorite class. Did you hear him the other day? He's lost a bunch of other jobs."

Art was her refuge. Suzie was glad Jason shared the class, but also enjoyed having Cronk for a teacher. There was something childlike, almost innocent about the Death who had brought her to this world. She didn't blame him either, after all it had been his job, a job he had now lost. "Well, you told us he was the Death who brought you here. I can't imagine what he did to lose that. Bring the wrong person?" Jason laughed but Suzie stayed silent. Was that possible? She was the only female in a million years. However, Athanasius had expected her, and she had lost most of her weight.

"I like the clay thing you're working on," he added.

"It's supposed to be metaphorical. It'll make more sense when it's done."

A 'Mental came to take her dish.

"Thank you," said Suzie. "It was delicious."

"Of course," said the 'Mental.

"What's your name?"

"Korik," he said looking around. He hurried away.

"Not supposed to talk to them," said Frank.

"Why not?"

"I told you," said Billy, "Deaths don't mix with 'Mentals. They serve us food, and we leave them alone. They probably like things better that way."

Something flashed in Frank's expression but vanished. She sensed he wanted to say more, but he picked up his bag and headed out of the Hall.

She walked to Art with Jason.

"G-g-g-good afternoon."

"Hello, Cronk." She walked to the back and got her project out: a large shallow bowl. She walked to the clay and broke off several small pieces, sticking them up in positions along the rim.

Cronk came by but said nothing, he only smiled.

"It's a metaphor," said Suzie. For loneliness. She guessed Cronk understood.

She and Jason didn't speak much, but concentrated on their projects. Jason painted while she sculpted. One Death in the back spent the class staring into space, claiming he needed time to develop inspiration. Cronk smiled at him too. He smiled a lot.

The class passed far too quickly. Suzie had barely started when it was time to clean up.

"Always too short," said Jason.

"Yeah."

She walked to Applications. Frank greeted her with a training scythe.

"We're getting beginner's blades today," he said.

"Are they mortamant?"

"Not pure, but they've got mortamant in them, yes. This is what Monday's test will use."

"Great."

"Try not to sound too thrilled." Frank rolled his eyes.

"I'll do my best."

She finished stretching and grasped the training scythe.

"No," said Billy. "Remember, right hand high and steady, left hand is a guide. Tense the right but leave the left loose."

"That's what I'm doing."

"You're not. Here, like this."

He moved her hands a few millimeters if anything.

"Now get ready," said Billy. "I'm going to come at you, and you need to block."

"What? We haven't practiced fighting. Aren't scythes just for transport?"

"They are," said Frank, "but learning to swing in combat will help prepare you for the real thing. Besides, Billy wants to get in some last-minute practice for boskery."

"You can go next," said Billy. "When I learned how to swing, the Death I was paired with taught me like this. Are you ready, Susan?"

Hann walked behind Billy, an amused grin on his face.

"I'm ready," she said.

Billy lifted his training scythe and whirled it around himself in an arc. The plastic blade whizzed forward and she raised her own scythe. Billy's trainer struck hers and bounced off. He spun again and the blade whizzed toward her a second time. Suzie tried to block again but turned the blade too quickly and lost her balance. The training scythe fell to the ground and Billy's plastic blade slapped her leg.

Hann laughed and walked away.

"Try again," said Billy. "You started well, but remember to guide with your left and swing from your right. The real scythe won't let you make a false swing, it's too smart."

"Why not give her the beginner's blade now?" asked Frank. "Show her the difference."

"She's not ready," said Billy.

"She's as ready as she'll be," said Frank. "Maybe if she learns how a blade responds she'll understand why we're being picky about how to hold the scythe."

"But—"

"Billy, it's Thursday. The test is Monday. I'm going to get the beginner's blade."

Billy nodded and Frank walked away. Across the room, Luc waved a massive scythe through the air. Frenchie smiled and then looked up at her. She looked away.

"Here you go," said Frank. He held out a scythe, resting it on the ground. Suzie looked up at the immense blade.

"This is a beginner's scythe?"

"Yup."

The handle of the beginner's scythe, a pole of polished black wood, stood six feet tall, rising well above her. A two-foot arc of silver extended from the top of the pole. A small red flag hung opposite from the blade.

"It's enormous," she said. "It's bigger than I am."

"It's regulation," said Frank. "Supposed to be bigger than you."

"But, I can't use that."

"Suzie," said Frank. "You can do this. You're ready."

"Go on," said Billy. "Hold here, like I showed you on the trainer."

Suzie counted down from the blade, placing her hands where she had practiced. Frank held the top of the pole.

"Little lower with the left," said Billy. "Bigger pole, but same idea. Try holding higher with your right, and keep the left hand low."

Frank let go, and she lifted the scythe on her own.

"It's light," she said.

"That's the idea," said Billy. "This blade is only ten percent mortamant. The rest is a light plastic. The pole is pure ash, but 'Mentals do something to take the weight away. Give it a try."

The handle of the scythe was cool in her hands. The wood tingled as she moved it through the air, as if hiding some great power. She lifted the blade above her head and lowered with a hesitant swing. The blade caught on the air and jerked backward. She stumbled and dropped the scythe.

"Suzie," said Hann, walking toward her with a snide grin. "I do trust you'll take better care of our scythes."

"I'm sorry, sir," she said, picking up the scythe. Hann chuckled, walking away.

"It's okay," said Billy.

"What happened?" she asked.

"You were too nervous," said Frank. "The blade's got enough mortamant to sense you, and to guide you. This scythe can't cut through dimensions, but still has a will."

"It's metal and wood, the scythe can't think." Even while she spoke the words, the pole in her hands tingled in a different way. Was this scythe alive?

"It's not alive," said Frank, "but you still need to tell it what to do. The beginner's blade will stop if you don't swing right. A real scythe is even more delicate: any hesitation and it'll stop, or bring you to the wrong place. Mastering scythes completely takes years of hard work."

Suzie gritted her teeth and practiced during the rest of class. With each swing, the beginner's scythe jerked out of her hands or stopped. Frank and Billy kept adjusting her hands and the way she swung, but she couldn't get it. She glanced at Luc again. He swung his beginner's scythe with ease, leaving a light trail of green light.

"The light's what we need." Billy sighed. He took the scythe from her, adjusted his hands, raised the blade, and swung. A trail of green light followed the scythe in an arc, lingering in the air for a minute.

"I'm trying," she said.

"We'll keep trying tomorrow," said Frank. He took the scythe from Billy, who followed him toward the equipment lockers. Luc walked over.

"Don't worry," said Luc.

"What?"

"You're a girl," said Luc. "You'll never do anything right." He walked away, laughing.

Suzie dragged her feet leaving the class. Outside, the sun hung low in the sky. She heard a crow caw above her. People shoved by her, joining a crowd surging toward the boskery fields. Suzie didn't see Frank or Billy.

"Hey," said Jason, running toward her. "How was Applications?"

"Same as always, Frank and Billy spent the whole time teaching me to do something I couldn't do."

"Scythe trouble?"

"I can't get it," she said.

"Neither can I," said Jason. "Everyone else got the green streak, but mine kept jerking at nothing."

"Honestly?"

"Yeah, and we have a test in a few weeks."

"A few weeks?" asked Suzie. "Ours is Monday."

"Monday? Man, I'm glad I'm not in your class."

"I'm going to fail."

"Suzie, even if you don't get pass, you'll keep trying. It's one test. Remember, we're only here a year."

Suzie looked up and forced a smile. "I guess you're right."

They let the crowds pull them along, away from the buildings of the College, and through the Ring of Scythes. South of the Ring stood an immense stadium Suzie hadn't noticed before. Jason led her through the crowds, past the stadium, and toward a small field surrounded by sparse trees.

Groups of boys stood in the center of the field talking. Frank and Billy stood near Frenchie at the edge of one of the groups.

"Any idea how this game is played?" Suzie asked.

"None," said Jason.

"It's not a game," said a voice behind her. A short boy with beady eyes pressed his way next to her.

"I'm Karl," he said. "I'm a third year, and you're Susan Sarnio. Are your friends trying out?"

"Yeah," said Suzie. "I don't want any trouble," she added.

"Don't worry, I'm not one of the girl-haters. I feel sorry for you."

"I didn't ask to be here."

"Neither did any of us, but here we are. Who are you here for?"

"My housemate," she said, "and a friend."

Billy, Frank, Frenchie, and two other Deaths separated from the main group and put on black padded suits. Jason pushed past some of the crowd to get a better view.

"How do they play?" asked Suzie.

"Four teams try to score points with a ball," said Karl. He glanced at her and raised a bushy eyebrow. "But they won't be doing that today. This will be pure scythe work, trying to pick the best players. I'm already on a team. This is mostly for second years or those who didn't place last year. You used a scythe yet?"

"Sort of, but not successfully."

"Well, a boskery blade is different from other blades. It's a different blend of metal, different feel. I think the 'Mentals make 'em. Whatever they are, they're some of the toughest scythe blades to wield."

Frank and Billy emerged from the crowd and each picked up a scythe. But they weren't normal scythes. Each boskery scythe had two enormous blades curving from either end of a single handle, like an enormous "S". Frank spun the handle, and the blades whirled like a circle of steel. Billy swung his toward Frank, and Frank blocked one of Billy's blades with his own.

"Those are the scythes?" asked Jason, turning back to her. He gave Karl a puzzled look.

"Yes," said Karl. "The try-outs will be the captains trying to get past the newbies. If they can block long enough to stay on their feet, they'll at least make the first cuts."

The Deaths on the field formed lines. A stocky Death Suzie didn't recognize went first. He swung the scythe in a circle, like Billy had done. As he swung, Frenchie and another tall Death ran toward him, swinging their blades. The boy blocked a few swings, before Frenchie's blade hit him on the leg. The stocky Death collapsed on the ground without moving.

"Next," said Frenchie.

"What did they do to him?" she demanded.

"He'll be fine," said Karl, "though he won't make these cuts."

Billy was next.

Suzie pushed her way through the crowd. What had happened to the first boy? His body still lay on the ground. Billy stepped over him, walking to a clear part of the field.

"Somebody help him," she yelled. "He's hurt."

No one listened to her. The crowd roared for Billy. He raised his scythe and swung, forming a circle with the blades. He danced from side to side as the two Deaths charged him. The Death on the ground wasn't breathing. Would that happen to Billy?

"Stop!" Suzie screamed. She broke through the crowd and ran onto the field. Karl and Jason tried to grab her, but she pushed past.

Everything seemed to freeze. Frenchie raised a hand and the Deaths stopped. Billy watched warily, still swinging his scythe. A moan escaped the body of the stocky Death, who rolled on the ground where he had collapsed.

"What's this?" shouted Frenchie. He glared at her, his dark face flush with rage. "The damned bitch wants to stop the try-outs? Who told the slut to come onto the field?"

"Go back," mouthed Billy, lowering his scythe. She glanced at Frank.

"Look at me when I'm talking, *girl*," snapped the bully.

"Leave her alone," said a voice in the crowd. Was it Karl?

"Who said that?"

No one responded, and every eye turned to her. Where were the teachers? Where was Sindril? The only adult around was Stevens, sleeping in the stands.

"That's what I thought." He snarled, motioning the other tall Death to come over and the two whispered to each other.

"He's hurt," said Suzie. "Someone wake Stevens. We need to help him."

"Stay still, slut," said Frenchie. "If you're on the field, you must want to try out. Here." He took the scythe away from Billy and handed it to her. Billy looked stunned. He wants to make the team; he won't say anything because of that. The idea flitted into her head, but didn't give her any comfort.

Suzie put her hands on the scythe. What choice did she have?

Be strong. The words reverberated like crystal, ringing in her head. Her body warmed with gentle flame. No one else had heard. In the back of her mind, a flash of fiery green eyes appeared for a moment.

She gripped the scythe, and tried to spin it like Billy. The handle was heavy in her hand, but the blades didn't resist her the way the beginner's blade had. In fact, the entire blade spun easier than she had expected.

Frenchie lifted his own double-bladed scythe, took one swing, and struck her leg.

Be strong. She heard the voice again, but far away, like a distant echo. The world exploded into pain. She saw nothing, sensed nothing. Her body fell to the ground, shriveled and useless, every muscle writhing in agony.

"Stop," someone said. Bodies above her moved in slow motion, dancing through a fog. Was that Frank? Someone was fighting Frenchie. People were yelling. People were laughing.

Each beat of her heart brought new pain. Her blood poured through her veins like rivers of fire, burning their way through her enfeebled body.

Her corpse.

She had died. The Land of the Dead. People came here to die. Death was painful. And the noise.

"Suzie?"

She opened her eyes.

"You okay?" Frank held out a hand.

"What happened?"

"You got nicked by a boskery blade. They paralyze you for five minutes. It'll hurt for a while, but the worst is over."

"The try-outs?"

"Canceled," said Billy, leaning down. His eye was blackened.

"Your eye."

"At least I didn't get bladed like Frenchie. He's still down. All hell broke loose when Frank tried to stop him. We've both received an invite from the Gray Knights, a different team. The Dragon Seekers aren't taking anyone."

"I'm sorry I messed things up." She groaned, trying to move her leg. Her skin was heavy, like it was covered with tar. Every inch of her body hurt.

"Stay still," said Frank. "Go slow for now. You did us a favor. We're both on a team and don't have to play with that jerk."

"Besides you made him look pretty bad," said Billy, "like the idiot he is."

"What is going on?" shouted a deep voice.

"It's Hann," said Frank.

"Great, *now* the teachers show up," muttered Billy.

Suzie closed her eyes again. The world didn't make sense, but at least Billy and Frank were happy. She floated down a river of pain. Her body ached but her heart beat with a new vigor. She was weak, she was alone, but she had friends.

She looked up through a strange haze of fire and shouting. Far above her, looking down, was a pair of glowing green eyes.

Be strong, the eyes seemed to say.

I'm trying, she whispered back. *I'm trying*.

CHAPTER NINE

The Albino

Suzie awoke the next day with a splitting headache. Her legs moved slowly, and her entire body throbbed with pain. She stumbled into the kitchen and poured a glass of juice.

"I'll get that," said Billy. A dark circle ringed his eye. "Sit down, and try to go easy. You might want to skip your morning classes."

"My leg," she groaned.

"Getting your first boskery blade is tough," he replied.

"Frenchie's a jerk."

Billy laughed. "Yeah, I guess he is. He wasn't so bad last year, but seeing his brother here changed him."

Jason yawned, sitting down with them.

"Hey Suzie," said Jason. "How're you doing?"

"I'll live. Did you guys come straight here after the try-outs?"

"Had to," said Jason. "Frank carried you. You were out cold."

"Here," said Billy, handing her some toast. "Eat and lie down. You're allowed to stay here if you're sick."

"I'm not sick."

"No, but you're hurt. Same thing," said Billy.

"When you play boskery, does it always hurt like that?" asked Suzie.

"Yes," said Billy. "But once you've been bladed a few times your body gets used to it. First time's always the worst. I could barely walk for a day and a half after my first time last year."

"Last year," said Suzie. "Were you sad when you... When you had to stay?"

"This place is my home now." He paused. "Yes, I was sad. Jason and I should be getting to the Hall soon. Try to get some rest."

"I will."

Billy and Jason left and Suzie sat down on her bed. She closed her eyes but couldn't sleep. Reaching over, she pulled out her Theory book.

Turning to the index, she searched for information on boskery. Who came up with such a painful game? Skimming past the rules, she looked for more about the boskery blade. A metal designed to cause pain and temporary paralysis. She cross-checked under "metal" but didn't find anything new. Her eye went up the page to "'Mental, see Elemental." She flipped to the section on Elementals.

She found less than she wanted, and nothing on why they were servants, but a lot of information about their abilities. The first Elementals developed the ability to manipulate elements with their minds. Today, Elementals controlled things from animals to colors on a painted wall. Each had a different ability, but according to the book, their powers were outlawed in the College.

Maybe Billy was right. Maybe the Deaths kept 'Mentals as servants out of fear. But why did the 'Mentals go along?

While Suzie read, she heard a knock on the door.

She rose and opened it.

"You embarrassed my brother," said Luc. He glared at her from the hall. A tall man stood behind him; a large hood covered the stranger's face.

"Luc? What do you want?"

"I want you to suffer," he replied. "No one makes a fool of Francois. We're the only pair of brothers in this damned world. Our parents were devastated when he went missing. He was even worse when he saw me here. Now we stick up for each other."

"Frenchie attacked *me*. I skipped class because I'm in too much pain."

"You made him look weak," replied Luc, his eyes narrowing. "He hates that. What are you, anyway? A girl. A true weakling. A pathetic excuse for—"

"Stop. I'm sick of your taunts. Grow up."

"My brother was right about you. We might be the only brothers, but you're worse. You don't belong here at all."

She wanted to shove him into the wall and slam the door but the tall hooded man stepped forward.

"It's time you met my friend," said Luc. "Francois found him, but never had the opportunity to try him out."

"What are you talking about?"

The man pulled back his hood. His eyes glowed blood-red, and his skin was whiter than bone. His ears pointed on either end. The albino was perfectly white, especially next to Luc's black skin.

"He doesn't talk much. He don't need to." Luc took a step backward and the albino opened his mouth.

The world vanished for a moment. When the room stopped spinning, the albino and Luc were gone. An enormous white wolf with blood-red eyes snarled at her. Suzie screamed.

The walls closed in and the wolf pounced. She ran.

Her body still ached with pain, but her heart thundered in her chest, pounding with complete fear. The wolf howled and another white wolf appeared, with the same blood-red eyes. She sprinted away.

She didn't remember going outside, but the walls were trees. The trees grew dense, a forest closing in. She ran and ran, faster and faster. The wolves howled behind her. More white wolves lurked ahead.

Wolves everywhere. Far behind her, she heard Luc laughing.

One of the bone-white wolves snarled and leapt for her throat. She fell back and rolled. The wolf turned toward her and vanished.

A massive white cobra with blood-red eyes hissed at her. She scrambled to her feet and ran again. Panting hard, her legs in agony, she couldn't think. Her only emotion was fear. Fear surged through her body, giving fleeting strength to her aching legs.

The ground opened and she fell. Down and down until she landed hard on something moving. Spiders. Thousands of bone-white spiders with tiny red eyes. Crawling. She screamed until the sound caught in her throat.

The cobra re-emerged, hissing.

Suddenly she understood. The cobra hissed at her again, its red eyes glaring at her.

"You're a 'Mental, aren't you?" she asked the giant snake.

Luc yelled something behind her. The snake vanished.

For a strange moment, the world cleared. Suzie looked around. The Ring of Scythes surrounding the College stood in the distance. She had run away from the school and collapsed in a field. Behind her, a real forest loomed.

"Not me, you imbecile, *her*." screamed Luc. His dark face tightened, and he yelled at some invisible threat. The albino man, the 'Mental, stood near him. Luc yelled in terror and ran back toward the College.

The albino turned toward Suzie.

At once all sensation was gone. This time she didn't see wolves, snakes, pits, or spiders. This time, she saw nothing.

The attack was swift and precise, cutting her deeper than a scythe.

Fear.

Pure, unfettered fear. Fear deeper than terror, darker than nightmares. Fear filled with horrors, too terrible to deny.

Fear swept through every cell in her body.

Suzie tried to fight. She tried to scream. Finally, she started to run again. She ran into the forest, tripping over roots. The albino followed her, and the forest darkened.

Crows cawed at her. If she turned, they'd attack. The trees reached down to grab her, but Suzie ran until she reached the other side of the woods. She collapsed.

Deep in the forest, far behind her, someone was crying.

* * * *

Suzie didn't move. She didn't open her eyes. Trying not to breathe, she waited.

The world quieted. Suzie sensed a change in the air, and the menace faded. The albino was still in the woods. He hadn't followed. But where was *she*?

The sun was high, probably near noon. She looked around. The forest stretched behind her. A path led away, and the gnarled silhouette of West Tower writhed in the distance. She wouldn't have to go back through the forest. The path extended toward more woods in the other direction. Near her feet, gnarled tree trunks crept out of the dirt, wrapping around a ruin. Suzie walked to the building.

A house, or what was once a house, lay hidden in the overgrowth. It seemed ancient, far older than the College buildings. The door stood ajar.

"Hello?" she said in a voice scarcely louder than a whisper. A tinge of fear crept into the back of her mind. She had to hide, in case he was still trying to find her. She walked through the door.

Dust and cobwebs covered the walls. Parts of the floor looked clean; the wind had blown the hardwood bare. A movement made her freeze. She held her breath as a tiny mouse scampered across one of the patches of light streaming from the windows. The mouse wasn't bone-white, it was brown. She exhaled slowly.

Large bookcases lined the walls. Ancient-looking volumes with torn but colorful spines filled the bookcases, adding color to an otherwise bleak room. One of the bookcases jutted away from the wall in an unnatural angle.

She heard something far behind her. Was the albino still looking for her? Was Luc back? She walked to the angled bookcase and it swung forward. Expecting a secret passage, she was surprised to find a wall with two large words "Librvm Exelcior" in gold writing. She touched the letters and her hand sank into the wall. She pulled her hand back.

Trying again, she touched the letters, and her hand passed through them. She took a deep breath and stepped through the wall. Behind her, the bookcase slammed shut. She turned and peered back. She saw straight through the wall and over the books of the bookcase. One book with a red cover leaned toward her, while the others leaned away. She reached through the strange wall and pulled on the red book. The bookcase swung open. She stepped out into the room. Suzie pulled on the same book and walked through the wall again, closing the bookcase behind her.

Behind the wall, a staircase led downward. A thick layer of dust covered the walls and stairs; she couldn't stop coughing. White flowers on either side of her lit up with a faded light, as if they hadn't illuminated for many years. Dust and cobwebs covered each flower, muting the dim light even more. She walked down the spiral stairs, holding her sleeve over her mouth.

At the base of the stairs, she came to a large open room with a vaulted ceiling. The room must have been beneath the house, and was older than anything she'd seen since she fell into the ruins on Widow's Peak. Strange paintings on the walls of the chamber reminded her of the pictures of Dragons and Lovethar, though these were paintings of Deaths. More white flower-lights, each covered in dust, struggled to light the room.

Stacks of books covered the floors and lay in heaps. Some old bookcases leaned against the far walls, but most had fallen over.

"It's an ancient library," she said to herself. Books were everywhere, many torn. Loose pages crumpled under her feet. To her left were scrolls, like the one she had signed. Behind piles of books to her right, she found heaps of stones covered in strange runes. Stones, scrolls, and books lay in pieces on the dusty floor. Many of the books had scorch marks.

"Someone tried to destroy this place," she said. Her voice echoed in the chamber and something screeched back. She ducked when two bats flew toward her, landing somewhere in the dome above.

She'd found an ancient library, but why here? Why put a library outside the College, beneath an old abandoned house? And what had happened here?

Suzie pulled a scroll from one of the piles. The smeared writing was in a language she couldn't read. She tossed the scroll back and reached for a book. When she opened it, the binding snapped and pages scattered onto the floor. She started to pick them up but stopped herself. No one had been here in years, if not centuries. What did it matter?

She glanced at one of the fallen pages, and read a list of names followed by dates. It meant nothing to her. She let the page fall and made her way across the paper-covered floor. She lifted a piece of carved rock. An image of a Dragon's wing covered one edge, with flame images visible on the other side. She put the rock aside and lifted another piece of stone. This one showed Deaths in a boat, holding scythes. Floating above them was an image of a key. She peered closer.

The Deaths were crudely drawn stick figures; a child could have etched them. Yet the key above them was intricate and covered with tiny curves and filigree. A hint of color stained the rock around the key as well.

She put the stone down and glanced at a large stone lying in the floor. She saw another picture of the war between Deaths and Dragons. Deaths stood on one side with Dragons on the other, and flames in the middle. She started to turn away when she noticed something drawn in the middle of the flames. She walked up and rubbed away the dust. An intricate key, identical to the one on the other stone, had been carved in the midst of the flames and the battle. Odd.

She looked through books and stones until her stomach growled. She needed food. The albino must be gone by now. She turned and walked back toward the stairs. She would have to come back to this strange library sometime. Maybe she'd show Billy and Frank. Maybe.

Suzie walked over loose papers and started to wonder. Maybe she shouldn't show this place to anyone. Luc had found where she lived. He'd attacked her in her home, a place she was supposed to be safe. But where could she go in the College? Sindril had claimed he'd help her, but had done nothing. They distrusted her. Billy, Frank, and Jason were friends, but they were still boys. They'd never completely understand.

Now here was a place only she knew about. A place filled with forgotten books, forgotten stories. A hidden place. Suzie smiled as she climbed up the stairs. She took a last look back at the library. At *her* library.

When she reached the top of the spiral stairs, Suzie stopped to catch her breath in the tight, dusty air.

"No, they will never suspect."

Suzie froze.

"Yes, yes my lords, of course."

The voice came from the other side of the wall. She peered through the wall, over the books of the bookcase. She prayed it wasn't the albino.

"She is here now. As you requested, the girl is a Death at the College."

Suzie almost fell backward. Girl? They were talking about her. She peered over the books again but couldn't see anything. The room on the other side was empty. The open door, the dusty bookcases, and nothing else.

"What of the girl herself? Do you need her alive, or just the body?"

Suzie's heart skipped a beat. What were they saying?

"She's been attacked already," said the voice. "But I will try to keep her safe. You will have her for yourselves."

No, this is wrong. Someone wanted to hurt her. Maybe even kill her.

"I will deliver the girl as promised. It will be ours soon."

Suzie started to back up as she heard a faint grumbling. Someone was answering the voice, but she couldn't make out the words. Should she hide in the library? Who was speaking? The voice sounded familiar.

"I understand," said the voice. Something moved between two of the bookcases. A curtain pulled back and a Death strode into the room. He glanced around, and Suzie held her breath. The face looked around the room. She gasped when she recognized him. Couldn't he see her? The Death pulled his robe close and hid under his black hood.

Headmaster Sindril turned and left the house.

Suzie didn't move for what felt like an hour. She stayed behind the bookcase, looking through the wall into the open room. She expected Sindril to return, or someone to come from the curtain. If they came now, she'd be trapped. She had to get out before they found her.

After she couldn't wait any more, Suzie pulled the red book. The bookcase slid open and she sprinted through the wall, out the front door, and toward the College.

She skirted the woods, still running. Fear ebbed into the back of her mind, but was it the albino or her fear of being found? Should she be afraid? Sindril had offered to help her.

Panting, she passed the dark, twisted trees. She saw the Ring of Scythes far in the distance. Yes, Sindril had offered to help her, but Sindril had been acting as Headmaster in the College. The man she had watched was terrified. He had been wearing a black robe, probably hiding, hoping people didn't recognize him. Suzie leapt from theory to theory, her mind filled with dark plots and conspiracies. What was going on?

She reached the Ring of Scythes and kept running.

Wham!

Suzie flew backward through the air. She landed hard, rolling on the dirt. She got up and stared at the Ring. The scythes looked like they always did, enormous arches of metal surrounding the College. She walked to the ring and put her hand out. Her fingers halted in mid-air.

The Ring of Scythes was shut. She was locked out of the College.

CHAPTER TEN

Suspicion

Suzie ran down the Ring, but an invisible wall sealed each archway. She remembered the villages, but wasn't sure which direction to walk. Finally, she started to yell.

"Hello? Can anyone hear me? I'm trapped out here."

She continued to yell off and on for several minutes before a tall man with bright green hair walked to the Ring.

"What are you doing outside?" he said.

"Please, sir," she said. "I walked out for some air. When I tried to get back, the Ring had shut."

"It's a drill," said the man. His eyes glowed like fire. He must be a 'Mental. "It'll be over tomorrow. Come back then."

"I don't want to be here all night," said Suzie. "Please, can you send someone for help?" She pictured Sindril sneaking out of the strange house. Had he locked the Ring, afraid people might follow him?

"I'm only a servant," said the 'Mental.

"My housemates Billy and Jason, can you get them? I live in Eagle Two, room six."

The 'Mental shrugged and stared at her.

"Please, sir, get them for me."

"You are a Death," he said. "I am yours to command." He nodded and walked away.

Suzie didn't understand, but didn't care either. She hoped the 'Mental brought Billy back. This was Luc's fault. She hated the fat bully more than ever.

She sat down on the grass outside the Ring, looking up at the stone mounds and massive mountainous towers of the College. The forest stood far too close for comfort; the nearest trees grew less than twenty yards away. She suspected the albino was lurking in the forest, still waiting for her.

The sun passed behind a cloud, darkening the sky. It must be about three or four in the afternoon. A raven cawed high above her, swooping over the Ring of Scythes and toward the towers of the College. Shafts of sunlight slipped out from the cloud behind her, reaching down toward the trees. Rays of light lit up the bottom of West Tower, while the top grew dark. A cool breeze blew from the forest.

"Hey, it's the girl," shouted a familiar voice.

She looked up.

Frenchie stood on the other side of the Ring with some of his friends. She didn't see Luc.

"What're you doing?" taunted Frenchie.

"I wanted some air," she mumbled. She refused to mention Luc.

"They don't open the Ring 'til tomorrow," he said. "And it's supposed to get nice and cold tonight."

"If the wolves don't get her," laughed another Death.

"That's right," said Frenchie, "you've got more to worry about than the cold, with the forest lurking right behind you."

Luc had told them. He must have. Yet she refused to give in to their taunting.

"I'm stronger than I look," she replied.

"She didn't seem strong at the field," said another Death. Frenchie turned and glared at him.

"Let's get out of here," he said, walking off. The try-outs must still be a sensitive subject.

As they left her view, Jason ran up to the Ring.

"Suzie," he said. "You okay?"

"Yeah," she said. "But I'm stuck out here."

"We know," said Jason. "What're you doing outside of the Ring?"

"Never mind that, can you get me in?"

"Billy's talking to Headmaster Sindril now."

Sindril again.

"Did the 'Mental tell you I was here?"

"Yeah, I was checking on you before our final classes. I found Billy and told him. He told me to come here and went to find Sindril."

"Well, thanks, Jason."

"What *are* you doing?"

"I'll tell you on the other side," she said.

She heard a commotion behind Jason and watched a large group of Deaths walking toward the Ring. Headmaster Sindril, in his purple robe, walked at the front of the crowd, followed by Billy. Sindril held out a scythe with a golden blade and lowered it slowly between the blades of the outer Ring. The air shimmered. He held the golden scythe in place.

"Susan, my dear, you may come in now." He extended an arm through the ring and grinned at her.

Suzie walked through the Ring. Sindril pulled the golden scythe back and the air shimmered again. The way must have resealed.

"My dear," he asked through his grin, "What in the world were you doing outside of the Ring during a drill?"

The sight of him made her sick. Had he seen her in the house? Had he guessed someone was there and closed the Ring? Did he want to kill her? What was going on?

"I needed some fresh air. I wasn't feeling well today."

"I'm sorry to hear that," said Sindril. His smile oozed like slime. He reminded Suzie of a snake.

"We'll take her home," said Billy. He put a hand on her shoulder, leading her through the crowd.

"Lucky for you, I was able to open the Ring," said Sindril behind her back.

"Thank you, sir," said Billy, turning over his shoulder.

"All right, the rest of you get back to class, this isn't a show," snapped Sindril. "And Susan…" He moved fast for someone his age. He leaned over her. "Do tell me if there's anything else I can do to help you. The first female Death in a million years, and the first time we've needed to open a sealed Ring, even partially, in as long as I can remember. Times are surely changing."

Sindril spun on his heels and walked away, his purple robe flapping behind him.

"Let's go home," whispered Suzie. "I have a lot to tell you guys."

* * * *

Jason sat at the kitchen table, watching Suzie. She finished her gorger and looked up.

"Took me a while to find him," said Billy, leading Frank into the room. Suzie hadn't told them anything yet; Frank was her friend. It didn't seem right to exclude him.

"Billy told me you were outside the Ring," said Frank. "I guessed you were skipping some classes 'cause of what happened at try-outs. You okay?"

"I'm fine now," said Suzie. She glanced at the door behind Frank. Luc wouldn't come back, not now. Would he?

"What happened?" said Billy. "Don't tell me you were getting some air."

"No," said Suzie. "I was attacked." She took a deep breath.

"Attacked?" asked Billy.

"After you guys left, Luc knocked at the door. He blamed me for embarrassing his brother."

"Frenchie embarrassed himself," said Frank.

"He had a man with him, I'm pretty sure he was a 'Mental. An albino, with white skin and red eyes." She shuddered. "He terrified me."

"What did he do?" asked Jason.

"I'm not sure exactly. Wolves and snakes appeared, and I ran from them. He seemed to turn on Luc at one point, right outside the Ring of Scythes. He chased me into the forest, and I felt terror. He didn't do anything. I just had to get away. I've never been more afraid in my life."

"A fearmonger," whispered Frank.

"A what?" asked Billy.

"Fearmongers," said Frank, "are 'Mentals who manipulate fear. They were killed off a long time ago. We learned about them in class. Apparently there's one still around."

"And Luc just happened to find this fearmonger 'Mental?" asked Billy.

"I suppose," said Frank. "If he did, he was trying to scare her out of the Ring. He probably wanted to get her outside the Ring before the drill."

"And he succeeded," added Billy. "She was outside, but we didn't find out about the drill until breakfast at the Hall. Did Luc plan this?"

"I didn't believe any fearmongers were left," said Frank. "Not any more. What happened to him? How did you get away?"

"I kept running." She hesitated. She had to tell them about Sindril but didn't want to reveal that she'd found the old library. These were her friends, but they were still boys. She was still alone, and she needed a place to get away. However, if Sindril had been in the house, how could she go back?

"Suzie," said Jason, putting a hand on her arm. "You can trust us."

Sindril hadn't been in the library, only in the house. The library would still be hidden. Still, her place was vulnerable.

"Suzie?" asked Billy. "It's okay if you don't want to talk. You're a girl, and the only one. I can only imagine what they might do. If this albino hurt you, or touched you in any way—"

"No," she said. "It wasn't like that. I got away from the albino. I found an abandoned house past the forest. I hid." She paused again.

"And?" asked Jason.

"Take your time," said Frank.

"A man was talking, but he didn't see me. He was doing something secretive. He kept talking to someone but I didn't see anyone else. He asked if he needed *the girl* alive. I think he wanted to kill me."

"Who was it? Did you recognize them?" asked Billy.

"Yes," said Suzie. "Headmaster Sindril."

She expected them to look surprised, but no one moved.

"Okay," said Jason, "the headmaster was in the house. I'm sure he goes out of the College at times."

"You don't understand," she said. "He didn't want to be caught. He was in a black robe, not his usual purple robe. And the conversation he was having…he was plotting something."

"If he was in black, are you sure it was him?" asked Frank.

"I saw his face clearly. It was him."

"You saw him, but he didn't see you?" asked Jason.

"Are you sure it wasn't part of the fearmonger's attack?" asked Frank.

"I'm sure. The albino terrified me, but didn't follow me out of the forest. Since the College closed up, he's probably still in the trees. No, I definitely saw Sindril, I'm completely sure. Trust me. He was hiding something secret, something important. He definitely has some plan, and it involves me."

"Something about you?" asked Jason.

Suzie shrugged.

"This doesn't make sense," said Billy.

"Did anything else happen?" asked Frank.

"No. I hid in the house until he left. I waited for a long time, before running toward the College. I didn't realize the Ring would be shut."

"I don't remember when the drill began," said Billy. "But Sindril wouldn't be outside when it started."

"If she waited long enough, he could have come back and sealed the Ring of Scythes," said Jason. He sounded skeptical.

"When he let me in, I believed he had sealed the Ring on purpose, in case anyone had followed him."

"No," said Billy. "They seal the Ring a few times a year, to make sure it works, and protect us if the Dragons ever attack."

"Or 'Mentals," muttered Frank. "Dragons would fly over."

"Sindril himself announced the drill," said Billy. "In the Hall this morning, he told us to stay within the Ring today."

"But maybe…" Suzie paused. "Maybe he scheduled the drill thinking no one would catch him. Maybe he planned to visit that house and didn't want anyone else to follow him."

"That's a big stretch," said Billy. "We don't have any evidence to support that. Honestly, even if it was him, who's to say he's planning anything bad?"

"Why wouldn't he wear his purple robe?" asked Suzie. "Why meet someone in an abandoned house?"

"Maybe it wasn't anyone," said Frank. "If you did encounter a fearmonger, it could easily have been in your head. It's nothing to be ashamed of, they're terrifying. At least, I've heard they are."

"Is it possible?" asked Billy. "Is it even *possible*? Can Sindril be involved in some terrible plot involving Suzie?"

Frank, Billy, and Jason looked at each other. She could tell they didn't believe her.

"It's possible," said Frank. "But it's more likely the fearmonger."

Was her imagination going crazy? Could the albino have followed her out of the woods? No, they were wrong, she'd seen Sindril. The announcement of the drill and his appearance in the abandoned house; this was not a coincidence. Or was it? Was she looking for something to keep her mind off her loneliness, her complete isolation? Was the mystery real or imagined?

"No," she said at last. "It wasn't the albino. Something is going on with Sindril, and I'm going to find out what."

Billy shrugged. "We'll help," he said. "We are your friends."

Frank and Jason nodded.

Suzie smiled, but they still didn't believe her. She wasn't sure she believed herself anymore.

CHAPTER ELEVEN

Mysteries

The test in Applications came far too soon. Suzie's weekend had been a blur. While working on assignments for History and Theory, she'd been obsessed with thoughts of Sindril and her secret library. She needed proof and wanted to learn more about what he'd been doing. She hadn't been back yet, though Frank had gone into the forest on Saturday.

"The fearmonger won't bother anyone anymore," he'd said after returning. His face was ashen, and he spoke with finality in his voice. She didn't ask what had happened, and he didn't volunteer to tell.

"Line up," shouted Hann, snapping her back to the present. Suzie stepped behind Frank and Billy. They'd get one shot to demonstrate their skill with the beginner's blade. She'd missed an entire day of practicing, but Billy had snuck her into the room over the weekend. A few other first years had the same idea, though thankfully Frenchie and his brother Luc hadn't been around.

Sam, a second-year Death and friend of Frenchie's, went first. He took the beginner's blade confidently, swung the scythe downward, and slit the air. A green swath of light trailed the blade, vanishing like steam on a cool day.

"Good," said Hann. He marked something on a clipboard. "Next."

One after another they went. Every second and third-year student created a green light, as did most of the first years. Luc stepped up.

Since the attack, he'd been quieter around her, but she sensed he was biding his time. He swung and a green light appeared, fading like vapor.

"Good," said Hann.

Billy and Frank went soon after, both making the green light appear.

"Next," said Hann.

Suzie walked forward. Frank handed her the blade.

"You'll be fine," he whispered. "Don't over think. Hands apart."

Suzie grasped the long handle. Her right hand slipped on her own sweat. The beginner's blade was light, but the weight was deceptive. She sensed the familiar tingle as the blade touched the air.

A blade with only a tiny fraction of mortamant imbued in its metal, yet a blade quivering with life. A blade that understood her strengths and fears. A blade similar to the blade that had bit into her thigh on the boskery field. The blade would determine if she passed or failed.

She'd practiced over the weekend, even when the class was closed. Billy had worked with her. She'd never succeeded. She'd never created a green light.

She raised her arms and adjusted her grip on the handle. She swung down. The blade sliced the air. The tingle on the handle intensified and she held her breath. The metal pushed its way downward, guiding but still resisting her. The smug metal that realized she'd fail.

The scythe finished its arc. No light emerged.

"What I'd expect from a girl," said Hann. "Next."

"I'm not the only one who failed," she said. "You don't have to be sexist."

Hann looked up, surprised. Suzie was the only Death who'd spoken back to him. The class stared at her.

"Give the blade to Nicholas," said Hann.

"Just because I'm a girl, doesn't mean you have to treat me differently."

"That is more than enough. I will talk to you after class, Ms. Sarnio. Now give the blade to Nicholas."

Suzie handed over the scythe. She'd probably gone too far, but so what? She was tired of second-class treatment. She hadn't asked to be in this world, and she was doing her best.

Class progressed in silence. Everyone after her passed.

"You were right," whispered Frank when the class ended. "If he tries to give you grief, stay strong."

Suzie walked to Hann's desk at the front of the room. The senior Death waited for the rest of the class to leave before frowning at Suzie.

"Do you have anything to say?" he asked.

She shook her head.

"I don't like being challenged in class," he said. Suzie met his eyes, refusing to look away or apologize. Hann sighed.

"I'm sure the class has been difficult," he said after a moment. "Your partners, Frank and Billy, are they helping you?"

"They're helping me a lot."

"But they are your friends, aren't they?" asked Hann. "Perhaps they've been too soft on you. Maybe you'd do better working in another group."

"Sir," she said. "I don't want to work with another group. Please."

"Are you sorry for what you said in class?"

She hesitated. "No," she said.

He smiled. "I thought not. I will let you continue with your friends, provided you pass the next test, which will be in a month."

"Sir?"

"I'll see you tomorrow, Suzie."

"I'll do better next time," she said.

"I'm sure you will."

She walked away, puzzled. Glancing back, she saw Hann sigh as he closed the door behind her.

Why had Hann forgiven her? It was another mystery to unravel. Didn't she have enough? She was done for the day, but didn't head for Eagle Two. She needed more time to figure things out. She wanted to go to her secret library, but wasn't sure she was ready yet. The last time had been stressful, and too many questions still lingered.

She stumbled down the hall without looking, turning into one of the few bathrooms assigned to her. She walked past the urinals and tripped over a string. She looked down, smelling something strange. A burning smell hovered in the air.

One of the stalls exploded in front of her, throwing pieces of plaster across the floor. Water spread out from the broken toilet, covering her feet. She frowned and left.

"One of the toilets exploded," she told a 'Mental with long pink hair.

"I'll fix it," he said in a high voice.

"Thank you," said Suzie. She looked at the 'Mental. Something about him was odd. His features were fair.

"Excuse me," she asked.

The pink-haired 'Mental turned.

"I'm sorry to ask, but—"

"Yes?"

"Are you female?"

"No," he said. "It's the pink hair, I get asked sometimes, but they don't let girls inside the College."

"Other than me, you mean?"

"Yes, miss. I'm sorry, let me fix the toilet. You probably want to change." He nodded at her pants, which were soaked from the calf down.

"Yes, of course," she said. She nodded as he left.

No females worked in the College. She remembered learning about female 'Mentals. Where were they? Another mystery. Her head hurt.

East Tower loomed on the far side of campus; a pair of windows near the top glowed like eyes looking down the face of a dark, gnarled giant. She passed the Examination Room, the cube of perfect black: unlit and unwelcoming amid the stone mounds of the College. Every Death here older than the first years had entered the room and failed. What sort of test awaited her? Another mystery. She kept walking.

Her own world seemed far away. Like a different life. Like a dream.

No, this wasn't a dream, and she *would* get home.

Sindril, the secret library, even the 'Mentals didn't matter. In the end, what truly mattered was passing the test and getting home.

"You *will* get home."

Suzie looked around in a panic but no one was around. The wall beneath her heated up and suddenly the sky above melted into crimson light.

Fire. She was on fire.

He's found me. The albino. Frank didn't deal with him at all.

Pieces of the burning sky fell around her, as the world collapsed. Two green eyes appeared, staring at her.

"No, Suzie. I'm not going to hurt you."

The words burned into her mind, searing her flesh. She cried out and fell. She smashed into the ground hard, and the fire vanished. It was evening, the sky was dark overhead. She reached her hands to the wall behind her.

"Stay strong," a voice whispered. Another faint flash of green eyes emerged, but they disappeared.

"Wait," she said aloud. "Who are you?"

No response.

Great. Another mystery.

Suzie stood up and headed home to Eagle Two. She wouldn't share this one with the others. Like the library, this would be a secret.

* * * *

"What happened with Hann?" asked Frank. He and Billy were waiting for her in the kitchen. Jason was out, probably at the Hall.

"I'm not sure," she said. "He asked me to apologize, said he doesn't like to be challenged."

"Okay," said Billy, "you apologized."

"No, I didn't."

"What? What do you mean?" asked Billy.

"I didn't apologize. I didn't do anything wrong. I wasn't going to lie and say I was sorry. If he looked bad, he made himself look bad, like Frenchie at try-outs."

"But Hann's a teacher," said Billy.

"No, she's right," said Frank. "He was sexist, and she called him out. Good for you."

"What happened when you didn't apologize?" asked Billy.

"That was the weird thing. He let me go. He threatened to take me off of your group, but he didn't."

"Strange," said Frank. "I wonder why he backed down."

"He's not the only sexist," she said. "Someone blew up a toilet in one of my bathrooms."

"What?"

"Yeah, I headed to the bathroom after dealing with Hann, tripped on a string, and boom. I soaked my feet, but walked it off."

"Is that why it took you this long to get back?" asked Billy.

"Yeah." She didn't mention the vision. She seemed to keep having them, and always with sensations of fire. They didn't believe her about Sindril, why should they believe her about anything?

"What'd you do about it?" asked Frank.

"I told a 'Mental. I learned there are female 'Mentals, but they're not allowed on campus."

"Deaths are afraid of girls," said Frank. "Of course they wouldn't let female 'Mentals in."

"No one here is afraid of me."

"Oh no?" asked Frank. "Why do they keep teasing you? Why did they blow up a toilet? Why'd Frenchie attack you at try-outs? Or Luc with the fearmonger? Why did Hann snap at you during the test? They're all afraid of you."

"Don't be ridiculous," she said. "They hate me because I'm different."

"Yeah, that's part of the issue," said Frank, "but you're the first female Death since Lovethar, and we learned how that ended up. They fear what you'll do to this world. You're a loose end, a mystery they don't want to solve."

Suzie laughed. "Me, a mystery? What's mysterious about one girl?"

"To a world of boys and men," said Frank, "you're the biggest mystery they've ever dreamt of."

"I'm not sure I agree with him," said Billy. "But you are definitely different. Many Deaths are nervous about you. They haven't met a girl since they left the Living World. To them you're probably a reminder that they're stuck here. Plus, we've been taught Deaths are great the way we are, and there aren't female Deaths."

"Until now," said Frank. "Suzie, it's amazing you stood up to Hann, Frenchie, and Luc. Don't you understand, you're starting to change things?"

"I don't want to change things. I want to get through this stupid year and go home. My life feels like it was long ago, and far away. At times…"

"What?" asked Billy.

"At times, I can't tell which world is real anymore." She sat down at the table and put her head in her hands.

"Let's get you some dinner," said Frank.

* * * *

"Hello Su-su-su-Suzie."

A week had passed since Hann's test. The visions had stopped, though she often woke in a sweat remembering dreams of fire and green eyes. She still hadn't been back to the library and was itching to go. Even if Sindril was in the house, what would that hurt? Maybe she'd discover what he was plotting.

"Hi, Cronk," she said, putting down her bag. Jason smiled as they sat down. Cronk brought her latest project to her desk.

"I lo-lo-lo-loved your l-l-last d-d-d-drawing." Cronk pointed to the picture, now hanging on one of the walls. A solitary girl surrounded by black, her picture of loneliness.

"Thanks," said Suzie, "but I've moved past it." She looked at Jason, who smiled again.

She dabbed her paintbrush into colors and started to paint. The brush flowed against the paper, swirling into random patterns. She wasn't painting anything in particular; the final piece would be a mystery. She let the paintbrush dance across the page, following the ever-shifting patterns of her mind. This world was a mystery, filled with mysteries, and according to Frank, she was the biggest mystery of all.

She continued to paint, letting her mind wander. The class ended, and she looked at what she had painted. Men in robes held scythes, flames flickered on the bottom of the page, and a man wore a purple robe. Colors swirled around the figures, leaping from the flames toward the top of her paper. In one corner, she had dropped two splotches of green paint. The splotches stared at her, like the green eyes from her visions.

"L-l-l-looking quite n-n-nice."

"Thanks," said Suzie. She nodded to Jason and continued through her day.

Applications was tense. She expected Hann to pull her out of Frank and Billy's group, but he said nothing to her. They practiced more with the beginners' blades, but Suzie was still unable to produce the green light.

After class, she pretended to head toward the bathroom. Instead, she walked a long, winding route through the College. She didn't want anyone to follow her. Slowly, she made her way toward the Ring of Scythes.

She passed the Examination Room and turned down an alley. The rocky mounds and mountainous towers of the College reminded her of canyons and caves. Ribbons of red, maroon, yellow, beige, and other earth tones snaked around her, forming the rough sandstone walls. Narrow windows in the stone opened on either side of the alley, and she walked quickly past them. She turned into a courtyard of weeds and cobblestones, surrounded by uneven rock walls and immense arched windows. She walked through a doorway, around a corner, and came to the Ring.

The forest stretched on the other side of the Ring, only a few yards from the College. The road circled the Ring, branching toward the trees. She reached out her hand, and it passed through. She glanced around but only a handful of birds watched her. She stepped through and broke into a run.

Not glancing at the tangled trunks of the forest, Suzie ran down the road. She turned back but no one was following her. She rounded a bend and the College vanished behind the trees, but she continued. The road split, and she followed the left fork. Then she left the road and walked into the trees near the edge of the forest.

She stopped. A hill covered most of the house, and foliage covered the rest, making the house invisible from the road. She had first encountered the house from its exposed side, which faced the heart of the forest. She circled around a hill, but paused. Was Sindril here? Had he ever been here? She had to find out. She stood behind a tree and counted to ten. She walked to the door and waited again. Silence. She pushed the door open and held her breath.

The house was empty. The floor was dusty, but she couldn't seem to make out any footprints. She walked around the room slowly. Three other bookcases like the one she'd gone behind stood around the room, but did not move when she tugged on them.

She held her breath as each beat of her heart seemed to thunder loud enough for anyone to hear. The slightest sound: a breath, a footstep, and she'd run. Nothing. She walked the room again.

A second room, one she hadn't entered yet, stood to the side, behind a curtain. Whoever Sindril had spoken to sat here. A worn table sat in one corner, covered in dust. She circled the room, pressing on the walls. The dust on top of the table was smudged. She saw no other exits, and no footprints.

She sighed. She had no proof, and if she brought her friends here, they'd be even less likely to believe her. She considered. It *had* been Sindril, and he *had* mentioned her. She was sure, but doubted it nonetheless.

Had it truly happened? Maybe the albino had affected her mind. Maybe Sindril had never been here. After all, the Ring of Scythes had been sealed.

Suzie circled the room again. She gave up, walking to the bookcase. If Sindril had never been here, then this place truly was safe and was hers alone. She pulled the red book, and the bookcase swung open. White light flowers came to life in the stairway, casting a dim glow behind the bookcase. She walked down the steps and kept going until she reached the library.

Nothing had changed, which was a relief. She'd half wondered if the books would be gone, or if someone else would have come in, but that was ridiculous. What was happening to her? She'd been focused on getting through the year and now was caught up in a maze of conflicting thoughts.

She picked up one of the books and started flipping through. Names she didn't recognize. Words like *Donkari.* Nonsense. Pictures that meant nothing. She tossed the book aside and picked up a second. She needed answers, anything.

She read for about an hour, flipping through book after book. Nothing seemed interesting until she came to a leather-bound green volume. She leafed through its yellowed pages until she came to a full-page drawing of a key. Filigree and jewels covered its handle. She recognized the same key she'd found drawn on the stones, and the same key she'd drawn on her own painting. Beneath the drawing, someone had written "Dragon Key."

Dragon Key? The next few pages in the book were torn out. She rubbed her finger on the torn edges and looked farther. The next page talked of flames and war. She skimmed the description of bloodshed until she came to a familiar name: Lovethar. She read on.

"I can't believe what they've done," she read. "They've taken him, they've taken him away. Lovethar will not forgive them, she will join the Dragons. And what do they intend to do with it now?"

Suzie turned the page again. She found another picture, this one of Lovethar herself, clutching a package to her chest. Flames surrounded her with Deaths on one side and Dragons on the other. She turned to the last page of the book and frowned. The same image, only someone had hand-drawn something above Lovethar's head: an ornate key.

Now Suzie had another mystery. She sighed.

This mystery didn't matter to her now. It had been long ago. She wasn't Lovethar. However, it was strange. Mystery surrounded the only other female Death.

Suzie took the book and left the library. She couldn't deal with these mysteries by herself. She closed the bookcase behind her and walked through the empty house, toward the door.

A pair of green eyes watched her leave.

CHAPTER TWELVE

Observing

"Prepare for your first foray," announced Hann.

Three weeks had passed since Suzie's failed Applications test. She'd been to the library four more times, but hadn't found a trace of Sindril. She was starting to lose confidence in herself, though she was growing more curious about the Dragon Key. Every time she found it mentioned in a book, she found torn pages and often hand-drawn additions. Lovethar's name was almost always nearby as well. More than a dozen books mentioned the key; many of them now sat in the corner of her closet. She perused them every chance she got, but the mystery had only deepened. She still hadn't shown anyone else the library, and though Frank and Billy had pledged to help her, they'd been busy with boskery.

"Miss Sarnio, are you listening?" snapped Hann.

"Yes, sir." She stopped her thoughts from drifting and focused, her heart beating faster in anticipation.

"This isn't some joyride. That goes for all of you. This is dangerous work. First years will do *nothing*. I repeat: *nothing* while in the Mortal World. You will observe. You will not even carry a scythe this time."

Suzie was glad they wouldn't get scythes. She'd gotten to the point where she could produce a green flash. The secret had been to let the scythe fall, hardly swinging. The green appeared if she let the blade do the work. However, her flashes always seemed small, as if the scythe was humoring her.

"We travel in our teams. Full Deaths work alone, and juniors in squads of two, but you students, you are going in your group of three. Luc, what does that mean?"

"We have to be careful not to be seen."

"Exactly," said Hann. "This is a high-risk excursion, but a necessary one. We will begin regular forays into the mortal world soon. We need to practice Reaping. For now, I am designating one student in each group to Reap, one to be a lookout, and the first years... Susan, what will first years do?"

"Observe."

Suzie knew how to observe. She'd been watching the other Deaths for a month. She'd been watching Luc and Frenchie torment her in hundreds of small ways. Nothing like the albino, thank God. Still, plenty of things had come up: from crude signs drawn on the bathroom wall to a snake left in her bed. They'd never leave her alone.

"Correct," said Hann. "If I discover you've even touched a scythe, you will be in bigger trouble than you can imagine. I can even guarantee that you fail your Final Test, the one in the Examination Room."

Suzie's eyes grew wide. This was the first real threat Hann had made, the first she'd heard from a teacher. She had to pass the test, or she'd be stuck in this world forever.

"You appear scared, Miss Sarnio," said Hann, seeming to sense her thoughts. "Don't worry, you only have to observe. All right, places everyone."

Suzie stepped toward Billy, who held a large scythe. This was no beginner's blade. Even a foot away, she felt power coursing through the sleek black handle and energy rippling through its blade. The light split at the point of the sharp blade, it looked like the air itself would tear. Frank smiled at her, he would be lookout.

"Reapers raise your blades and ready yourself."

Billy grasped the handle in both hands and readied himself. Frank snapped a cord to Billy's waist, to Suzie's, and finally snapped himself on, tethering the three of them together. Power flowed through the tether, bouncing around her and away from the scythe.

"After delivery, return here immediately. You have one hour. Good luck," said Hann. "Go."

Billy raised the scythe. The tether tightened and the blade fell. The world tore open as light and sound screamed into a tunnel of pain. Suzie's waist pulled her through the portal as the tether hurried to keep up. Darkness and colors bled into each other. The familiar smell of strawberries, present everywhere in the World of the Dead, seemed to fester and boil, exploding into sour fire around her. Everything vanished.

A pair of green eyes appeared, wreathed in a ring of flame.

"You are strong," said a voice. It was strange, and yet somehow familiar.

The eyes vanished.

Reds, yellows, hots, colds. Sensations blended and faded. Suzie's head spun in a whirlwind of sensation. Two suns appeared for an instant, and she watched the building where she'd signed the contract. Athanasius, the first 'Mental she'd met, seemed to smile at her, and then was gone.

Stars burned her.

Oceans drowned her.

Clouds suffocated her.

Noise deafened her.

The tether slackened. She opened her eyes.

Billy still held the scythe; the blade dripped with tiny beads of white light.

"You okay?" asked Frank, turning.

"Yeah," she said. "Are we there?"

"Yes," said Frank. "We're in the Mortal World. The scythe will never bring you anywhere near anyone you ever met here. That's one of the rules, but we're here. This is the closest to home most of us will ever get." His voice trailed off, and he looked away. Suzie patted his shoulder. She could imagine his pain.

"We're not here to talk," said Billy. "The target will be here in a minute."

"The scythe tells you the target as you cross the portal," explained Frank.

"They explained in Theory class," she said. "But it's still weird to be here."

She looked around. They stood in an alley, with gleams of starlight visible above them. Flies buzzed over a trash can, overflowing with pizza boxes. A cool breeze blew candy wrappers across the pavement, to graffiti-covered walls. Behind her, a cement building rose, with barred windows. In front of them, a larger street met the alley, with part of a neon sign glowing around the corner. It smelled like urine.

She heard shouts in Spanish from a dilapidated cement building with iron bars. More shouts and someone pleading. Then a gunshot and the shouts moved away from them.

A young girl staggered into the alley. Suzie was about to speak, but Frank shook his head.

The girl fell onto her face, a pool of blood leaking out from under her. In the distance, Suzie heard another gunshot.

"We have to help her," said Suzie.

"It's too late," said Frank.

The girl lay motionless. Time seemed to stop. Suzie had never witnessed someone's death. Who was this girl? Who had shot her?

Even as the questions started to form in her mind, the girl sat up and stared at them. Suzie started to move, but Frank grabbed her arm, holding her.

"Where am I?" said the girl.

She was sitting up, but she was also laying face first on the ground. The sitting girl looked at Billy with terrified eyes and struggled to her feet. Suzie realized they were each wearing black robes; even with their training badges, they must look frightening. Billy still held the scythe.

"Is this a joke?" said the girl. "I'm not dead—"

"You are," said Billy.

The standing girl had no gunshot wound in her chest. Her dress seemed to shine as she moved a step away. She never looked down at her own body, or the blood continuing to run.

"Who are you three?" asked the girl.

"We're in training," said Billy. Suzie admired how calm his voice was. He was cool and collected, while she wanted to yell.

The girl took another step back and tripped on something. She tried to get up again but Billy held up a hand.

"Please," he said. "Allow me."

He raised the scythe and let it fall. The girl screamed, and Suzie screamed as well.

The girl stood up again and looked at her body. Frank touched her hand, and Suzie stopped screaming.

"I'm dead," said the girl.

"I'm sorry," said Billy.

"And now?" said the girl.

"It's time to go," said Billy. "Hold my hand."

Billy grasped the girl's hand and raised the scythe, letting it fall in the opposite direction. Suzie jerked forward, pulled by the tether. Light and sound converged, this time screaming even louder. Tears flowed, time slipped, and worlds passed.

"You are strong, do not forget," said a voice. A pair of green eyes flashed.

Stars became twin suns. Suns became one. The familiar smell of strawberries returned. The tether slackened and she opened her eyes.

"Where are we?" asked Suzie. Nothing looked familiar. Behind them, a cliff face rose into the sky for thousands of feet. The stony surface was craggy but rose at a perfect right angle to the ground. The wall of stone stretched impossibly high, masking the sun. The cliffs stretched beyond the horizon in each direction. She'd never imagined anything this massive.

"The door to the Hereafter," said Frank. "This is where we bring the souls of the dead."

They stood on a narrow beach of sand and pebbles. The beach ran the length of the cliff face, going to the ends of her sight. On the other side of the beach, a great sea roared. The water flowed away from the beach, and about a hundred feet into the ocean, the water shot into the air.

A wall of water, taller than the cliff face, stretched across the waves. Water pounded in her ears, rushing skyward. The beach was the bottom of a chasm between sea and stone, a chasm reaching beyond her sight and extending to infinity.

In front of Billy, a stone bridge extended over the waves. An enormous metal door, thirty feet high, stood in the middle of the gushing wall of water.

"I'm not ready," said the dead girl. "I want to go back. Please."

"There is nothing else," said Billy. Sadness lingered in his eyes, but his voice was firm. "We will stay here. Cross the bridge and enter the door."

As he spoke, the metal door opened a crack. White light streamed from the other side.

"We don't even know her name," said Suzie.

"I'm Julia," said the girl. "Please, miss, I don't want to die."

"You already have," said Billy. "Don't make this any harder."

"Strawberries," said Julia. "I never dreamed Heaven would smell like strawberries."

"This isn't Heaven," said Billy.

"But I've been good, you don't mean it's—"

"No," said Billy. "This is nowhere. Go through that door, and you will get your answers. I don't know what will happen, but it's my job to bring you."

Julia took a deep breath and laughed.

"I guess I don't need to breathe anymore," she said.

"Habits die hard," said Billy. He gestured with the scythe. Its blade caught the reflection of the waves, glistening with an expectant air.

"What will happen to me?" said Julia.

"You're about to find out," he replied.

Julia nodded, stood straighter, and walked onto the stone bridge. The metal door opened another crack. She started to walk, but turned back and looked at Suzie. Tears flowed down both of their eyes.

"Thank you for asking my name," said Julia.

"Good luck," said Suzie.

"You too."

Julia turned and walked to the door. It opened, and the air around the bridge blurred. Suzie couldn't see anything. The blur faded and

Julia, the door, and even the bridge vanished. The wall of water pounded skyward without pause.

"Let's go," said Frank. "Only a few minutes left. Don't want to be late."

Billy nodded and raised the scythe again. It fell into a swirl of colors, and they were back in the classroom. The trip was over.

Frank unfastened her tether and Suzie sank to her knees. Billy handed the scythe to Hann.

"How'd she do?" he asked.

"She did well," said Frank. Suzie wiped the tears from her eyes. She wouldn't show weakness, not here.

Hann raised an eyebrow and walked to the next group.

"You okay?" whispered Billy.

"I shouldn't be upset," she said. "It was supposed to happen. It was too—"

"Too real," said Frank. "It's tough, seeing your first Reaping."

"I've never seen someone die before," she said. "We don't know anything about Julia, but she looked scared."

"Everyone dies," said Billy. "Our job isn't to get involved. I usually speak to them as little as I can."

"She's a human being," said Suzie, rising to her feet. "How can you be this callous? She was an innocent girl shot down in a street. Don't you care about what happened or who she was?"

"No," said Billy. "I don't. We have a job to do. Our job is transportation, and that's it. We don't need to make friends with the cargo."

"*Cargo?*" Suzie's face flushed.

"Billy's trying to keep his distance," said Frank. "Your empathy isn't bad, if you stay strong enough to keep doing your job."

"I care," said Suzie. "I care about people. I care about people dying and suddenly realizing they're dead. The least we can do is be nice to them and ask their name."

Luc stood and his brother nodded, pointing at her.

"Sounds like someone's getting a bit attached," he said. Luc walked over to her. The class quieted while even Hann looked on.

"This isn't a job for softies," he continued. "That's why girls ain't welcome."

"I'm not soft," said Suzie. For a moment, she worried that he'd continue, but Frenchie beckoned him away.

"Luc is right," said Hann. "This is not a career where your emotions can be involved. Reap your souls, and bring them to the Hereafter. Do not stop to chit chat." He looked at Suzie. "Do not worry about their fate. What happens will happen." He glanced at the hourglass on his desk. "Class is over; we will continue our discussion tomorrow."

* * * *

Suzie walked back to Eagle Two, trailing Frank and Billy.

"You did well," said Billy. "My first Reaping was a mess. Someone spotted us, and we had to flee before cutting the soul loose. They had to send in a real Death to clean up the mess. I'm glad Hann let me do this one, good way to start the year off."

"You've been to those places before?" she asked.

"If you mean the Mortal World and the door to the Hereafter; then of course I've been. Have to for the job."

"Is that what this is? A job? We're bringing souls of the dead to... well, to what?"

"Not our business," said Billy.

"Like it's not our business to ask why the 'Mentals are servants, or why there's never been a female Death for a million years?"

"Those are different," said Billy. "Back me up, Frank."

"There are some things no one should know. Like where exactly we're bringing these souls," said Frank. "I believe if we found out, it'd make what we do even harder."

"But what about the other things?" said Suzie. "I'm sick of questions, I want some answers. Why was Sindril in the old house? Why'd Hann let me off easy after challenging him? How did Luc find the albino? What's the real deal with the 'Mentals? Why are Deaths afraid of women? And why are the pages torn after any mention of the Dragon Key?"

"Wait, what?" interrupted Frank. "What was the last one?"

"I was only wondering."

"You've heard of the Key?" asked Frank.

"Sort of."

"What're you talking about?" asked Billy.

"Lower your voice," said Frank. "I'll tell you at home."

Billy paused for a moment before describing his last boskery practice with Frank. Suzie half-listened. They walked through the courtyard and into Eagle Two.

"All right, have a seat," said Frank. "Both of you."

"What's going on?" asked Billy.

"Suzie mentioned the Dragon Key. The last time I spoke to anyone about it, they disappeared for a month. When he showed up again, he couldn't remember where he'd been. His memory had a month-long gap in it. I've never spoken about this to anyone since."

"Wait, someone got kidnapped and you didn't tell anyone?" asked Billy. "Who?"

"You probably never met him," said Frank.

"Try me."

"Cibran Alfar," said Frank.

"Who?" asked Billy. "That's a weird name. I'd remember a Death named Cibran."

"He's not a Death."

"But you said—"

"Cibran is a 'Mental. He used to work here at the College but now he's returned home."

"You were friends with a 'Mental?" asked Suzie.

"I didn't say we were friends," said Frank. "But to be fair, yes, we shared some moments. He was kind to me when I first came to the College. I'm sure you can relate. You understand what it's like to be alone."

She nodded.

"This 'Mental," said Billy. "Cibran. You and he talked about the Dragon Key and he was kidnapped? This still doesn't add up."

"I wanted to go home," said Frank. "Like any first year, I didn't want to be here. I was complaining to Cibran about the contract and the Final Test. He told me about a third way to leave, a secret he'd overhead."

"The Dragon Key," said Suzie.

"Supposedly," said Frank. "He claimed he'd heard a few senior Deaths talking while he was planting some new lights. They got angry when they realized he'd heard them and cut off one his fingers as a warning."

"Wait, what?" exclaimed Billy. "Who would do that?"

"He didn't say. But he was missing his pinky finger on his left hand."

"No way," said Suzie. "I didn't suspect this was serious."

"Cibran took me aside. He made me swear never to tell a soul about the Dragon Key, and never to breathe a word. I promised. We were in the Great Hall, a service entrance near the back, and I think someone spotted us leaving. Cibran vanished the next day, and I didn't see him for a month. When he finally showed up, he was packing his stuff and getting ready to leave. I asked him what had happened, but he had no idea who I was."

"He didn't remember you?" asked Billy.

"He didn't remember anything. I asked if they'd taken him because of the Dragon Key, but he didn't have any idea what I was talking about. He told me to pick on someone else. I asked him about his missing finger and he told me a dog had bitten him as a child. That was the last I saw him. I'd almost forgotten about the Dragon Key, until you mentioned it, Suzie."

"Before he vanished," said Suzie. "Did he tell you anything else about the Key? You said it was a way to get back to the Mortal World. But how?"

"He'd heard the key was a way back," said Frank. "I'm not sure if he believed it himself, but the thing sure scared him. Whatever he heard was serious."

"And now you found out about the same thing?" asked Billy, looking at her. Suzie blushed.

"I found some books," she said. How could she hold out any longer? These were her friends, and she needed the help. Her time at the library hadn't answered anything, only created more mysteries. "Wait here," she said. "I'll be right back."

She went to her room and pulled out two of the books from the library.

"I have more in my room," she said, putting the books on the table.

"What are these?" asked Billy.

"I found them," she said. "Look. This page has a picture of the Dragon Key."

"Where did you get these?" asked Frank.

"Remember how I ran from the albino and saw Sindril, before the Scythe Ring closed on me?"

"Yeah," said Frank.

"You said it was Sindril," said Billy, "when you heard someone."

"It was Sindril. I also found an ancient library, hidden behind a bookcase. I found these books, and there are thousands more still in the library, probably tons about the Dragon Key."

"You found Sindril in that library?" asked Frank.

"No. I was coming back. I heard a voice and hid behind the bookcase. The wall hides it, almost like magic. You can't see behind the bookcase from the room. Sindril was talking to someone. He never noticed me. It's true, I swear."

"I believe you," said Frank.

"I don't know," said Billy.

"I can take you," said Suzie.

The door opened and Jason walked in.

"Hey guys, what's happening?" he asked. "How'd the trip go? I'm nervous about mine tomorrow."

"Sit down," said Suzie, "and promise you'll never mention to another soul what we tell you."

"What?"

"It's for your own good," said Frank.

"We're in this together now," said Suzie. "And this weekend, I'd like to take you somewhere."

"The library you found?" asked Frank.

She nodded. "It's not my secret to keep anymore. Whatever's going on, we're in this together."

"And what if Sindril shows up again?" asked Billy.

"I'm not afraid of him," she said, trying to sound brave.

CHAPTER THIRTEEN

Styxia

"This one's got nothing new," said Billy. He pulled another book from the pile. Jason was staring at a rock with images on it. Frank sat in the corner of the library, looking at scrolls.

"I've got another Dragon Key drawing," said Suzie. "But nothing new here either."

"We've been looking for over a month," said Jason. "When you first showed us the library, it was the coolest thing ever. But now—"

"It's like we're not looking for anything," said Billy. "We're just looking. Frank and I should get going soon, we have a game tomorrow."

"We're trying to figure out what the Dragon Key is," said Frank. "We need to find out if it's why Sindril was here, and what this has to do with Susan."

"It has nothing to do with her," exclaimed Billy. "I'm not even sure Sindril was ever here. We've been coming to the library as a group ever since you showed it to us, Suzie. But come on, what have we found?"

"Lots of drawings of the Dragon Key," added Jason. "We've seen lots of torn pages and many references to Lovethar."

"Yeah, and it's fascinating," said Billy. "It is. But it's almost Styxia. We've been spending too much time down here. Let's take a rest until the new year."

Frank sighed. "Maybe Billy's right," he said. "We have no real proof Sindril was ever here. And all we learned about the Key is that lots of people draw it."

"And tear out pages," said Suzie. "Don't give up now. Remember Cibran."

"And look how he turned out," said Jason. "I'm ready to go, at least until after the holiday."

The holiday. Suzie had been in the World of the Dead for three months. It was November back in Maryland. Had Mom and Dad given up hope of finding her? Did they assume she was dead? What about her friends? Suzie found she was starting to forget details. What did Joe used to say when she forgot something? She couldn't remember. The Living World, the home she was trying to get back to, was fading into a blur. It frightened her to imagine a day she might not even remember home. No, she'd get back. She'd go home to Mom and Dad after she passed the Final Test.

"Suzie, we should head out," said Billy.

"They're right," said Frank. "Things will quiet down after Styxia. Once we get through midterms, we can focus on these mysteries." He smiled.

Suzie wondered why they were here. The Key interested Frank, but they'd found nothing. Billy and Jason always came along, but not out of curiosity. Maybe they wanted to watch her fail. No, don't start thinking like that. They came because they're her friends.

"We'll come back after Styxia," she said. "Let's go."

Styxia. The one holiday on this world. Styxia commemorated the victory of the Deaths over the Dragons in the Great War. In History, they'd spent three weeks talking about the great revolt, when the Deaths won the right to transport souls of the dead to the Hereafter. The role had previously belonged to the Dragons. Lovethar tried to help the Dragons, turning on the Deaths, and her capture was the turning point in the War. Suzie had heard the story week after week, yet something always seemed false. She wasn't sure why.

"You'll like Styxia," said Frank. "We have a big parade and a banquet. Everyone gets dressed up."

"Not to mention the boskery finals," said Billy. "First time the Gray Knights have made the finals. The team that wins is guaranteed placement in the Upper College, which would help down the road."

"It'll be tough," said Frank. "Giant Tamers and Widow Makers should neutralize each other. It's the Dragon Seekers I'm worried about. Will you come Suzie?"

Suzie hadn't been to a single game, and now the final one was approaching. All four teams would face each other in the final boskery match, as part of the Styxia celebration. She'd been avoiding the field, ever since her embarrassment during try-outs. Billy had pressured her before every game. He and Frank would return from their games with the Gray Knights limping and bruised, but smiling. She'd said she'd go to several games already, yet always snuck off to the library instead.

"I'll be at the game," she said.

"Sure you will," muttered Billy.

"You should," said Jason. "The last game was amazing. You should've seen Frank jump over a guy to score. He looked like he was flying."

"I've been silly," she said. "Try-outs were a long time ago, and these are the finals. Besides, if this is required after first year, then someday I might have to play." No, she'd only be here a year.

She put the last book down and started up the winding stairs. The library looked nicer than when she'd first found it. Jason had swept the stairs and around the corners, getting dust off the flower lights. Billy and Frank had straightened up the books, organizing things into categories. This way they'd remember which books they'd already looked at.

"Quiet," whispered Frank, turning suddenly. He put a finger to his lips. The others froze on the stairway behind him.

"What—" Suzie started to say, but Frank shook his head. He walked to the bookcase and looked out, without opening it. Billy crept to his side.

"I understand," said a low voice. Suzie barely heard it through the wall. She couldn't see a thing. Frank and Billy watched, while Frank held out a hand, telling them to remain still. Time froze as Suzie tried not to breathe. A tiny piece of paint fell from the ceiling, flittering past

Jason's head and landing on the steps by her feet. Her heart beat loudly, pounding against her ribs. She expected Frank to tell her heart to be quiet. Minutes passed.

"He's gone," whispered Frank. "But let's wait a bit." Suzie ran her sweaty palms over her pants. Her heart thundered in her chest.

Billy nodded first, and Frank pushed the book. The bookcase swung open, and they walked into the house.

"Who was it?" asked Suzie. "Was it Sindril?"

"Couldn't tell," said Billy. "They had their back to us the whole time. The robe was black."

"Sindril was in a black robe when I saw him," she said.

"I never fully believed the story until now," said Billy.

"I believed you," said Frank, "but this was still big. We caught him, Suzie. He's planning something."

"We saw someone," said Billy. "They could've been doing anything."

"But now we have proof something is going on," said Jason. "Maybe we should stop looking for this Dragon Key stuff and start focusing on whoever was here. We shouldn't come back. We don't want to be caught."

"I want to learn what they're planning," said Suzie. "I showed you the other room, but can't figure out who else was in the house." She walked to the small side room again. It was empty except for the dusty table. A fresh smudge about the size of her fist sat in the dust on the center of the table.

"Maybe he's using some device," said Jason. "Maybe he puts something on the table and talks through it like a phone."

"Do you have phones in this world?" asked Suzie.

"No," said Billy. "They don't use electricity the way we do in the Living World."

"It could be something we don't understand," said Frank. "The Council has items and powers they hide from everyone else."

"That's a rumor," said Billy.

"You see that smudge," said Frank. "Open your eyes. Sindril was here, and he was talking to someone by putting something on the table.

He's trying to keep it secret. That's why he does it here, and in disguise."

"I gotta admit, it's sounding possible," said Jason. "He's up to something."

"Even if he is," said Billy. "What are we supposed to do? You want to risk him finding us here?"

She paused. It was risky, but she had to find the truth.

"We do nothing for now," said Suzie.

"Suzie," said Frank. "You're the one who—"

"I want to learn what's going on as much as you guys, but we need proof. We need to figure out what's happening and why."

"Why did you say we do nothing?"

"We've been looking through these books for weeks and have nothing. We find Sindril, or someone, at the house, okay. Who cares? I saw Sindril here and it didn't change anything. We need a new game plan, a new strategy, and you guys are right, for now we need to wait until things quiet down. Let's wait until after the holiday."

"Then what?" asked Jason. "How is waiting going to make a difference?"

"It might not," admitted Suzie. "But you guys were ready to give up a few minutes ago. This doesn't change things for me. Billy's comment bothered me the most."

"What did I say?"

"You said you never believed my story until now. If you didn't believe something was going on, why'd you keep coming here? Why'd any of you come here for that matter?"

"Suzie," said Frank. "Calm down, we're here to help you. We're your friends."

"Friends believe each other."

"Suzie, I'm sorry," said Billy. "I didn't mean—"

"We need a break," she said. "We need a break as a group. After Styxia, we'll reorganize and come up with a new plan. For now, let's remember what happened, and remember that sometimes even *girls* know what they're talking about."

"Hey," said Billy. "You're being completely unfair."

"Let's calm down," said Frank. "Suzie, I'm surprised at you. This was what we've been waiting for, and you flip out and get mad?"

Suzie walked out of the house and the others followed her.

"I'm not mad," she said. "I'm tired. Tired of coming up with nothing. I'm tired of being the only damned girl in this whole world. I'm tired of being alone." Tears were forming around her eyes, and she walked faster hoping they wouldn't notice. She didn't care what they thought now. They'd never believed her; they'd needed to see Sindril himself. Even now, Billy doubted it had been him. These were her friends? No. Who was she kidding? She didn't have any friends here.

As she hurried away, the ground gave way beneath her. The sky turned orange, and around her flames sprang to life. Her body burned as a pair of green eyes opened and stared at her.

"Go away," said Suzie. "Leave me alone."

"Suzie, you will never be alone," said the voice.

The flames grew stronger, and her skin started to melt away. Her flesh dissolved into a heap of steaming blood, and her bones collapsed into ash. Her soul stood alone. Stripped of her flesh, she was completely exposed: more naked than she'd ever dreamt possible. The green eyes looked at her. This must have been what Julia had felt like before her eyes. Yet she remained calm.

"Suzie, these are your friends," said the voice.

"Are they?"

"You are strong," said the voice. The flames turned from orange to blue. "But you cannot win this fight on your own. This is a battle far bigger than you realize."

The naked purity of Suzie's soul stood amid the blue flames, surrounded by doubt, but also by warmth.

"Who are you?" she asked.

"I am a friend as well," he said.

Blue flames swam upward, shooting toward the sky. They leaped higher and higher off the ground, running together. Behind her, the earth folded skyward into a cliff. The flames parted in a sliver of light, at the base of the waterfall.

She opened her eyes.

"Suzie?" Frank leaned over her, his face full of concern. "Are you all right?"

"Frank?"

"You were annoyed at Billy and stormed off, but collapsed right outside the house."

"How long was I out?"

"Only a minute," said Billy. "I'm sorry again."

"Me too," she said. "Sometimes I forget."

"Forget what?" asked Frank.

"That I'm not alone in this world."

* * * *

They hadn't spoken about Sindril. Frank and Billy were too busy with boskery, and Jason seemed to have other things on his mind. She'd bring it up after the holidays. Suzie didn't tell the others about her visions, but they seemed to be growing more frequent. Flames and green eyes haunted her sleep, though she no longer feared them while awake. In a way, the strange images comforted her. She glanced at the calendar on the kitchen wall. Friday, December 17th: the big day had arrived.

Red and white streamers now covered the rocky College walls. Teachers and students wore red ribbons on their robes, commemorating the blood shed in the Great War. Even the scythes in the Ring glimmered with blood-red light. A large mural, painted by Cronk's art classes, hung across the back of the Lower Hall. Suzie had painted Lovethar, while other Deaths had painted Deaths and Dragons around her. In Lovethar's hand, Suzie had painted a smudge. It represented the Dragon Key, though she'd told Cronk the smudge was a mistake.

"You ready?" asked Jason, straightening a red ribbon on the front of his robe. Suzie wore a similar ribbon and a second bright ribbon in her hair.

"I am," she said. A constant noise streamed in through the windows, as Deaths headed toward the Ring for the Styxia parade, marking the beginning of the three day holiday. The boskery match would be tomorrow, and the festivities would end at the feast on Sunday. School was suspended for the entire week, and that suited her fine. Forays into the Living World had also stopped, but Hann had announced a second trip immediately following the holidays. Combined with the stress of dealing with Luc and her teachers, as well as an upcoming report due in Theory, she was glad for this vacation.

She straightened her robe and glanced in the mirror. A Death looked back. A pretty Death with dark, curly hair, a red ribbon, freckles, and lipstick gazed at her from the mirror. She'd decided to look feminine. They had to wear their robes, but commemorating a day associated with the negative aspects of Lovethar had given her the idea to accent her femininity. It was a bold move, one Frank encouraged, though Billy disagreed.

"Let's go," she said. She walked out of Eagle Two, followed by Jason. Billy and Frank would meet them later, they were in the parade. They joined a crowd of Deaths young and old, wearing robes and red ribbons. Her thoughts turned to Billy and Frank.

Billy was the first friendly boy she'd met here. He was fun to live with, but lately she'd started to have mixed feelings. At the start of the year, he'd excited her. Maybe, she blushed to think, maybe she'd even had a slight crush. But then she'd seen Sindril the first time. He'd been the most hesitant to believe her. Every time she brought up the conspiracy, Frank had been supportive, while Billy had doubted. Frank, the boy who'd sought her out on his own to introduce himself. She liked Frank a lot. When they played boskery, would she be cheering Billy or Frank?

"This is insane," muttered Jason. The throng grew around them.

"I've never seen this many Deaths," she said.

"It's not only the College," he replied. "The nearby towns have emptied out. All of the Deaths are here for Styxia."

A loud horn blared through the strawberry-scented air. The sun shone high above them, casting light onto the crowd of black robes. A cool breeze blew overhead, but the air was warm from the assembled bodies. Strange how even Deaths are warm. As they came to the Ring of Scythes, Deaths leaned out of windows waving down. Someone threw a bucket of confetti, showering the crowd with scraps of red. Suzie wiped confetti from her shoulders.

A tall, portly Death shoved his way past Suzie and Jason, wiping sweat off his brow.

"They've moved the location," he muttered. "We have to hurry. Damn 'Mentals." He hurried away from them.

"Everyone's in such a rush," said Jason.

"That's odd," said Suzie. "He mentioned 'Mentals."

"And?"

"In this huge crowd I haven't spotted a single 'Mental."

"Suzie, listen to me. You over-think *everything*. I'm sure the 'Mentals are keeping out of the way of the crowds."

They came to a stop about three yards outside of the Ring of Scythes. The throng stopped, and a smaller crowd of Deaths stood a few yards farther away, with a path for the parade between them. The path surrounded the entire campus of the College, circling the Ring. The air sizzled with excitement. Behind them, the mountain of West Tower shot into the sky, draped in blood-red banners. The stone didn't appear festive, it looked frightening. The sun slipped behind a cloud. The horn blasted again and the noise grew to a roar.

"The parade's starting," said Jason. "Look." He pointed. A procession of Deaths marched around the crowd to their left, circling the Ring of Scythes. The parade would make a single large lap, starting and ending near West Tower, and she wouldn't be able to leave until the parade was over. This wasn't simple entertainment, but an obligation; a responsibility for every Death in the entire world. Suzie sighed.

The teachers marched first. Hann stood at the head of the line, followed by a group of Deaths Suzie didn't recognize. Dr. James smiled as he marched, arrogant like always. Professor Stevens struggled at the end of the group, leaning on Cronk as he walked. Cronk looked nervously at the crowd.

The four boskery teams marched next. The Dragon Seekers walked first. As they passed, Frenchie turned and spat at her.

"Hey," yelled Suzie.

Frenchie turned, but didn't stop marching.

"You're a jerk," she said. "And you're going to lose the match."

Jason put a hand on her arm.

Frenchie muttered something and continued to walk. A few of the other Dragon Seekers shot dirty looks her way, but the parade was moving. The Giant Tamers and Widow Makers followed. Suzie recognized some of the faces.

She cheered as the Gray Knights came into sight. Billy and Frank waved.

"Don't skip the game tomorrow," said Jason.

"I won't." She meant it.

After the boskery teams, two horse-driven carts rolled past. Green shapes sat on the carts, covered by red cloths.

"To symbolize the dead Dragons," said Jason, "killed in the War."

Behind the carts, a Death marched. His hood was down. He wore a blonde wig and bright red lipstick. At first, Suzie wanted to laugh, until she realized whom he represented. The Death pretending to be Lovethar turned to the crowd and screamed. Then he fell and burst into flames.

Suzie screamed, and even Jason looked shocked. The flames vanished and the Death stood up. A man wearing blue pants and no shirt extended his arm toward the fake Lovethar.

"It's a 'Mental," said Jason. "They used a theatrical effect to show the punishment of Lovethar."

The fake Lovethar stood, adjusted his wig, and waved to the crowd. The Deaths around him applauded, but Suzie only stared. He moved on, followed by the 'Mental. Two Deaths stood on either side of the 'Mental.

"He's chained," she whispered. "Jason, look at the 'Mental." The Deaths pulled on the chains as he walked past them.

"He made a Death catch fire. It's probably to keep him under control."

The fake Lovethar screamed again, replicating his act for the next part of the crowd. The 'Mental raised his hand. He paused right in front of Suzie, and a tear fell from his eye. The Deaths tugged on his chains. He continued to walk past them.

The next group was the most shocking.

A dozen 'Mentals marched next, each wearing blue pants and no shirt. They stared at the ground as they walked. Collars of iron chained their necks together. Black-robed Deaths held each chain.

"What the—" started Suzie.

"It's symbolic, like everything in the Parade," said Jason.

"Symbolic of *what*? The 'Mentals aren't slaves. They're servants."

"True," said Jason, shrugging, "maybe it has to do with the Great War."

The 'Mentals marched by. She recognized them; each had served her at least once in the hall.

"This is wrong," she said. What could she do? She started forward and raised her hand.

"Out of the way," shouted a voice. She jumped back into the crowd as a team of horses pulled the final cart in front of her. The Council of Twelve, each in their purple robes, waved to the crowd. Sindril glanced down at her as the cart passed by. He smiled, but his eyes glittered with menace. A thirteenth chair on the cart, taller than the others, was empty.

"Where's Lord Coran?" she asked, after the procession passed. They would have to wait until the parade circled the entire College, before they could leave.

"Haven't you heard?" asked Jason. "They say he's starting to fade."

"Fade?"

"He's been a Death for over ninety years."

Wait," said Susan, "he did look old, but—"

"Michael, in my Applications class, said a Death faded last year, one of his teachers. They had a big ceremony like he died, and even wrote his name on some monument near the Examination Room."

"I sort of remember Athanasius, the 'Mental who gave me my contract, mentioning this. He said it's better to fade. If you get killed, you stop."

"You *cease*," said Jason. "That's what they say. No one remembers, and you just vanish. If you fade, you go to…well, you've been to the wall of water and the big doors?"

"Yeah. They called it the Hereafter."

"Whatever it is," said Jason. "Maybe Deaths who *fade* end up on the other side of the doors. But Deaths who *cease*—"

"They stop. They never existed. Everyone forgets them."

"Right," said Jason.

Suzie realized something. "But wait a second," she said. "Lovethar was a Death. A true Death. And she was killed. They keep telling us how she was executed for treason, but we remember her. She didn't cease."

"Maybe she wasn't certified?"

"The pieces don't add up," said Suzie. "She was killed, but didn't cease. We'd forget her completely, unless—"

"Unless she faded," said Jason. "But the story about her—"

Some of the Deaths around them had grown quiet. Too quiet.

"Yeah, what a silly joke," laughed Suzie, suddenly nervous. "When we get home I'll tell you one of mine. It's about two Deaths who walk into a bar."

Jason gave her a strange look but stopped talking. This was dangerous. If Lovethar had been killed, no one would remember her, but everyone did. What happened a million years ago? Why was Lovethar's death played out repeatedly in history books, and even in the Styxia parade? What was the connection, if any, to the 'Mentals? Whatever was going on, she'd need to talk to the others in private. She remembered Frank's story about Cibran and shuddered.

"Are you cold?" asked Jason, who seemed happy to change the subject.

"It is a little chilly out here."

"How about the 'Mental who set the Death on fire? Pretty neat effect, right?"

"Yes, pretty neat," she said. *And pretty horrible how the 'Mentals were in chains. What was happening here?*

"Reminded me of your part of the mural," continued Jason. The Deaths near them were talking about other things, but Suzie remained watchful. Tension hung in the air.

"I'm glad we're in Art together," she said. *Keep it simple, keep it innocent.*

The chatter continued for another hour. She avoided mentioning Lovethar, Sindril, or even the 'Mentals. Several times, she found her thoughts drifting to Athanasius, the first 'Mental she'd met. It seemed a lifetime since she'd met the strange goat- man. Cronk had brought her to that in-between place and he'd given her the contract.

She blushed. She'd completely forgotten the cake. How much had she been through already? She reached into the pocket of her robe and found the small bag. She'd thought she might need it on her first day of school, but hadn't had a piece since Widow's Peak. She pulled out the pouch and looked at the cake. She broke off a small piece and popped some in her mouth. She had nothing to be frightened of now, no reason to indulge, but having a piece now made up for the times she hadn't eaten. They'd thrown rocks at her, sliced her with a boskery blade, and even frightened her with the albino. She'd suffered through fiery visions, burning questions, and painful ridicule. She deserved a small bite of strength.

As the cake dissolved on her tongue, courage and comfort welled up inside her heart. She stood up straighter, unafraid to confront this World of Death and its mysteries; this world where even though she was alone, she'd finally made friends. She glanced at the pouch again. A single piece of cake remained. She folded the pouch carefully into her pocket.

"Sneak that from the Hall?" asked Jason. The horn blew, and they finally started to leave the parade route, heading back into the College.

"It was a gift," she said.

"Oh?"

"From a friend."

CHAPTER FOURTEEN

Boskery

Suzie looked down from the stands. A crowd of Deaths surrounded the circular boskery field, filling six enormous grandstands. More Deaths stood around the field itself. Chalk crossed the field, dividing it into four equal quarters, each a half-acre large. In the center, a smaller circle stood. A few trees dotted the field, and a small canal, shaped like a river, cut across three of the quadrants. A twelve-foot wooden tower stood at the edge of each quadrant, forming four distant points around the field's perimeter. Ladders covered the sides of the towers, and a platform with a bucket stood atop each one.

The four boskery teams walked around the center of the field, each staying in their assigned quadrant. Suzie could hardly make out which team was which. The Gray Knights were in gray, in the nearest quadrant to her grandstand. The Dragon Seekers, wearing bright red were opposite; the orange-clad Widow Makers and blue Giant Tamers paced in the other quadrants.

"You understand the rules, right?" asked Jason, who'd been coming to the games.

"Sort of." She glanced at the double-bladed boskery scythes in each player's hand. With ten players on a team, eighty blades gleamed in the sunlight. She remembered the blade Frenchie had used to attack her during try-outs. The memory stung, even if the wound had healed.

"A referee will drop a ball into the center. That ten-yard wide circle in the center is no-man's land, a free-for-all area. Each team has to try to get the ball out of that area and into the other team's goals. If you get it in a tower other than yours, you get one point. If your team makes all three of the opposing goals at least once, you win automatically. If no one gets the other goals, the team with the most points after three hours wins."

"All right, I get that. But why four teams at once?"

"To watch more players at one time; don't forget that the older kids have to do this to prove their scythe mastery. Besides, having four teams at once is fun. Teams can join forces against other teams, as part of their strategy. Each team puts one player at the base of their tower. They're like the goalie, they protect the tower. If no one scores and time runs out, or if time runs out and it's a tie, the four Protectors face off in the center. The last one standing wins the game for their team."

"Last one standing?"

"Boskery blades paralyze you for ten minutes if you get hit. Like what happened to you back at try-outs. That's what makes the game tough. Every player has a double-bladed boskery scythe; one hit from any of them, and you're down."

"Those things hurt like hell," she said.

"I've heard," said Jason, "and one last rule. You can be in your quadrant or the center any time. After the whistle blows, you can only have four Deaths in an opposing quadrant at any time. That's a big challenge, and I've watched a lot of penalties. When a player breaks that rule, they lose their scythe for ten minutes."

"You mean they have to play without a way to defend themselves from the other blades?"

"Exactly."

Suzie's respect for Billy and Frank grew. This was a painful, difficult game. It might be required, but they'd still made it this far.

"Frank and Billy will be trying to score goals on the other towers?" she asked.

"Billy will. Frank's the Protector."

A whistle blew and the stands quieted. A referee wearing white and yellow rode to the center of the field atop a large white horse. Suzie recognized his dour expression. It was Hann. Other mounted referees stationed themselves around the massive field.

"Here we go," said Jason.

The four teams readied their scythes. Suzie couldn't tell who was who, but she saw the blades glinting, eager to strike. One player from each team moved toward their home tower. As he came closer, she recognized Frank. He looked nervous, though perhaps she only projected her own apprehension.

Hann yelled something she couldn't hear and blew his whistle again. He tossed a large ball into the air and spurred his horse away. A group of players raced toward it, their blades whirling in a circular motion. One of the Giant Slayers fell to the ground, and a Widow Maker picked up the ball. Two Dragon Seekers darted forward, catching the Widow Maker between their blades. He fell with a scream, clutching his side. The Gray Knights started forward but fell back as four Dragon Seekers stormed into their quadrant. A fifth Dragon Seeker ran into the Knights' quadrant followed by Widow Makers and Giant Slayers.

Hann rode over, blowing his whistle.

"A foul this early?" asked Suzie.

"It's strange," said Jason.

One Dragon Seeker waved at the crowd as he handed his scythe to Hann. One of the other players tossed the ball to him, and the group of five made their way into the quadrant. Six Knights started attacking, but a group of Widows and Giants struck back. In minutes, a dozen Deaths lay sprawled on the ground and the Dragons were running toward the Gray Knights' tower.

Now the action was closer, and Suzie saw faces. Frenchie ran with the ball, holding no scythe. Two Dragon Seekers flanked him, another ran in front. A Widow spun his scythe behind Frenchie, but one of the Giants knocked him to the ground. Frank braced himself, spinning his boskery blade, as the group approached. Billy and two other Knights circled around, but a group of Giants and Widows were attacking each other. Frank leaped in the air, swung the blade, and a Dragon Seeker fell to the ground. Frenchie put a hand on a ladder. Frank spun around, but another Dragon had hidden himself on the other side of the tower. He cut Frank's leg, opening a gash. Frank yelled and fell to the ground, clutching his leg. The Dragons flanked the ladder as Frenchie climbed.

Billy broke free from the melee but it was too late, Frenchie scaled the tower and tossed the ball into the bucket. Hann blew his whistle and everyone stopped. The players started back toward the center, looking suddenly tired. Fourteen stayed where they were on the field, still paralyzed.

"A point that soon," said Jason. "That's unusual, and a bad sign for us."

"He got the penalty on purpose," said Suzie. "That was planned."

"I agree. They've come to win."

Hann rode to the center, still holding Frenchie's scythe. The paralyzed players, including Frank, hadn't risen yet. Hann blew his whistle and tossed the ball into the air.

"We might have a chance here," said Jason. "Frenchie's still in penalty."

Billy seemed to be thinking the same thing. He ignored the ball, and struck two Dragon Seekers down, running toward Frenchie. He spun the scythe, whirling the blades into a circle of silver. Frenchie ran away, tripped and fell. Billy snapped the scythe right onto Frenchie's back.

"Yes," yelled Suzie.

"No," said Jason. "They're distracted. This is bad."

He was right. The Giants grabbed the ball, deep in Widow territory. The Widows had taken the heaviest toll from the first brawl, but now two of them staggered to their feet. The Gray Knights continued to attack the Dragons as the Giants stormed farther into the Widow quadrant. Two Widows ambushed the ball-carrier at the canal. He collapsed into the water, but managed to throw the ball to a teammate before he fell. Another Giant slashed one of the trees. A branch fell onto a Widow Maker, and the Giants walked to the tower. Only their Protector remained, against three of the Giant Slayers.

"Slayers. Slayers," chanted a group in the stands.

The Protector spun his scythe, lunging toward the Giant with the ball. He tossed the ball to one of the other three, as the third nicked the Protector's foot. The Protector fell to the ground and the Giants scored a goal. Hann blew his whistle and the Deaths started back toward the center.

"Slayers one to Seekers one," said Suzie. "Knights aren't on the board yet."

"Maybe that'll change, look at Billy."

She followed Jason's outstretched finger and looked at her friend. Billy stood on the far side of the field, huddled with two Widow Makers. "What's he doing?" she asked.

"I'm guessing he's trying to form an alliance. The two teams that are down, against the two leading teams."

Hann dropped the ball in the center of the field. Frenchie still lay face down, and the others walked around him. A Giant grabbed the ball and tossed it to his teammate. Three Gray Knights converged, and tossed it to Billy. Billy threw the ball to a Widow.

"Did he throw the ball away?" asked Suzie.

"I don't think it was an accident."

The Widows withdrew into their own quadrant, where all of their players ran. As they approached their goal, the Widow Protector tossed the ball to Billy, who grabbed it, leaped onto the ladder, and scored an easy goal.

"Knights will probably do the same thing in reverse now," said Jason. "They're trying to even the score."

Frenchie rose as Hann dropped the ball. He took his scythe back from Hann and started running. Dragon Seekers and Giant Tamers shouted to each other. The Knights withdrew to their quadrant, with a small group of Widows, but the play didn't go as planned. Seven of the Dragons, followed by seven of the Giants, stormed into the quadrant. Hann rode after them, but three players from each team dropped their scythes and kept running.

Billy turned around, holding the ball, frowning with confusion. He started to throw to one of the Widows, but the scythed Giants and Dragons were too many, they mowed down the Widows and half of the Knights. Billy broke into a run, toward the empty Giant Tamers' quadrant. A pack of Deaths sprinted after him. Frank shouted something to the team. Four other Gray Knights ran after Billy. Hann rode over, carrying a pile of boskery scythes. He took one of the scythes from a Knight, but the remaining three ran into the crowd of still unarmed Dragons and Giants. Many fell. Billy reached the Giant's tower, held the ball in one hand, and swung his scythe. It hit the Protector on the foot and he went down. Billy scaled the tower and scored.

"We're winning," said Suzie.

"By accident. That play was designed to be a freebie. Now the alliance is over. We'll find out what happens next."

It was gruesome.

It was heart-wrenching.

She loved every minute.

Play continued for another two and half hours without a break.

The Deaths stopped running and started to walk, sometimes even crawling toward the towers. Three times Deaths were stopped on the ladders, too tired to climb. Many hid in the few trees around the field, throwing the ball to teammates when they could.

The Gray Knights scored four goals, two in the Widow quadrant, and two in the Giant's. They were never able to score in the Dragon Seeker's tower. The Dragon Seekers scored three goals in the Gray Knights quadrant, and one in the Widow Maker's.

"It's tied," said Jason, as Hann blew his whistle.

"Game time has ended," shouted Hann. "No team was able to score in the three opponents' towers. The score is Widow Makers: one, Giant Tamers: two, Gray Knights and Dragon Seekers: four each. We'll have a five minute break, before the final elimination match."

"I can't believe it," said Jason. "We might actually win the championship."

"What happens now?" asked Suzie.

"They break and clear the field while the two Protectors square off in the no-man's land in the middle. Last one standing wins the game for their team."

The crowds in the stands grew quiet for the first time in hours. Billy patted Frank on the back, whispering something in his ear. The other players trailed off. Frenchie spat as Hann rode to the center of the field.

"Frank can do this, right?" asked Suzie.

Frank hobbled to the center. Blood ran down the side of his face and covered his leg.

"I hope so," said Jason. "He got hit a lot, when they kept ganging up on him. Don't forget they scored three goals on us, and we haven't even touched their Protector."

"Who is he? Their Protector?"

"That's David Overby," said a Death next to Jason. "He's one of the best Protectors to ever play the game. Seekers will win without a doubt."

"Look at his opponent," laughed another Death. Suzie couldn't match the voice to a face. The crowd around her laughed as Frank paused, dropping to one knee.

Jason took her hand in his. "It's only a game," he whispered.

"We'll win," she said.

She closed her eyes and concentrated. *Be strong, Frank. You can do this. We're all behind you.* In the distance of her imagination, a pair of green eyes watched.

Frank rose as Hann blew the whistle and spurred his horse out of the way.

David ran toward Frank, his boskery blade spinning into a perfect circle of metal. How the boy had any energy left after the three hour game was a mystery.

Frank held his position, turning his double-blade slowly back and forth. David swung and Frank took a step back, dodging. The Dragon Seeker lost his balance and Frank poked his scythe into the whirling blades. Blade met blade in a clash that reverberated around the field. No one in the crowd spoke. The other players stood on the field, forming a ring outside of the central no-man's land. Billy was the first to break the silence.

"Come on Frank," he yelled.

The crowds erupted. The lower stands ran out toward the field. Hann waved at them, warning them to stay back. Suzie and Jason ran forward with the crowd. She jostled her way to the front of the line, right behind Billy.

Blades smashed into each other again and again. Sparks flew as the two scythes met. David kicked Frank's bad leg, and Frank fell to the ground. David raised his scythe, spinning it. Frank grabbed his own scythe, but David slammed his blades down, knocking it away. Frank was unarmed.

David's face grew wild.

"Finish him!" screamed Frenchie.

"No, Frank," whispered Suzie.

Frank backed up toward the canal.

David smiled at the crowd, milking the attention. He stood, waving his boskery blade in a wide, slow circle.

A handful of mud flew into David's face. He stumbled backward as Frank threw a second handful. Frank staggered to his feet and ran into David's legs, tackling him. The blade fell, and both David and Frank collapsed onto the ground.

"What happened?" asked Suzie, starting to move forward.

"Stay back," warned Hann. "Match is still on."

"The blade hit both of them," said Jason. "Now whoever gets up first will win."

"But Frank was hurt bad."

"Nothing we can do now."

The ring around the two Deaths froze, watching.

Ten minutes was never as long.

Frank struggled to his feet. David remained on the ground.

"Gray Knights are the winners!" shouted Hann.

Suzie ran forward with the crowd, tears flowing freely down her face.

* * * *

The party lasted for hours. Frank was the hero, cheered by everyone. Suzie joined in the celebrations held in the Lower Hall. Food, music, and applause continued without end. Even Hann gave a speech praising the Gray Knights for their performance.

Finally, Suzie staggered home with Jason and Billy.

"That was amazing," she said.

"I'm glad you came," said Billy. "That championship will be hard to top. I couldn't believe when Gary ran into the tower the first time. And that finish with David and Frank."

"Good job," said Jason, "but I think I'm ready for bed."

They entered Eagle Two and Billy flopped on the couch.

"Only one more day of Styxia left," he said. "Suzie, I told you this world wasn't too bad. We have fun here, like anywhere."

"Today was a lot of fun," she admitted. "I'm with Jason though, it's almost five, and I'm exhausted."

"Sleep well." Billy got up and kissed her lightly on the lips.

Suzie's face turned beet red.

"I…"

"Good night," he said. He smiled and walked to his bedroom, closing the door.

"Good night," she whispered.

Suzie's heart raced. Her first kiss. Did it even count? She hadn't been expecting it, and Billy was probably tired. Maybe he didn't realize what he was doing.

Her first kiss. Her first kiss was Billy.

She closed the door to her room and sat on the bed. The room was warm and wet.

Wet? No, it wasn't the room. A trickle of moisture ran down her legs. Was she that excited? She had actually wet herself?

Suzie hurried to the bathroom, pulling off her robe and pulling down her panties. She almost fainted when she saw the blood.

CHAPTER FIFTEEN

Blood

Suzie frowned. She hadn't been sick since entering the World of the Dead and had started to wonder if illness even happened here.

She looked down again.

She was bleeding between her legs. She felt for a cut, but if there was one, it was high inside her. She didn't want to go to a doctor. She was the only one. The only girl in the entire world.

Suzie couldn't think straight. Her head spun from exhaustion. Surely, it could wait until the morning. That's when the realization hit her. Her first period. Here, in a world with no other women.

Like a wall slamming into her heart, she suddenly missed her mom. With no women here, no one would understand. She couldn't even go to a store to buy pads. It was the morning now. It could wait until after she'd slept. However, what if she kept bleeding? The Mortal World was so far away, like a dream.

She clumped a wad of toilet paper and used it to stop the blood. It lessened, but she still worried. The Deaths had stolen clothes from the living; surely they'd get her some tampons? She should visit a doctor, at least they'd be able to get her something. Did they have doctors here? In her time at the College, no one had mentioned a doctor or a nurse, but she had to ask.

"Billy?" she called, knocking on his door.

"Thought you went to sleep," he said, opening the door. He still wore his robe.

"I'm hurt," she said. "I'd like to see a doctor."

"I'm the one who was in the game," he teased. "You got hurt in the stands?"

"I want to see a doctor, Billy."

"Now? It's like five in the morning."

"I want to get this taken care of. I won't be able to sleep."

"All right, all right. I guess we can take you to Doc Harman. He helps us out when we get hurt in boskery."

"Thanks, Billy."

She gave him a hug and they headed out. After the earlier festivities, the College was eerily silent. The air smelled of strawberries, but also of dew. Overhead, stars twinkled in a cloudless sky. West Tower loomed above them, cutting a writhing black swath into the night. The crescent moon hung low on its side, like a scythe reaping a field of diamonds. To the east, slight hints of gray hung at the edge of the sky, preparing for the morning.

"Doc Harman is in East Tower," said Billy. "I've only been to his office once."

"What happened?" she whispered, but her words still sounded loud against the silence of the sleeping College.

"I had just started boskery and fell out of one the towers. Broke my leg. Doc fixed it up pretty good."

She nodded and they walked on. The blood started to trickle down her thighs again. Had they actually kissed? Was he only tired, or did he like her?

They crossed through the center of campus, passing cold, unlit buildings. At night, every mound looked as black as the Examination Room. Half of the year was over. In a few months, she'd take her test and finally go home. A bird cawed in the night, and in the distance she heard a low howl.

"Are there wolves here?" she asked.

"Probably. Outside the College I've heard of all sorts of beasts," said Billy. "But don't worry, only Deaths can get through the Ring."

"And 'Mentals," said Suzie, "and don't forget the albino that attacked me."

"Yeah, 'Mentals can cross through, too, but wolves can't."

Another howl rang out and Suzie shivered. They continued toward East Tower. In one courtyard, they passed a few Deaths sleeping, covered in confetti from the boskery win. Billy walked on without stopping.

"I hope he's up," said Billy when they reached the base of East Tower.

"Wait a second," said Suzie.

"What for?"

"Shhh." She paused and listened. Someone was approaching, whispering something. Suzie pressed herself behind a corner of the door. Billy did the same, but gave her a questioning look.

The door to East Tower swung open and three Deaths walked out. She didn't recognize them.

"At the banquet?" said one of them. They walked away from Suzie and Billy without turning around.

"We'll show them," said another.

"They'll be sorry. The way they treat us."

"After the outrage at the parade."

The trio continued to whisper but disappeared around a bend.

"Who was that?" whispered Billy after a minute had gone by.

"I've no idea," said Suzie, "but they were mad about something."

"Well it's none of our business. C'mon, I'm tired. Let's find Harman and go home."

"Of course," she said.

Billy pulled on the massive doors, and they swung open. A flower Suzie didn't recognize lit the inside of East Tower. It hung on the walls like ivy, but had petals like tulips. The light cast by the flowers shone dim and blood red. Red, like the trickle of blood between her legs.

"This way," said Billy. He led her down the hall and up a flight of stairs. She wondered where Sindril's office was. Much higher up, she supposed. He probably watched the College from the top tower, peering down at the Deaths.

They walked around a bend and Billy stopped. A sign outside the door read "Sidney Harman, Doctor to Deaths."

Billy knocked on the door. After a minute, he knocked again.

"Who's there?" called a voice from the other side.

"Billy Black. My friend is hurt."

"Give me a minute."

Suzie heard muttering from behind the door and began to wonder if this was a good idea. Why was she visiting a doctor? With no other girls here, would they even know what a tampon was? No, she was being silly, they went to the Mortal World, and they'd seen girls before. Besides, she didn't want to keep using toilet paper, and she couldn't steal from the living herself.

The door opened with a creak. The other side was lit by white flowers, which grew brighter as the door opened. Suzie wondered how the flowers shined and dimmed. The ones in her room always darkened when she closed her eyes to sleep.

"Black, huh?" said Harman. The Death was thin and wiry. A thick moustache covered the bottom of his lean face. "Watched you in the match. You did a fine job."

"Thank you, sir."

"Your friend's another Gray Knight?"

"No, it's Suzie here."

Harman paused and squinted at her. She smiled.

"The girl," muttered Harman. "Come in, Suzie. Black, you too. You can wait in the front room here." He gestured to a couch on the other side of the door. "Suzie, follow me."

He led her through a door in the back. Two small examining rooms met the hall, each with a bed and a curtain in front. At the end of the hall stood a tall bookcase filled with books.

"When they got your clothes, they brought some literature for me. Never had a female Death, but don't worry, I'll help you. Have a seat, have a seat."

He waved her to one of the beds and she sat nervously. He pulled the curtain closed. This wasn't an ordinary doctor; it was a Death, one who had never worked with a girl before. How would he respond to this issue? Would she have to strip for him?

Harman opened the curtain and entered with a clipboard and a handful of books. He set the books at the foot of the bed and sat on a stool. She glanced at the stack. The top book said *FEMALE*

ANATOMY, and one under it said *An Idiot's Guide to Girls*. She wasn't reassured.

"What seems to be the problem, Suzie?"

"I'm bleeding," she said.

"Okay, where is the cut?"

"I don't have a cut. It's my first period. I need someone to get me tampons or pads from the Mortal World."

Doc Harman's face reddened and he stood for a moment in awkward silence. He then spent twenty minutes reading the books. She sensed that he was more embarrassed than she was, but left with a promise that pads would be delivered soon.

The Living World felt far away. She'd signed her name four months ago. She'd been back, but only to help reap souls. She was a Death now, a female Death. The *only* Death who'd ever need to worry about periods.

"You okay?" asked Billy. "You were inside a long time."

"I'm fine," she said. "Thanks for bringing me."

"You come any time you need to," said Harman, escorting them out. He closed the door and she heard him sigh.

"I freaked out the doctor a little," she laughed.

"You are a girl," he said. "But you're sure not scary." He smiled and touched her shoulder. For a moment, she thought he would kiss her again. She blushed and looked away. "You want to tell me what was wrong?"

"Nah, scary girl stuff." She laughed and he laughed too.

They walked out of East Tower. Behind the bulk of the Tower, pink light warmed the edges of the sky. The moon hung low to the side of West Tower. The College was still quiet.

"That wasn't too bad," she said.

"I'm glad Doc Harman could help."

"No, not that. I mean East Tower. I pictured some sort of fortress where the bad Deaths went."

"Yeah, I'd say that's accurate." Billy laughed again. "Man, I am tired, can we go home now?"

"Yes," she said. "Let's go back to Eagle Two."

She watched the dawn light strike the black of the Examination Room. Would she ever go *home*?

* * * *

"I'd like to propose a toast," shouted Hann, yelling over the noise.

Deaths filled the Lower Hall, crowding the long tables and standing around the room. The full council sat at the far end. Lord Coran, dressed in white, sat on a throne at the head of the room. He seemed to be sleeping, but Suzie could barely tell, he was far away. Sindril and the other eleven council members sat on either side of him, wearing their purple robes. Tables stretched toward Suzie. The faculty and oldest students sat near the Council. Suzie and the other young students sat at shaky tables outside the hall.

She glanced into the hall again. A wall had been opened on the side of the hall closest to her, which apparently happened during every Styxia Feast. Four massive outdoor pavilions stood side by side next to the open hall. A series of microphones and speakers connected the podium in the hall to the pavilions, letting everyone hear. She couldn't spot Hann; he must be somewhere near the purple robed council.

"To the Gray Knights," said Hann. A cheer went up from the hall and Deaths raised their glasses. She wished she could find Billy and Frank, but the guests of honor, including the Gray Knights, sat near the head of the hall.

The toasts continued. At each, the Deaths stood, cheered, and then sat as they drank. The Deaths in the hall had breads and cheese along with their drinks. Suzie glanced at her empty plate.

"I wish they'd bring us some food already," said Jason, "even if it's a gorger. I'm starving."

"No food for the pavilions 'til they've toasted everyone and everything," said a second year sitting across from them. "Last year took over an hour."

"It's been that long already," said Suzie. Her stomach growled like a tiger. She wondered if Jason could hear her hunger.

"And another toast to our amazing Lord Coran." She didn't recognize the voice on the speaker, but the Deaths stood and cheered. The pavilions didn't have to toast. This meant no food either.

A gong rang.

"Finally," said the second year.

"Are they done?"

"Almost," he said. "First each of the council toasts, and then Lord Coran gives the final one."

Ten of the council members toasted the Deaths of the College, and one toasted the four finalist teams of the boskery match. Sindril was the last council member to speak.

"To Susan Sarnio," he said, "the first female Death in a million years."

The Deaths got up, but no one cheered. In the pavilion, Deaths turned to stare at her. She looked around in awkward surprise. The moment passed and Lord Coran spoke.

"To Deaths," he said, in a thin, high voice. "And let the feast begin."

Everyone cheered when 'Mentals streamed in from every side, carrying large trays. They set the trays down, and for a moment, all was calm. The moment ended with sudden shouts, running, and screaming.

"Fire!"

"Stop them!"

People ran out of the hall. The pavilion above her shook.

"Run, Suzie," said a voice to her side. She turned and was startled to find the goat-face of Athanasius. His yellow eyes flashed.

"What's going on?" she asked.

"Fire," said Jason. He grabbed her arm, pulling her away. A crowd of Deaths ran toward them, shouting.

A 'Mental with pink skin and wild, purple eyes jumped onto the table. He held out a hand and purple flames shot toward the Deaths. Two young boys screamed as their cloaks caught fire.

"Not this one," said Athanasius. He raised his hoof-like hands. The pink-skinned 'Mental glared at him and then jumped into the crowd of Deaths with a snort.

"Quickly," said Athanasius. "This way, before it gets worse. I'm glad I found you, Susan."

Suzie and Jason followed him. The pavilion erupted into chaos, and smoke billowed from the direction of the Hall. She heard Sindril yelling orders over the static-laden speakers. Deaths ran away from the chaos, while 'Mentals seemed to be running toward it.

Boom. The sound thundered around them, making Suzie stumble. Jason caught her, keeping her from falling.

"They've closed the Ring," said Athanasius. "We've got to hide now. Come on, I'll bring you to safety."

He darted away from the stream of running Deaths, toward a wall. He tapped on a white rock and a section of the wall slid open.

"In here."

They ducked into a low passageway and the wall slid closed behind them.

"What the hell is going on?" screamed Suzie.

"Quiet," said Athanasius. "We don't want to be found."

Another thunderous crash erupted outside.

"What's—" she started.

"It's a revolt," replied the goat-faced 'Mental. His gold eyes caught the light of a flower starting to glow. They crouched in a narrow hallway with bare, clean-swept walls. The hall extended toward a row of white doors.

"Where are we?" asked Jason.

"An access hall," replied Athanasius. "Elementals use thousands of these to serve the Deaths." He sighed. "Help us stay out of sight. We're treated like slaves."

Suzie remembered the 'Mentals she'd watched paraded in chains. "Is that what's happening?" she asked. "The 'Mentals are fighting back?"

"That's right," he said. "The plan was to attack the Council and set the hall on fire. They wanted to capture Coran alive and hold him hostage. I doubt they've done anything of the sort, the Elementals were too angry."

"I can't believe it," said Susan.

"You haven't seen Plamen have you?" asked Athanasius. He looked nervous.

"Who?" asked Jason.

"My assistant," said Athanasius. "Another Elemental. I thought Susan might have remembered him. He's been missing for some time."

"I haven't seen anyone," she said. She vaguely remembered Athanasius's assistant, but her head spun and she couldn't focus.

"Why should we trust you?" said Jason. "You said the 'Mentals attacked the Deaths."

"He's not here to hurt us," said Suzie.

Athanasius turned his wide yellow eyes toward her, his goat-like features melting from fear into a smile.

"Thank you. Susan," he said.

"And thank you for the cake and for being kind to me. Jason, we can trust him. If he's brought us here it's to keep us away from harm."

"The Elementals are furious about the Deaths, and I've heard rumors that a new war is coming. Fires have been spotted in the mountains."

"What fires? And what Mountains?" asked Jason.

"The Mountains of the Dragons," said Athanasius. "The Dragons are waking. Something has happened, or someone." He looked at Susan.

"The Dragons?"

Jason seemed confused, but pieces were starting to fit together. Could Sindril, the mysterious meetings outside the Ring, and the strange fiery visions all be connected? Maybe they were connected to Dragons.

"Coran sent a hundred Elementals to search the Mountains. They were due back two months ago, but none returned. The leader of this revolt, a young hothead named Lyrus, is the son of one of the missing hundred."

"That's terrible," said Susan. "Why do the Deaths treat you poorly?"

Athanasius laughed, and for a moment, a far-away glint came into his eyes. "Fear," he said. "To explain more would take longer than we have, we should move." He listened but the hallway was still. The tumult outside seemed farther away.

"Why are we in this corridor?" said Jason. "Why Suzie and me?"

"Susan," said Athanasius, "is far more precious than you realize. She is—"

He stopped suddenly and turned his head, but it was too late. A scythe flew through the air and landed in his neck. Athanasius fell to the stone floor in a pool of blood. "No!" Susan screamed.

"It's all right, you're safe now," said the calm voice of Sindril. He stepped from the shadows. Deep splotches of blood-red stained his bright purple robe. A smile stretched across his face like the reddened blade lying in Athanasius's neck.

"That 'Mental was trying to kill you," said Sindril. His voice slithered through the silent corridor like a snake.

"No," said Suzie. "What have you done?" She backed against the wall of the corridor in terror.

"Suzie, he was part of a coup. Two of the council are dead. I'm glad I found you before he killed you too." Sindril turned to his right and shouted down the darkened hall. "Two in here, including the girl."

The girl. Athanasius had tried to warn her; she was important to them. Everything was a blur. Something was terribly wrong on this world. War was coming. Dragons were back, and she was in the middle of it.

"Suzie," said Jason. "Come on, let's get out of here."

Two Deaths stood beside Sindril. She wasn't sure when they'd arrived. She wasn't sure of anything anymore. This morning, she had only wanted to go home. However, where was home, and why was she important to them? What had Athanasius tried to tell her, and how had Sindril found them?

The Deaths led them through a pair of doors, down a corridor, and to a wall. They tapped and it slid open. As they exited, she turned and saw a Death talking to Sindril.

"We almost lost her," said the Death.

"That was too close," said Sindril. He noticed her and spun back into the corridor. The door slid closed again.

CHAPTER SIXTEEN

A World on Fire

For the first time since she'd arrived, the World of Deaths did not smell like strawberries. A rancid burning smell hung in the air, mixed with the smell of blood.

Athanasius fell to the floor of the corridor.

Blood.

Blood spurted out of his neck.

Blood.

Her own scream froze in her throat as the kind and caring Elemental collapsed, his golden eyes staring at her in horror.

Blood.

The scythe blade turned red. Her eyes were mirrors to a scene she didn't understand.

Blood.

Sindril, smiling his blood-scythe smile. Eying her like some treasure he needed to protect.

For the first time since she'd arrived, Suzie wanted to stay. She wanted blood. She wanted Sindril's.

"I'm going to kill him," she muttered. "I'm going to kill Sindril."

"Suzie," said Jason. "He saved us from that crazy 'Mental. You can't believe what one of those creatures said. Look what they did."

She looked around the College. Everything around the Hall smoldered. Many of the tall stony walls looked less like canyons and more like Swiss cheese, pocked with holes. Rubble lay strewn around the ground. Yet it was eerily silent. The Deaths and 'Mentals had either fled or been taken away.

Suzie closed her eyes for a moment and the scene repeated. The blood splattered, she heard the scream, and Sindril stood over the broken body of her friend.

"I saw," she said.

She didn't speak again until they reached Eagle Two. The two Deaths who escorted them through the College never spoke, but one glanced back at her every minute. Neither Death seemed to care about Jason. Was she saved from a coup, or was she Sindril's prisoner?

The Deaths gave her a curt nod and ushered them inside. She closed the door.

"Suzie, you're all right." Frank rushed over and gave her a hug.

"I'm fine," she said, more icily than she intended.

"Is Billy here?" asked Jason.

"Yeah, I brought him back," said Frank. "He's in his room, but he's burned pretty badly. Good thing the season's over."

"Did you bring him to the doctor?" asked Suzie. Had that only been today? It seemed like a year ago.

"They have doctors here?"

"Of course, this morning I went to doctor, um…" What was his name, and why couldn't she picture him? She *had* visited a doctor hadn't she?

"Can't remember?" asked Frank. "He might have been killed. When a Death is killed here, they are erased from existence. It's like they never came to this world."

She closed her eyes. The blood and the scream. Athanasius's terrified golden eyes.

"It's not true for 'Mentals," said Jason. "We watched one get killed. He had kidnapped us."

"He saved us!" she yelled. "And you never believed him." She grabbed Jason and threw him against the wall.

"Hey, I was—" he tried to say, but she slapped him in the face.

"Suzie," said Frank, pulling them apart.

"What's happening?" asked Billy. "Is Suzie home?" He stood in his doorway clutching his side. Suzie's anger evaporated as his face came into view. An open cut ran down one of his cheeks, beneath his eye. The right side of his face was blackened, and his robe was torn.

"Billy, you're hurt," she said. She went to him, tears forming in her eyes. She took a cloth and held it to his face. He winced as she put her arms around his shoulders. Billy, her first kiss. Sindril would pay.

"Gently," he said, wincing as he spoke. "I got beat up a bit."

"We need to swap stories," said Suzie, "but not here, and not now." She glanced at the door. Were the Deaths still listening? Was Sindril monitoring them?

"Write down what happened if you need to," she said to Jason, glaring. He hadn't understood. He had been there, but was too afraid to *recognize* the truth. Was he blind?

"We'll talk about it here in the kitchen in a couple days, once things have settled down." She motioned to the door and raised her hands to indicate someone was listening. She grabbed a piece of paper and started scribbling.

Trust no one, she wrote. *They are listening. The four of us will meet in the library. Understand?*

The other three nodded and Billy staggered back into his room. Jason gave her an uneasy shrug. Suzie went to her room and shut the door. She looked in her bathroom for anything to help Billy. She started toward the door, but a knock stopped her.

Frank entered.

"You free?" he asked.

"I'm scared," she whispered.

"Tell me," he said. "Tell me what happened."

She didn't want to tell him, but he looked at her and her resolve melted. She was angry, terrified, upset, and confused. A tear fell from her eye and suddenly she was sobbing in Frank's arms, telling him everything. When she was done, he leaned over and kissed her on the cheek. Suzie blushed.

"Athanasius was a friend of mine," he said at last. "I'm sorry to hear this." For a moment, moisture welled in Frank's eyes, but he turned away. "Don't take it out on Jason. He's scared, like all of us."

"You know more about the 'Mentals than you admit, don't you?" she blurted out, trying to choke back the tears. "You got that albino, and you always have a far-off look when I ask about them. Did a 'Mental hurt you too?"

"Yes," said Frank. "But, I'll tell you another time. I wasn't surprised at this revolt. If anything, I'm surprised it took them until now."

"What's going to happen?"

"I don't know, Suzie. It'll be a while before school goes back to normal, and if what Athanasius said is true, war is coming."

"I won't be able to go home will I?"

"Suzie, this is home to me. Maybe it's meant to be home to you as well."

"I can't think. Everything's confused. Maybe I should stop trying to figure things out and should go along with whatever Sindril wants."

Frank laughed. "Suzie, you're upset and in shock. But the day *you* stop trying to figure stuff out? Well, I'll believe it when I see it."

Frank rose and went to her door. She didn't want him to go, but wasn't sure how to ask him to stay. She remembered her kiss with Billy and felt her cheeks turning red.

"You try and rest. I'll stay here tonight, it's crazy out, and everyone's on lockdown anyway. They're probably looking for the last 'Mentals."

"I hope they don't find them."

"Me too," he said.

"Frank," she paused. "Thank you."

He nodded and opened the door.

"First time the world doesn't smell like strawberries," she mumbled as she lay down.

"What?" he asked.

"Strawberries."

Frank gave her a confused look; then left her room and closed the door.

She stared at the ceiling.

Blood.

She could still see it. Still hear the scream. Her own scream.

Blood.

The grin on Sindril's face, his teeth forming a bloody blade.

She closed her eyes.

* * * *

The College burned.

Deaths ran screaming around her, fleeing massive shapes with leathery wings.

"Run," screamed Athanasius.

She turned to the 'Mental. His face was burning. Fire licked her heels, tracing tongues of orange heat onto her legs. She should be afraid.

"Run!" he screamed again. His head fell off into a pool of blood.

The flames crept higher, dancing between Suzie's thighs, setting her clothes ablaze and leaving her naked.

A pair of green eyes emerged from the inferno.

"Be strong," said Billy.

The ground vanished in a river of blood.

The eyes stared at her, watching her through flames of orange and gold.

"Be strong," said Frank.

The sky burned into a cloud of ash.

One of the green eyes blinked.

Blood soaked her feet, hissing where it met the fire.

"Be strong," said Athanasius.

The eyes watched her, she knew those eyes.

The green eyes.

Her own eyes.

Suzie awoke covered in sweat.

* * * *

Most of the College had been unaffected by the 'Mentals' revolt. Only the buildings near the Hall showed noticeable damage, yet the entire campus was quiet. Young Deaths hurried to their classes without looking up, whispering to each other in hushed voices. She hadn't seen Frank, Billy, or the others since the morning, but hoped they would come. She snuck out of the Ring of Scythes, grateful it was open, and walked to the library.

When she entered the dusty old house, she ran straight for the bookshelf and pulled on the red book, jumping through the words "Librvm Exelcior" when the bookcase swung open. She ran down the spiral staircase as the white flowers slowly began to glow behind her. Sindril might know about the house, but not the library. She hoped that was true. This was still her place, her sanctuary. The only place she felt safe.

Light came from the library beneath her, and she stopped on the staircase until she heard Frank's voice.

"She'll be here soon," he said.

"We shouldn't be here," said Jason. "What does she hope to gain?"

"I want Sindril to pay," she said, walking into the library. Frank, Billy, and Jason sat at a table covered in old books. The room felt more like home than Eagle Two.

"We should start with what happened that night," said Frank. "The Styxia feast was five days ago. We've waited until now to tell where we were. We're all worried, but we need to trust each other."

Suzie glanced at Jason. She couldn't help it. Did he honestly believe Sindril had tried to save them, or had it been an act?

"Suzie, you asked us to come," said Billy. "What do you think we should do?"

"Frank's idea is good. I want to hear what happened to everyone the night of the feast." She glanced at Jason again and he turned away.

"It's still a blur," said Billy. He forced a smile at Suzie. The side of his face was bright red, with tinges of black in parts. Dried blood and early scab tissue covered the cut beneath his eye. It would leave a massive scar. If he wasn't her friend, his face might have frightened her. Looking at him, she understood that he was more than just a friend. She wasn't repulsed. She only felt sorry for him, and wished she could reach out and touch that kind face, one of the first to smile at her in this strange world. The first boy to kiss her.

"Frank and I were in the hall, up near the front," he continued. "The speeches were droning on and on, and all of a sudden Frank leans over and points out that the 'Mentals were missing."

"The servants," interjected Frank. "I noticed they were gone, which was strange. Then Sindril got up and started talking. A 'Mental ran into the room with bright red eyes. He yelled something and shot fire right out of his hand. The table where the Council was sitting split in two and suddenly twenty 'Mentals were yelling and running everywhere. They started shooting flames in every color, and one of 'em honestly looked like he was flinging icebergs through the air. Deaths I didn't recognize were hit and vanished. The Council was screaming and I turned to look, when a blast of fire hit Billy. He's lucky it wasn't any worse."

Suzie's heart caught in her throat, imagining the pain he must have endured.

"When I woke up," said Billy, "the place was deserted. I staggered to the side and found Frank. I don't remember how I got the cut. Frank helped me home and I fell asleep. When I awoke, you two came in, looking scared as hell."

Suzie walked to Billy and embraced him. He patted her back, but she knew he was embarrassed. When she let go, he fell backward, breathing hard.

"I'll take him to get help," said Jason.

"No," said Billy. "I'll be fine. I've been hurt worse in boskery. Let me stay a few minutes."

Suzie doubted he'd ever been hurt like this, but she didn't want him to go until they'd formed a plan. She looked at Frank, who was staring into space.

"You okay?" she asked.

"Yeah," said Frank, nodding. "But it was bad. The 'Mentals poured out of the wall, probably through a hidden entrance. I think some of them got into the Council's heads, sort of like the albino did to you, because the Council started screaming. Sindril was one of the first to grab a scythe and he started swinging like mad. I tried to pull Billy under the table, but a blast of flame hit him before we made it. I pulled him under after that and we hid until the fighting died down. I think they tried to attack Lord Coran himself, but the 'Mentals never got close. A couple of the Council were hurt, and a ton of other Deaths died, but the Council got away."

"Which Deaths died?" asked Jason. "Is it anyone we know?"

"Couldn't tell you," said Frank. "I watched a few die myself, but I have no idea who they were. When a Death is killed in this world, it's as if they never existed. Their entire existence is ripped from the universe, even from memory."

"Has it always been like that?" asked Suzie. "What about Lovethar? The one other female Death? If she was executed, how do people remember her?"

Frank laughed. "She wasn't executed, obviously, or at least not on Widow's Peak like they say. It's not what actually happened to her. It's just a story. She wasn't killed, not in this world anyway."

Suzie had already guessed the Lovethar story was made up. Did it connect to what was happening now? Why would they lie about the only other female Death?

"Never seen 'Mentals this angry," said Frank, continuing his story. "But the Deaths were even worse. Hann looked like he wanted to kill everyone, and a few Deaths started swinging their scythes, hitting everything in their way. I was watching from beneath our table when a 'Mental swung his arm and snapped the table in two. Samuel, one of the Gray Knights, got a scythe and swung it like a damn boskery blade. He tripped and the blade opened up Billy's face before I dragged him to the side of the room. I had to fight off a couple of guys myself. Used my fists, since I didn't even have a scythe, but luckily the roof gave in and helped me out. Part of it fell on one of the guys I was fighting, and I was able to drag Billy away."

Frank's scratched face looked tired. Next to Billy's charred face, Frank looked fine.

"If Billy got killed," said Jason. "We wouldn't remember him? Like he never existed?"

"It's weird," said Frank, "but that's how it is. The Curse of the Deaths they used to call it."

"I'm glad you both made it out all right," said Suzie. "Jason and I were together, but I'm sure we remember things differently." She had toyed with the idea of letting Jason tell the story first, but she didn't want to hear it. She told them everything, starting with Athanasius's strength cake, which she still had one piece of left, and ending with Sindril's murder of the 'Mental. She even told them about her dream, and the visions she'd been having of fire and green eyes.

"A 'Mental with green eyes worked for Athanasius," she said. "I had forgotten until a couple of days ago. In my dream I thought they were my own eyes."

"Most 'Mentals have strangely-colored eyes," said Frank. "It probably is related to a 'Mental."

"I didn't want to believe Sindril was a murderer," said Jason. "He seemed to save us. I hadn't met Athanasius before, and in all the confusion, I—"

"Sindril's the original reason we formed this group," said Billy, wincing. "He was up to something. Suzie herself said he planned to kill her."

"He definitely wanted his men to watch us," said Suzie. "They stayed at the house for three days. No one followed me here, but it wouldn't surprise me if Sindril knew."

"But you came anyway?" asked Frank.

"Even if he's upstairs, he can't hear us," she replied. "If he was coming to the library, we'd hear the bookcase open and see the lights on the stairs. I'll go check now, to be double-sure." She walked up the stairs to the closed bookcase and looked through the invisible wall. The house was empty. She paused; her heart beat wildly against her chest, but the house was deserted. She turned and came back down. Billy looked around the room uneasily.

"He isn't here," said Suzie. "I think he hasn't found this library, and maybe he's stopped the meetings for now. Given what's happened, he's probably too nervous to leave the College."

"Maybe," said Billy. "But let's keep this brief. I need to rest."

"I didn't realize Athanasius was your friend," said Jason, looking uncomfortable. "Maybe I wanted to, I mean maybe I was—"

"It's okay," Suzie replied. "But I've had enough. I want to learn what's going on."

"Even if we found out, what would we do?" asked Billy. "We're two first year Deaths, and two second years. Nothing we can do if the head of the school's up to something."

"Yes there is," said Frank. "We need to take the fight to Sindril. We need proof he's been meeting someone and that he's involved in some plot. We break into his office in East Tower, and find the proof we need. Then make it public."

"Are you nuts?" laughed Billy. "He'll find us and kill us all, no one will even remember."

"What do you think is going on?" Jason asked Suzie. "You've been suspicious the longest. What's your theory?"

"I think Lovethar wasn't killed," said Suzie. "And she has something to do with the Dragon Key. She *had* a Dragon Key, and that's why the Deaths are afraid of her. That's why those pages about the Key are missing from the books. Sindril found out somehow, and now he wants to get the Dragon Key himself."

"A lot's missing from that," said Frank. "Like what it has to do with you, or your visions. Was the 'Mental revolt a coincidence, or is it related? Don't forget that Sindril was in this house, apparently talking to someone. I still say we need to get in that office."

"Maybe he was talking about the Key," said Suzie. "Maybe some 'Mentals found out and he punished them. Or maybe it had nothing to do with all this, though it happened at the same time. I'm not sure, but I agree with Frank."

"You what?" Billy stared at her. "You honestly expect us to march into East Tower, find Sindril's office, and search…for what exactly?"

"I'll know when I see it," said Suzie. "And I'm the one who has to go."

"Why you?" asked Jason.

"Because he invited me."

"He what?"

"The first day of school, when I was upset, he told me to come to him any time I needed help. I'm going to do just that."

"And then what?" asked Billy. "You ask him if you can search his office? Please, Headmaster Sindril, I suspect you of plotting something awful. I'd like to search around a bit?"

Suzie took a deep breath.

"I had an idea," she said. "It's honestly a long shot, but still might work. What's the one thing that would force Sindril out of his office?"

"The end of the world?" asked Billy.

"Close," she said. "The only thing that would get him out is another attack. Like the attack in the Hall."

"But the 'Mentals aren't even allowed to be servants now," said Jason. "You heard the announcement today. Besides, how would we get them to attack?"

"You remember how angry Sindril got," said Suzie. "When they attacked he went berserk. His scythe probably opened up Billy's face. We need to replicate that, and make sure it starts right when I'm in his office. I'll pretend to be afraid. I'll ask to stay, and remind him how I was…" She paused for a moment, trying not to picture Athanasius's blood. "How I was kidnapped, and he saved me."

"That's crazy," said Billy.

"Absolutely insane," added Jason.

"But it also might work," said Frank. "One group could attack, *if* we could find a way to get them on campus."

"Don't tell me you're friends with any 'Mentals," asked Billy.

"The 'Mentals who attacked were all men," said Frank. "And a lot of them were killed, and maybe even imprisoned. But they have to have families. Wives and relatives."

"You want to start a revolt with women?" asked Jason.

"Not any women," said Frank. "Female Elementals. Remember Cibran Alfar?"

"Your 'Mental friend," said Suzie, "the one who mentioned the Dragon Key."

"Before they stole his mind, Cibran told me a few things about the Elementals. He said women in his home were even more powerful than men. Suzie's plan might work, since we don't need a revolt to succeed."

"What we need is a distraction," said Billy.

"And while he's out of the office—" started Jason.

"It still sounds too risky," said Billy.

"Let's take one step at a time," said Frank. "If we do this plan, we need something big before we can even dream about starting. Hell, it might take us until the end of term."

"What do we need?" asked Jason.

"To find the 'Mentals," said Suzie.

CHAPTER SEVENTEEN

The Reaping

Suzie's excitement lasted for three months before it started to fade. The school was apprehensive, and she hadn't found a single opportunity to sneak away and look for the 'Mentals. They'd had meetings in the library twice more, but had only affirmed the plan. Even Jason and Billy wanted to help find the 'Mentals. Frank and Billy knew the general direction, but they weren't sure how far away they'd have to travel. If they left the College for more than a day, they'd be noticed. It was already March. They didn't have much time left.

Suzie suspected they'd be noticed whatever they did. She couldn't tell if Deaths were following her, but she did notice people watching her more than usual. Sindril wasn't letting down his guard. Every time she went to the library, she expected an encounter. Frank had suggested a new meeting place, but she refused to give in to fear.

The guard over the College was even worse. 'Mentals had been banished from campus, which meant no more servants at all. Everything took longer, as Deaths got their own food, did their own cleaning, and had to find their own supplies. Anxiety hung over the school. No one was sure who had died in the revolt, but some students whispered that as many as a dozen Deaths had been killed. No one asked how many 'Mentals had died.

"I understand your nerves," said Hann, "but this Reaping will be crucial."

Suzie tried to focus on the teacher, but kept drifting into fears about their plan. How would they find the 'Mentals? How could they convince them to help? She *had* to get into Sindril's office. Yet even if she did, what was she looking for?

"Suzie," said Hann. "Are you listening?"

"Yes, sir," she lied.

"You gonna let a girl like her Reap a soul?" said Luc. "She'll probably break down crying."

"I'm sure Suzie will be fine," said Hann.

"Hell, the poor soul will take one look at Billy's face and get freaked out. They'll tear themselves right off their corpse. Suzie won't even need a scythe."

Suzie was used to mockery and hated watching Billy suffer it. He looked at his feet while a few Deaths chuckled.

"That's enough, Luc," warned Hann.

Frenchie put a hand on his brother's shoulder and shook his head. He glanced at her, but she looked away.

"The Reaping begins tomorrow," said Hann. "Same groups, but the first years will do the actual act. This will be your only Reaping for this year. Make it count. Should any of you pass your Final Test, you will never have to Reap again. A year of your life traded for a single reaped soul. Of course, none of you will pass."

I will. And I'll bring down Sindril before I go.

* * * *

"You ready?" asked Billy. He wore a mask over his face, showing only his eyes. He had insisted on covering his face to help the soul feel at ease. If they were transporters, they didn't want to frighten their passenger.

"You can do this," said Frank. His calm manner reassured her. He looked at her with his deep brown eyes and freckled face. She nodded and straightened the sleeves of her black robe.

She walked to Hann who stood in the center of the class. He handed her a long scythe, even taller than she was. It was light in her hand; the handle danced with energy. The blade slid through the air like sunlight through water. Life flowed down from the blade, coursing through the handle, sending tingles into her arm. Sweat beaded in her palms and trickled from her forehead.

"Let the scythe do the work," reminded Hann, "and you'll be fine."

She nodded and walked back to her group. She tied herself to Frank and Billy using a tether. Then she held the scythe in her hands and paused.

This was ridiculous. She was a thirteen-year-old girl, a kid from Maryland, holding a scythe. Not some costume piece, but an actual, *working* scythe. Now she, Suzie, was supposed to Reap a soul. Even her mysteries with Sindril and the Dragon Key suddenly seemed trivial.

"Good luck," said Frank.

She adjusted her grip and adjusted again. The tingles in the scythe grew stronger, itching her hands and arms. *It's ready. It wants to swing; to do its job.* She moved her hands a third time and Frank glanced at Billy. Billy adjusted his mask.

"What's the matter," taunted Luc behind her. "Is the little girl scared?"

She clutched the handle and let the blade fall. She hardly moved, but the blade shot downward, slicing air, light, heat, even thought. For an instant, her arm was on fire and the world vanished into darkness.

The smell of strawberries exploded around her as color, form, and details blurred into a single, unending stream of confusion. She heard the sound of screams in the distance, and tears. The scythe pulled her down, down, down between the worlds. She slipped past the twin suns of the In-Between and watched the Mortal World approaching. On the edge of her vision, she glimpsed two bright pools of green fire.

"You grow stronger every day," said the eyes. "But the greatest challenge is yet to come."

She tried to turn, but the scythe pulled her onward. She coursed through stars and space, beyond time and emotion. Lighter than a daydream, she slipped through a crevice: the gap between light and shadow. The blade twisted, finding its way.

A face appeared before her: an elderly man she didn't recognize. Somehow, she sensed a name: Elias Stoneridge.

She landed hard, stumbling as her feet hit a tiled floor. Beads of white light trickled off the blade.

For a moment, she couldn't tell where she was. She heard beeps and the slow intake of air.

Frank patted her on the shoulder. "You okay?" he asked.

"Yeah."

"Remember, don't let anyone else see us," said Frank, looking around the hospital room.

Certified Deaths received special robes to help avoid mortal eyes. Ironically, the Deaths who'd inspired tales of the Grim Reaper throughout the ages had been students like her. Students *and ones who didn't make it back.* She shuddered, remembering her skeletal appearance. It seemed long ago.

A man lay in a bed, connected to an array of tubes and machines. Suzie walked to the foot of his bed and read the name on his chart. "Elias Stoneridge." The scythe quivered in her hand. The handle pulsed like a beating heart, or was that only her own heartbeat? No, the blade felt the soul, it was *hungry.*

"It's his time," said Frank, patting her on the shoulder. "Quickly, before someone comes."

Elias's eyes stared at her, but he seemed to look through her. He gasped for air and the machines behind the bed beeped.

"A nurse is coming," said Billy, glancing into the hallway. "She's only a few doors down."

Suzie didn't have time to think, but in a way, she didn't have to. She didn't even swing; she relaxed her muscles and stopped fighting the scythe. The blade leapt downward, straight through Elias Stoneridge. As it struck the weak stranger, she felt a strange sensation as the blade swam through the soul. For an instant, she swore she heard *chewing*, not from Elias, but from the blade itself. The scythe continued down through the floor, before swinging around. It pulled on her, jerking her into a stumble.

Elias sat up, his eyes wide with fear. His body lay on the bed and the machine let out a long, droll beep. The scythe tingled again.

"About time," said the soul of Elias Stoneridge. "Past few days have been awful. What kept you?"

"Sorry?" said Suzie.

"Quick, quick," said Billy.

The beeping and hiss of tubes grated on her. The blade at the end of her scythe turned slightly. Had she turned? No, the scythe was ready to go on. The tingling in the handle started to itch. Billy tugged on one of the tethers and waved his hands, telling her to hurry.

"Take my hand, please," said Suzie.

"You lot are dressed a bit dark for angels. And where're your wings?"

"Please, Mr. Stoneridge," said Suzie. "We have to go." She felt her strength failing her. She could barely stand. She was Reaping a soul. An old man she'd never heard of. A man she was taking from his family. She was taking him away to never come back.

Elias turned and peered at himself. "I am dead, right?"

"We are Deaths," said Frank. "And we're here to take you onward."

"Deaths?" Elias laughed. "You mean like the skeletal guy on the lunchboxes? You bunch of kids? Don't they teach angels better'n to lie?"

"Now, Suzie," said Billy.

The door to the room opened and a nurse entered. She screamed and collapsed on the floor. Frank pushed Suzie's hand into Stoneridge's. The soul felt warm, but at least she could hold it. She let the scythe drop and the hospital vanished.

The ride back was agonizing.

Colors tore through her like swords, tearing through her, clawing the ghostly soul from her fingers. She clenched her hand, but felt Elias slipping away. No, she couldn't lose him yet. No. Smells, sights, sounds, and sensations bombarded her in a whirlwind of confusion.

Two suns became two eyes of green flame, but they said nothing. Darkness clashed with light in a roar, and the student Deaths slipped between the lines of dreams. Suzie plummeted upward and downward, trying to break free. She held on as the manic scythe blade tore through time and space.

A whirlwind of confusion.

A world of lies.

Cool grass slid beneath her shoes, and beads of light dripped from the blade again.

"That was fun," said Elias Stoneridge. "But let's not do it again."

Behind her, the cliff soared impossibly high, cutting off half the world. The ocean stretched in front of her, flowing away toward the upward-flowing waterfall. The great iron doors in the center were closed, yet she knew Elias would be able to enter.

She'd only been here once before, but the place was unforgettable. The end of all things: the door to the Hereafter.

"Well if it isn't the bitch and her pups," shouted a voice. She spun around and Luc came toward her. He led a soul of his own, a middle-aged woman with blonde hair.

"Not now," she heard Frenchie say.

"I'll bet you botched it up already, didn't you Suzie?" taunted Luc. She didn't answer, though in truth he was right, they'd been seen.

"Finish the Reaping," said Frank softly. "Ignore them."

"How many Deaths we got here?" asked Elias. "Way I figure, you only need one."

"Mr. Stoneridge, you need to—"

Luc walked over, guiding the blonde woman. She looked like she'd been crying.

"That way," said Luc, pointing with his scythe. "Go die. You, too, old man."

"I want to—" started the woman. Luc smacked her. She started walking across the water. Elias said nothing, but clutched Suzie's hand.

"You gonna let him go?" asked Luc. "Or do I have to do it for you?" He raised his scythe.

"That's enough," said Frenchie, leaping forward. He pulled a dagger from his cloak and slashed at his younger brother. Luc vanished in a cloud of dust.

"I'm sorry," said Frenchie. He stepped away and Frank glared at him. Something glinted in Frank's hand. Did he have a dagger too?

"This wasn't supposed to happen like this," said Suzie, trying to apologize to Elias. He smiled and bent down, kissing her on the cheek.

"Most fun I've had in years, little angel. Er, Death. But I do think I'll be going now. Someone's waiting for me on the other side."

Suzie blushed and wiped away a tear as the old man walked across the water and entered the massive iron door. The door vanished and the scythe relaxed in her grip.

"What the Hell was that about?" demanded Frank. He pushed Frenchie, knocking the taller boy back a step.

"I stopped him," said Frenchie.

"Your brother raised his scythe. He was going to strike her."

"I told you, I stopped him," said Frenchie. "Suzie, can I talk to you in private?"

"Anything you have to say, you say in front of us," said Frank. Billy nodded.

"I'm gonna head back and talk to Hann," said the other boy on Frenchie's team. The short, wiry boy was still tied to Frenchie's waist with a tether. The third tether hung limply.

"I'll be back soon, Mark," said Frenchie. "Don't let him go easy on Luc."

Mark nodded and pulled a dagger from his robe. Its blade was curved, like a small scythe. Mark nicked himself and vanished in a puff of smoke.

"We all have 'em," explained Frank. "The older students have to carry them on Reapings in case of an emergency. They send you straight back to Hann."

"It's only us now, Frenchie," said Billy. "Start talking."

"I'm sorry for what he did. Luc shouldn't have done that."

"It's your fault," said Billy. "You've been egging him on."

"I'm trying to apologize." He paused, and Suzie sensed a great deal of turmoil in his expression. The way he looked at her, with longing in his gaze, like Billy's looks before he kissed her. Or was that how she imagined him?

"Spit it out," said Frank.

"You don't understand," said Frenchie. "When I first came two years ago, it was hard enough, but you can't imagine what it felt like to meet *him* here. My own brother. In the World of the Dead."

"You set him against Suzie?" asked Frank. "You had no right—"

"Everyone was against Suzie at the beginning. She was different. She was…convenient."

"Convenient?" asked Frank. "A nice target for you and your friends to bully? Is that what you mean?"

"It wasn't personal," said Frenchie. "She let me turn my anger somewhere. I was beyond anger. They brought two brothers here."

"We're all angry," said Suzie. "None of us want to be here. You had no right to treat me poorly. You've been picking on me the whole year. What have I ever done to you?"

Frenchie's mouth tightened. "Nothing." He looked at the ground.

"Say that again," demanded Frank.

"I said it once," said Frenchie. "But whether she did or didn't, my brother sort of snapped after try-outs. He wanted to literally kill you. He's not normally like this. Luc's a good kid."

"You hadn't seen him in two years," said Frank. "Maybe he'd changed."

"Maybe," muttered Frenchie, looking away. "He lost me. For years, I was gone. He'd probably given up, convinced I was dead and then finds me here. Whatever my disappearance did to Mom and Dad, he saw firsthand. I can't imagine what's going on in his head." Frenchie paused and looked up. Tears wet his eyes. Frenchie, who'd she always thought of as an enemy. This Death was only a boy after all, a scared and angry little boy. She pitied him.

"Listen," said Frenchie, "I'm not saying I did the right thing. I'm saying I'm sorry."

"Tell your brother to lay off," said Billy.

"He won't listen, but I'll try. I'll catch you guys later." He pulled out his dagger and hesitated.

"I might still act mean at times," he said, "but don't listen. You're not a bitch, no matter what they say." He nicked himself and vanished.

"No matter what *you* say, you mean," muttered Billy.

"C'mon," said Frank, "the Reaping's done, let's head back."

"We were seen," said Suzie. "Hann will know, won't he?"

"Probably. But it happens every year." Frank smiled. "They expect it. They used to let the first years have their Reaping right around Halloween, in case the living spotted them. Of course, the teachers complained because it was too much to cram in. Now they chalk it up to pranks or insanity. Not our problem."

"Hann will be annoyed," said Billy, "and as much as Frank downplays it, it's not good. Yet in your case, I wouldn't worry. He had Deaths sent back early." He took out his own small dagger. "Hann himself told us that they haven't had to use these in over a hundred years. He's got bigger things to deal with today."

CHAPTER EIGHTEEN

The Scent

Hann hadn't been distracted, he'd been furious. For two weeks after the Reaping he didn't even speak. A chubby Death named Professor Rayn discussed the need for *absolute discipline* during a Reaping. It was *unconscionable*, Rayn said, to interfere with a Reaping. If Reaping was a Death's primary role, to interfere with that role was almost as bad as slaying another Death.

Suzie felt conflicted. On the one hand, she was grateful Hann hadn't singled her out, and was instead punishing Luc's behavior. On the other, she was petrified. They couldn't even practice with the scythes. During two classes, Sindril himself had come in and scolded the class.

The only Death who seemed unfazed by the change in the class was Luc. Every day, Suzie came to Hann's class, sat, and listened as Rayn scolded them. Suzie glanced at Billy or Frank, but no one said a word. The class never moved or spoke until the period was over. The next day, they'd repeat everything. Hann stared at each of them, every day, sitting to the side of his desk. He never said a word, and never looked at Rayn or Sindril. He seemed totally lost.

He wasn't the only one who was lost.

Four months after Styxia, they were no closer to starting the plan.

"That was painful," said Frank as they left Hann's class. "How much longer can this go on?"

"Who is Rayn anyway?" asked Billy. "Why does he have to come in and lecture us?"

"Rayn? He's got nowhere else to be lately," said a third year named Jeff. "Since Styxia that is."

"What do you mean since Styxia?" asked Suzie.

"Rayn's the College expert on 'Mentals. With the 'Mentals gone, there's nothing for him to do except play the disciplinarian. They assume Hann didn't get through to us, and that an extra scolder will help. If I find out who messed up a Reaping, I'll kick 'em right in the nuts."

Suzie kept her mouth shut. Hann had never mentioned Luc, or even told the class exactly what happened. At first, she considered telling her classmates, but what was the point? Besides, if they discovered what Luc had done, eventually they'd find out she'd been seen.

"Rayn's a 'Mental expert?" asked Billy.

"That's what Joey said. He had a class with him, but it's suspended now. Seems they don't want to think about 'Mentals here. Not after what happened." Jeff shrugged and turned a corner.

Suzie glanced at Billy but couldn't tell what he was thinking. He wore his mask daily now, hiding the disfigured face.

"Meeting. Nine," she muttered. He nodded and walked away.

* * * *

"We need to ask Rayn for help," said Suzie, "to find out where the 'Mentals are. The Final Test is in six weeks. We do this now, or not at all."

Her eyes adjusted to the dim, dusty white light of the flowers in the library. A spider crawled across the table, and she flicked it away. It scampered under a book.

"What do we say when he asks why?" asked Billy. "What if he tells Sindril?"

"We have to take that risk. We have nothing, and I'm sick of going nowhere. I'm going to ask him tomorrow after class."

"No," said Frank. "I'll ask. You stand out too much Suzie. I'm just another Death."

"This is my fight," she said. "I'm the one who got you into this. I'm the one Sindril targeted, and Athanasius said I'm the one they're trying to keep safe. I'll ask."

"Frank's right," said Billy. "If one of us asks where the 'Mentals live, we at least stand a chance of Rayn not noticing."

They were right. They had to be cautious.

"Not Frank," she said. "It has to be a first year asking an entirely innocent question. To help with—"

"An art project," said Jason. "I see where you're going."

"But why—" started Frank.

"And Jason's not in our Applications class," continued Suzie. "Any question from him will seem unrelated to us."

"That sounds shaky."

"I'll do it," said Jason. "Let's meet back here tomorrow. Same time."

"Good luck," said Suzie.

Frank looked like he wanted to protest, but Suzie rose. The decision stood. As much as she needed her friends, she called the shots, which was a strange reversal. She'd been isolated, struggling to get them to believe. Now they followed her. Jason would ask.

As they left, Suzie waited an extra minute before opening the bookcase. No one was in the house. She nodded to the others and they walked out. They'd return at different times, by different routes. Were they being followed, or was Suzie paranoid?

She walked into the cool night air and glanced up at the crescent moon. A scythe of white sliced the souls of stars, cleaving the heavens. A cold crescent moon stared down; yet, for an instant, perhaps, she saw a smile.

The smile of Athanasius.

She smiled back at the sky.

* * * *

"It's the smell," said Jason.

He peered over the dusty table, tossing an old book to the floor. A pile of dust rose, catching the dim glow of the flowers.

"What smell?" asked Billy.

They'd met in the library two days in a row. Suzie's excitement had never been this high. For the first time since arriving in this world she had something to think about other than the Final Test. Sindril had brought her here, she was sure. Sindril wanted a Dragon Key, and somehow he wanted her to help find it. Sindril. She didn't even care what he wanted. He'd killed her friend. She couldn't leave this world until he paid the price.

"What did he say exactly?" asked Suzie.

"At first he wouldn't answer," said Jason. "I told him Cronk had mentioned he was the smartest Death in the faculty. You should've seen him perk up to that. I explained how I was doing research for a special portrait about the Revolt, but didn't know much about the 'Mentals."

"Smart," said Billy.

"Still wasn't easy," said Jason. "Tried to ask in the halls, but he was too busy. He brought me to his office at the base of East Tower. Man, that place is freaky."

"And?" prompted Suzie.

"You ever noticed how the World of the Dead smells like strawberries?"

"Yes," she said. "I've definitely noticed."

"Well, according to Rayn, it doesn't. What we smell is the 'Mentals. I stopped short of asking more and thanked him."

"You mean, if we can track the smell, we'd find where they live," said Suzie.

"How are we going to do that?" asked Billy.

"Deaths steal from the Mortal World," she replied. "They stole clothes for me, when I first got here. Maybe we could steal a dog?"

"That *stealing* you mentioned isn't easy," said Frank. "Only a certified Death can cross into the Mortal World without constant supervision. And if it was a living dog? I don't think it's possible. Besides, how long would it take to train? No, we need another way. Yesterday, I remembered Cibran mentioning his home village. It's north of the College, in the forest. If you head north and follow the scent yourselves, maybe you'll be able to find them."

Suzie sat for a moment. Would they be able to track the 'Mentals themselves?

"Maybe there's a map here in the library," added Billy.

They searched for hours, but didn't find one.

"We should still try," said Suzie. "I'll come back to the library every day and try to find a map, you guys can come too. We'll go in a week, whether we find one or not."

* * * *

Saturday arrived and they'd found nothing. She looked out her window as a gentle rain came and passed. Billy led her outside. The sun emerged from a cloud and a rainbow appeared, stretching behind West Tower. They sat together on a bench in a courtyard, looking up. He put an arm around her shoulder and she leaned her head against him.

"Has everyone noticed?"

"It's not a big deal," said Billy. "I'm okay with it."

"We'll go without one."

"Wait. What?" He turned to her. Without a mask, she saw his full disfigurement. Bruises and small cuts covered the right side of his face. The wound on his left side had healed poorly, and was scarred and surrounded by a brown tinge.

"You were talking about my face, right?" he asked.

"I was talking about something else," she said. "But never mind." She didn't want to say that they were looking for a map. Probably no one was listening, but still…

She looked up at the colors hanging in the sky. A bird flew overhead, crying out, and fluttering toward the mountain of West Tower.

"Tell me about yourself, Billy," she said. "We've been friends for months, but you've never said anything about your life *before*."

"Before I came to this world? Before I became a Death?" Billy laughed. "Seems like ages ago. A different life."

"Frenchie said his brother got pulled here. I can't imagine watching your brother go missing, only to find him here."

"Me neither."

"I had a brother named Joe who used to tease me a lot. I *have* a brother named Joe, I mean. He's still my brother. I will see him. I'll see my parents too."

"Maybe, but I'll miss you if you do."

"I'll miss you, too, Billy."

A cloud drifted in front of the sun, and the rainbow faded. A squirrel glanced at them and darted away. She didn't smell strawberries, which meant no 'Mentals around. She wondered if any remained in the College.

"I was lonely before I came here," said Billy. "My parents were divorced and I didn't have any siblings." He shifted on the bench and looked toward the red stone walls around them. "I had a dog named Comet. He was my best friend. We used to take a lot of long walks together, to get away." He pulled a long blade of grass from the ground and twirled it around his fingers. "I lived with my mom most of the time, but she started seeing other guys. Whenever my dad was around, they'd fight. I started failing school, but they hardly noticed. Even when I got skinny they thought it was a cry for attention." He tossed the grass away. "I ended up here. I'll be honest, Suzie. I never took the Final Test. I told them to fail me, and they did. Truth is, I couldn't imagine going back."

"Billy, I'm sorry."

"Heads up, one of your teachers is here," he said.

"S-S-S-Suzie, can I have a w-w-w-word?"

"What is it Cronk?" she asked.

"I've s-s-s-s-seen your T-T-T-Test."

A tear fell down his face. She'd met Cronk before any Death; she'd even seen him in her dreams before he appeared at her door. She stood and wrapped her arms around him. Out of the corner of her eye, she watched Billy turn away.

"You c-c-c-can pass."

"Thanks, Cronk. You're not just my teacher. You're my friend as well."

She watched Cronk walk away. Suzie turned and kissed Billy on the lips.

"I understand how you felt," she said.

* * * *

The plan was set. Suzie laughed aloud. For the first time since arriving in this world, she was truly happy. Even if it didn't work, she'd proven something she needed to know—*she had friends*. They'd never found a map, and had even spent an extra week looking, but they were out of time.

The plan is set.

Frank and Jason would stay at the College, and if anyone asked, Billy and Suzie were confined to Eagle Two with the flu. Jason would insist they were highly contagious, and would spend a few nights at Frank's house. Suzie hoped it wouldn't take a few nights to find the 'Mentals, but it was better to be safe.

The hardest part was leaving the College unnoticed. For a while, Suzie wasn't sure what to do, but fate seemed to be on her side.

"Everyone's called to the Hall tonight," read Billy. "They want to discuss how the College will function without the 'Mentals." He folded up the notice that had been slipped under their door. "Everyone will be there, and Jason will tell them we're sick. Guess they're realizing life's different without servants catering to you. It's perfect, Suzie."

"I'm glad you're going with me," said Suzie. Billy leaned over and kissed her on the cheek. She didn't blush. She was starting to like it when he kissed her.

Four long hours later, they heard hundreds of Deaths filing toward the Hall. Suzie and Billy waited another half an hour before leaving Eagle Two. Suzie snuck into the corridor and peered out the front door. In the reddish dusk light, the reds and browns of the earthen walls grew vivid. The College looked empty.

"Let's go," said Billy. He and Suzie ran toward the Ring of Scythes.

They ran through the Ring, and as they passed beneath the blades, the sky turned orange. Suzie felt a familiar tingle around her and paused.

"Suzie?"

An eagle flew in front of her and turned its head. The bird vanished, leaving only two eyes of swirling green flame.

"Suzie, we have to keep moving. What is it?"

You are going to my home, said the eyes. *And you are going to your home as well. The end of the journey is at the journey's beginning.* The world around her melted into flames. The fire didn't burn, it was warm and comforting.

"Suzie?" She felt Billy shake her, but she couldn't move.

The answer does not lie in a distant land. It lies in you; in who you are. Find the truth and save us. You are strong, Suzie. You are—

The eyes vanished. Suzie glanced around but they were still alone.

"I'm okay," she said. "I had another vision. Let's get out of here."

They passed the Ring of Scythes and walked north.

"Strawberries," she said.

"I don't smell it," said Billy.

"Me neither."

They followed the path uphill. Trees parted as they reached a small pond.

"This is the pond Cronk brought me to the night I first came to the Land of the Dead," said Suzie.

"I've been here a couple times," said Billy. "This is Silver Pond." He glanced at his reflection and shuddered. "If Cronk brought you here it was probably to show you that you weren't anorexic in this world."

"They did the same for you?"

"Yeah."

The two writhing towers loomed against the sky in the distance, covered in shadows. They passed Silver Pond and entered another forest, older than the first. Billy helped her climb over a few massive overgrown roots. At one spot, she tripped over a patch of roots and tangled thorns. Billy plucked two thorns out of her leg. Overhead, the sun sank beneath the canopy of trees.

"You think Sindril will figure out we've snuck away?" asked Billy.

"I don't," she replied. "He's got enough to worry about, and I haven't seen a guard on us. Besides, the Final Tests are coming up and he has no 'Mentals to help get things ready."

"That's probably one of the reasons they called a meeting."

"Right," she said.

The forest opened and a barren field of grass and rock stretched to the horizon. Suzie turned around. The forest ringed the horizon, with no sign of the College or its towers. No sign of pursuit either.

"It's getting late," said Billy. "Maybe we should set up camp here." He pulled his backpack off and opened it.

"I don't like being out in the open," said Suzie.

"You'd rather go back to the forest? If any animals are around, I'd figure the forest would be more dangerous for us."

"Deaths or animals," said Suzie. "I'm not sure which would be worse. Let's set up at the edge of the forest. We'll use that canopy Frank stole; try to make a tent out of it."

"Should we start a fire? If you're worried about being caught—"

"A fire will be okay," she said. She wasn't used to making decisions. Part of her wanted to remain hidden, but she thought about the green eyes and the surrounding flames. Fire was familiar and comforting. Besides, it'd keep away animals, which were probably more likely to be after them than Deaths.

"This is the craziest thing I've ever done," said Billy as he started setting up the tent. He gathered sticks from the edge of the forest and heaped them into a pile. He took a match and after several failed attempts, managed to set the pile on fire.

"What do you mean?" Suzie pulled out one of the gorgers they'd filched and broke it in two. She handed half to Billy and gazed into the flames. No eyes.

"We're running into the woods chasing a strawberry smell, and for what, to create a distraction for you to sneak into Sindril's office? Come on, Suzie, you have to admit, this is a bit nuts."

"Maybe," said Suzie between bites. "Don't tell me you're having second thoughts."

He laughed. "No, I'm glad I'm here. I've been a Death for two years now, and in all that time, this is the first moment I've felt *alive*. Never felt like that back in the Living World either. Thanks, Suzie, you're…you're a good friend."

"You are, too, Billy." She sensed he wanted to say more, but she wasn't quite ready to hear it. This was new to her too. "We should take turns sleeping. One of us will keep watch," she said.

"Why don't you sleep first," he said. "I'm not tired."

"Me neither," she said. "But I guess you can have the first watch. If anything happens, wake me. Run if you have to, but wake me first."

"Stars are coming out," said Billy, gazing out across the rocky field. Above them, millions of tiny lights glistened against a sea of black. The moon shone, almost full, like a watchful eye of silver, surrounded by attending stars.

"They're beautiful," said Suzie.

"You're beautiful," said Billy.

Her face turned red, and she moved a little away from the fire. Then she lay down.

"I'm going to sleep now," she said. "Wake me in two hours and we'll trade."

She closed her eyes and pretended to sleep. She sensed Billy was watching her, but she didn't open her eyes.

What were these feelings? Billy was her friend, but he was more. He was ugly, with his disfigured face. Yet, something about him remained unhurt. He was also caring. He'd always been on her side, even when the others had doubted her. Or had he? And he had failed his Final Test on purpose. That still befuddled her. In the Living World, he must have felt as alone as she felt here.

The Final Test. When the time came, what would she do? If she passed, how could she leave Billy, Frank, and Jason? How could she think of not leaving? She didn't belong here, none of them did.

Yet Billy had chosen to stay. There were other boys in the Living World, and other girls too. Still, no one had ever paid attention to her the way Billy did.

For the first time, she realized an advantage to being the only girl in a world of men. It meant she had no competition. No, don't be ridiculous. *You'll meet plenty of boys back home*. But where was home? She wasn't sure.

She didn't remember drifting to sleep, but the ground faded away and Suzie found herself flying through stars: tiny shining scythes grinning at her with hungry steel teeth. She kept flying and the stars crowded around her, trying to nip her with their blades. A gust of flame sent them scattering.

You are strong, said the green eyes. *You are nearly home.*

"Where is home?" she asked. "I'm not sure anymore."

Only you can answer that, Suzie. Look inside your heart and see. Look inside your heart and find the truth.

Billy rubbed her shoulder gently, waking her. She wiped her sweaty forehead and propped herself up. The fire had died down, but still burned enough to give both warmth and light.

Billy lay down and she watched him as he closed his eyes. In the flickering light, his face looked even more disfigured. Try as she might, she couldn't ignore the charred skin or ugly scar. She turned to the forest and rose.

Shadows lurked at the edge of the firelight, taunting her. They danced and moved with every flicker of flame. In the distance, she heard a wolf howl.

She sensed something watching her, but nothing emerged. She stayed near the fire and turned back to the open field. For two hours, she wondered what was in the woods. She remembered the albino 'Mental. Frank claimed he had "gotten rid of the problem" but what had he done? Was the albino dead?

The night passed without incident. Flames and riddles filled her dreams; apprehension filled her waking moments. At last, dawn broke on the edge of the rocky field. The fire had long since died out, but she kicked dirt on top of it and spread the ashes.

"Anyone who wanted to follow us would have," said Billy. He took out a gorger and split it with her. Instantly, her half took the flavor of hot eggs and bacon.

"Let's get moving," she said between mouthfuls. "Gather the stuff, and we'll go." Together, they finished breakfast and filled their backpacks.

"Strawberries," Suzie said. "I smell it faintly, coming from that direction."

"Looks like that's where we're headed."

"I'm strong," Suzie muttered to herself, echoing the words she'd dreamed too many times. If only she believed them.

CHAPTER NINETEEN

The First Female Death

Two days later, Suzie's legs throbbed in agony. They walked from dawn to dusk each day. They'd followed half-beaten trails and abandoned roads. They'd crossed fields and forests, even wading through two streams. They hadn't found anyone. Yet they were going the right way. Strawberries filled every breath. Ripe, delicious strawberries, mixed with smells of mashed strawberries and strawberries past their prime. In one of her dreams, the red flames faded into a field of vivid red strawberries.

"We need to head back," said Billy. "We're almost out of food." They'd tried a few berries in the forest, but spit them out. Suzie had split the final piece of her strength cake, but it hadn't filled their bellies.

"We're close," she said. "I can smell it."

"Me too," he admitted, "but that doesn't mean we're close. I'm sorry, Suzie. We tried. Maybe next time."

"There won't be a next time, Billy. If we turn back now, Sindril wins. He killed Athanasius, and he's been toying with me. If I do *one* thing in this world, I want to discover *what* is going on."

Billy stopped walking. "Suzie, I hear what you're saying, but we don't have enough supplies. I don't want to starve to death out here."

"We're already Deaths," she said, only half-joking. "Besides, the 'Mentals will have food."

"They might not be friendly," warned Billy. "Even if we *do* find them, what's to stop them from attacking us? The 'Mentals started the riot at Styxia, remember?"

Of course she remembered, but she said nothing. It was no good arguing. She started walking again, not turning to check if Billy was behind her. He'd follow, and she was weary. She stopped for a second.

The bush beside her rustled. She listened and heard the rustle again.

"Something's in the bush," she said. She put a hand on the leaves and the bush shifted, sitting up. She jumped back startled.

"Suzie, look out," said Billy, running to catch up.

Two eyes appeared in the top of the bush and the foliage receded. Leaves and stems pulled back into skin and hair. A woman with green skin and yellow eyes looked at her, clothed only in other parts of her bush.

"Two Deaths," said the bush-woman.

"We're friends," said Suzie. "Friends to the 'Mentals."

"Deaths are not our friends. Go away, before I call my sisters."

Sisters. This was exactly what Suzie had dreamt of. Other women, other females. The woman who stood in front of them was strange, yet somehow the most beautiful woman Suzie had ever encountered. It was impossible to tell where bush ended and woman began, unless she *was* the bush somehow.

"We've been looking for you," said Suzie. "I want to talk to you and your sisters. I'm Suzie."

"I know who you are," said the bush-woman. "Better than you do." She laughed. "You're not old enough. Come back in a few years." She turned and her hair flowed downward, sprouting leaves. Her skin grew branches, and she started to vanish into her own foliage.

"Wait," Suzie shouted. "Please, miss. We want to help you."

The bush laughed. "How can *you* help *us*?" Her voice was light and leafy, like a flower dancing in the wind. "No, Susan. It's *you* who need *our* help."

"That's true," said Billy. "Please—"

The foliage retracted suddenly and the green woman's face emerged, her eyes pulsing gold. She glowered at them.

"It has been one million years since a Death came into our village. Do you expect me to trust you?"

"No," said Billy. "You probably don't. But we're kids. We're not even full Deaths."

The bush turned away, and some of her leaves dropped. Stems and leaves moved inside her skin, until only a few twigs stood in her hair. The green-skinned woman glared.

"You stay here," she said to Billy. She put her hand up and vines sprang from the earth, coiling around his legs like chains.

"Hey," he shouted. "I didn't do anything."

"You alone may follow," she said to Suzie.

"I'll be back soon," Suzie whispered to Billy.

"Be careful," he said. "These guys are powerful."

"No harm will come to Susan," said the woman. "She is far too precious."

The leaves faded into her skin, and the woman turned and started to walk away. Suzie followed, glancing back at Billy, who'd sat on the ground, watching her. His disfigured face looked strangely handsome as she walked away.

"I am Lucina." The bushes receded into Lucina's skin, and Suzie realized that the green-skinned woman was nude. "The last Death who walked freely into our village was an ancestor of yours."

"An ancestor?"

"A female Death, like yourself."

"Wait, you mean Lovethar? She can't be an ancestor of mine," said Suzie.

"Her blood flows in you," said Lucina. "Though it is thin and flows in others. I cannot sense it, I am a Foliate Elemental." She turned to Suzie and smiled. Suzie glanced at the strange woman's green breasts; then looked up at her bright golden eyes.

"A Foliate Elemental?"

"Elementals have attributes, or abilities if you like. It is in our blood. My blood runs green. Like my parents and daughter, I am one with certain plants. Other Elementals possess different abilities. Kasumir, one of the Seers, first told of us of your presence in this world. She sensed a tie to Lovethar and her family."

They came to a small stream and crossed. The trees grew sparser as they approached a ring of small houses. Women clustered around the houses, pointing at Lucina. She didn't respond, but led Suzie to the center of the village, past row after row of houses. Some had quaint gardens; smoke puffed from small chimneys in thatched roofs.

Women, children, and men walked around the village, staring at Suzie as she passed. Each Elemental had eyes of strange colors. Some of the women were naked with bright green skin like Lucina's. Two boys with wings instead of arms ran into the street, waved their wings, and hopped away. An old man brushed past them. He turned to Suzie with a goat-like face and eyes like Athanasius's snake eyes.

"Look out," shouted a young girl. A massive rock flew through the air, and Suzie leapt out of the way. A second girl raised her hand, and the boulder froze in mid-air; speeding back toward the first girl. It looked almost like boskery, only these children weren't using a ball, they were using a boulder. Instead of throwing, they were using some sort of magic.

They kept walking and Suzie started when she saw an albino, who looked identical to the one who'd attacked her. The albino stared at her and Suzie froze. She remembered the terror, the fear in the forest... The Elemental turned away, walked into a house, and closed the door.

"Come, Susan," said Lucina. She led her to the heart of the village. A two-story wooden building with a thatched roof and large chimneys stood in the center of an open square. Lucina walked straight to the building, opened the doors, and ushered Suzie inside.

The air was stuffy inside the timber-framed hall. Two skylights let light in through the ceiling above, and large bouquets of white flowers glowed brightly. Lucina led her to the front of the room where three Elementals sat on chairs. A woman with ivory skin and eyes darker than coal smiled. Her entire eye sockets were pitch black, giving her an alien look. To her right sat a woman with light blue stripes across her skin. Her eyes were entirely white. A man sat on the third chair. His eyes were closed, as if he was asleep.

"May I present the female Death," said Lucina.

The man opened his eyes and Suzie took a step backward. His eyes glowed with green flame. The green eyes turned to her.

"It's you," said Suzie.

"I'm sorry?" said the man. "I've never met you before." His voice was high and shaky. It was not familiar.

"Your eyes," said Suzie. "In my visions—"

"Perhaps you have me confused with someone else," said the man. "But we will have time to discuss that. We have much to discuss, don't we Kasumir?"

The woman with black eyes rose. Her hair and skin were white, and she wore a white dress. When she closed her eyes, she looked like an ivory statue. When she opened her eyes, the darkness of her eye sockets overwhelmed the whiteness of her skin. Her eyes sank like two pools of shadow into her alabaster face. With a start, Suzie realized the woman reminded her of a skeleton. Was she an Elemental or a Death?

"Welcome, Susan Sarnio, daughter of three worlds," said the raven-eyed woman. "I am Kasumir, the White Seer, as some call me. This is my sister, Hinara, and my husband, Giri."

"Hello," said Suzie. The hall smelled overwhelmingly of strawberries; it made Suzie's head spin.

"We've been expecting you," said Kasumir.

"My friend," said Suzie. "My friend Billy was tied up and left behind. Why didn't you let him come?"

"No Death has entered our village in a million years," said Kasumir. "Not since Lovethar. I can't allow an exception for your friend. I am sorry. Yet you, Susan, for you alone we made an exception. We have much to discuss."

"No," said Suzie. She was in no position to bargain, but what did she have to lose? For some reason, the Elementals didn't frighten her. Even their strange powers were just another oddity of this strange world. "No," she repeated. "I'm not talking or listening until you bring Billy here. He's my friend, and he's here to help me."

"Suzie," said Hinara. "I don't think you understand. This is something we cannot do. The village—"

"I understand the 'Mentals hate the Deaths," said Suzie. "I watched at Styxia. Billy's face was disfigured because of it. I want to help you. *We* want to help you. We're Deaths. Not just Billy, but me too."

"You are a female Death," said Giri.

"I'm a girl, yes," she said. "Who cares? I'm ticked off. I'm tired of people taking advantage of me. You get Billy in here now, or I'm leaving. Whatever big thing you've been waiting for will have to go on waiting."

For an awkward moment no one spoke. Suzie feared she'd said too much. It was a bluff. What would she tell her friends if she left? She wasn't even sure why she'd insisted on getting Billy, but she hated to think of him tied to the ground. Had she offended the 'Mentals? Had she ruined any chance they might have?

"Lucina," said Kasumir. "Bring the boy."

"But, Madame Seer—"

"Bring him. *Now*."

"Yes, of course." Lucina bowed and ran out of the room.

Hinara chuckled. "I like you, Susan," she said. "The boy doesn't matter. You don't like being pushed around."

"Billy does matter," she started.

"Oh, I understand," said Giri, "and I sense you are troubled by me. You said you've seen eyes like these before?"

"Many times," said Susan. "Green eyes that tell me things. I have strange, yet recurring visions. But it's not your voice I hear."

"Only one other Elemental has eyes of green flame," said Hinara, "and he's missing."

"Missing?" asked Suzie.

"My son," said Giri. He glanced at Kasumir. "Our son. His name is Plamen. He wanted to work for the Deaths. It's good money, though they treat us like slaves. He went to work for an old family friend of ours, an Elemental named Athanasius. Yet even before the revolt, we stopped seeing him."

"I met Plamen briefly," said Suzie. "When I was first brought away from my world, they took me to an office where Athanasius had me sign a contract."

"It is standard procedure for all new Deaths," said Kasumir. "How is my son? How is Plamen?"

"I don't know," said Suzie. "I haven't seen him since that first day, unless he's the cause of my visions. I did see Athanasius during the revolt. I'm sorry to say he was killed."

"No," said Giri. "Athanasius is dead?" He grasped Kasumir's arm.

"Hundreds died in the revolt," said Hinara. "And many are still missing. Yet this is terrible news. Athanasius was my friend as well. He was a good man."

"Who killed him?" demanded Kasumir.

Suzie tried not to picture the hallway, the blood. She couldn't stop the screams.

"Suzie?" asked Giri. "Are you all right?"

"Sindril," she said. "Sindril killed him right before my eyes. Athanasius was trying to save me. He tried to tell me something, but Sindril came."

Kasumir turned away, her white hair bristling.

"But you swear you haven't heard from Plamen?" asked Giri.

"I still have visions," she said, "but I don't understand. A pair of fiery green eyes, like yours, always appears in them."

"Strange."

"Sir, if your son is the one sending me the visions, then *why* is he doing it? Why doesn't he find me and talk to me? And what is he trying to say?"

Kasumir faced her again. "I can answer that," she said. "It is an answer I have observed in my visions. The powers of an Elemental develop from birth and are hereditary. Plamen must have inherited some of my gifts, even if we did not foresee that. He must have realized some of the truth as well."

"What truth?" asked Suzie.

"You've heard of Lovethar?" asked Kasumir.

"The only other female Death," said Suzie. "They compare me to her. They say she was burned to death, but I thought if a Death is killed they fade from memory."

"You are wise," said the black-eyed seer. "Lovethar came to this world at a critical period. Since the dawn of time, the Dragons had been responsible for bringing souls from the Mortal World to the Hereafter. The Dragons, as a race, are older than the Living World, or any species here in the World of the Dead. They carried souls before man stood up in the jungles on your world. And it was that rise that changed them.

"With such a number of new souls, the Dragons needed a place to process them. They wanted a place for souls to wait, while they flew one soul at a time to the Hereafter. This was before that fancy door, the College, or the In-Between. The Dragons dreamed of all those things, but had no capacity to build. Thus, they created the Elementals. Using fire and magic, they formed living creatures to help build them a city, which is now the College. The Elementals built the World of the Dead, and the Dragons were happy for their help."

"I don't understand," said Suzie. "Where were the Deaths?"

"The Deaths," said Hinara, "came from the East, beyond the sea. How they came to this world is a mystery. Some suspect that the Dragons created them as well and forgot. Others say it was an accident, when a Dragon mistakenly brought a living man from the Mortal World. And others claim that whatever god created the Dragons, formed the Deaths as well."

"The men Hinara mentioned were called the Donkari," said Kasumir. "They were an ancient people from across the sea. The Donkari were all male, and vicious. Every few years, they raided villages in the Mortal World, recruiting new Donkari. They believed only males were worthy of being raised as Donkari. And as you've probably guessed, they crossed to the Mortal World using blades from their homeland, the first scythes."

"We didn't learn any of this in History," said Suzie. She found herself sitting, overwhelmed with new knowledge. She thought back to the ancient books in the secret library. She'd seen pictures of ships, and she did seem to remember the word Donkari. What did it have to do with her?

"I assure you, this will make sense, and it does connect to you personally," said Giri. She found it hard to meet his eyes. They were familiar, those twin pools of green flame.

"At first the Donkari wanted peace," said Kasumir. "But when they discovered the power of the Dragons, they became jealous. They renamed themselves *Deaths* and started a war. They could cross to the Mortal World, and they wanted to ferry souls. They believed if they transported souls, they would have the powers of the Dragons. They were wrong, of course."

"That's when Lovethar arrived," said Hinara. "By all accounts it was an accident. During a raid to get more Deaths, they accidentally snatched a young girl from a village, mistaking her for a boy. By the time she arrived here, it was too late. The Deaths raised her, even as they threatened war on the Dragons."

"They taught us a little about her," said Suzie. "They said she betrayed the Deaths, and that's why she was killed."

"In a sense she did," said Kasumir. "Yet her sin was the same as my own. She fell in love with an Elemental."

"Suzie, are you all right?" Billy's voice filled the hall behind her, and she turned to watch him come in.

"I'm fine," she said. "Are you okay?"

"Fine. Did you ask them? Are they going to help?"

"We will help," said Hinara.

"I—" started Suzie. "I didn't even have the chance. I mean, you were telling me."

"It is important that you understand where you come from, and why things have become tense," said Kasumir.

"Does this have something to do with the Dragon Key?" asked Suzie. "I keep hearing about it."

Giri looked at the other Elementals and then turned to her. His eyes blazed in a familiar, yet strange way.

"Perhaps," he said. "I have heard rumors, but nothing more."

"Tell her, Giri," said Hinara.

"Lovethar was a curious girl. As she grew older, she explored far beyond the College. She walked the same path you did. She met a young Elemental named Orryn. Orryn impressed Lovethar by making rocks fly through the air and stop suddenly. He had been practicing a game many of our kind play."

"They were playing when I was brought through the village," said Billy. "Looked like boskery, only magical."

"Magic," laughed Kasumir, "is a word used to describe things you don't understand. Yes, fire and magic formed the Elementals, according to the old songs. Yet, we don't think of ourselves as *magic*, simply

204 | CHRISTOPHER MANNINO

gifted with abilities. Orryn was an Earth Elemental and could manipulate stone and metal. He was also a threat to the Deaths, since Lovethar left the Deaths to live here. The Deaths accused her and Orryn of plotting with the Dragons. Some claimed that Orryn forged a Dragon Key, using stolen metal from a scythe and his own power as an Elemental. The Dragon Key was supposed to be more powerful than the scythes; it was supposed to even unlock the Hereafter itself." She laughed again. "No one has proof, and I doubt such a key ever existed."

"But the Deaths believed it did," said Suzie. "They wrote about it a lot."

"The Deaths cared about Lovethar," said Giri. "The war with the Dragons started, and she was here. Since the Dragons formed us, Deaths assumed we were natural enemies in the war. The Dragon Key story was an excuse to punish her. They captured her and did burn her on Widow's Peak."

"The story we learned is true?" asked Suzie. "But if she died—"

"She didn't die," said Hinara. "They tried to burn her, yes, but Orryn saved her."

"She was rescued?" asked Suzie.

"And she wasn't alone," added Hinara. "She and Orryn had a son: Gesayn. The Deaths tried to kill both in the flames. Orryn saved both his wife and infant son, but the boy was maimed. Gesayn lost a hand, but the family lived. They went into hiding, only emerging after the war."

"The Deaths won the war," said Kasumir. "Yet though the Elementals were neutral, we were treated as enemies. That is when the enslavement began, the hatred of my kind. Male Elementals were forced to work at the College for a million years, up until the Styxia revolt. A revolt you helped inspire, Susan."

"Me? I didn't have anything to do with it."

"News that a female Death had returned started the Elementals thinking. And I had a vision." Kasumir waved toward her darkened eye sockets. Did she have eyes, or were they holes?

"Lovethar's line did not end with her son, Gesayn," said Kasumir. "Gesayn's sons were forced to work for the Deaths. For a thousand generations, the Elementals continued to grow. Lovethar's blood ran thin. She was forgotten in all but name, as each new generation of male Elementals started their work with the College. Until a clever boy named Gesayni became frustrated. Named for a distant ancestor he himself had long forgotten, he disguised himself as a Death and joined the College. He eventually stole a scythe and escaped to the Mortal World. He lived and raised his own family there. Suzie, you are his granddaughter."

"What? That's impossible," said Suzie. She knew three of her grandparents. One had passed when she was young; a man she had heard was an orphan, a man named...

"Giuseppe Sarnio," said Hinara. "Who came to America as an orphan. In truth, he came to your world as a refugee: an Elemental seeking to escape the Deaths. His blood flows in you as well, Susan. It is no accident that you're here."

"But I belong in the Living World," insisted Suzie. "Even if everything you've told me is true and honestly, I don't believe it." She paused, her head spinning. "Even if it *is* true and I'm a descendent of Lovethar and Elementals, it doesn't matter. It doesn't mean anything to me. I want to pay Sindril back for killing my friend. I want to show the Deaths that he shouldn't be in charge, and I want to go home. We came here to ask for your help in that. This other stuff doesn't matter."

"You're wrong," said Giri. "We want to help you because of who you are. We want to take down Sindril for what the Deaths have done to us. Don't you understand? You can't leave. You belong in this world, Suzie. Our blood has come home. You must finish what Lovethar tried to do a million years ago, and bridge the gap between Elementals and Deaths. It's why you are here."

"I'm not here for some grand purpose," shouted Suzie. Her cheeks reddened. This hadn't gone the way she'd planned. The smell of strawberries made her sick, as did the three 'Mentals spouting nonsense in front of her.

"Wait," said Suzie. "Let me make this clear. I don't buy your story. I'm an ordinary girl. Sindril is a creep, and I want to make him pay. We're going to create a diversion, and I'm going to sneak into his office. I don't care about what happened a million years ago. Maybe I was curious when I first got here, but that's ancient history. Will you help me do something that matters *now* and stop worrying about the distant past?"

Billy took her hand and squeezed. The gesture was reassuring. Could she be part 'Mental? Is that why Cronk had brought her to the World of the Dead in the first place? Is that why Plamen, if it was Plamen, kept showing her visions? Maybe that explained why Athanasius had given her the cake and tried to help her during the coup. Many pieces made sense, and yet she couldn't believe it. She didn't belong on this world, she belonged with her parents.

"We will help you," said Kasumir. "What exactly is the plan?"

Billy smiled. She forced herself to smile back.

CHAPTER TWENTY

East Tower

"How'd it go?" asked Jason.

They'd snuck back during the night, following two Elementals who helped hide them. Given the overwhelming powers of the 'Mentals, Suzie didn't understand how they'd ever been subjugated, although the scythes were powerful as well. She shuddered as she thought of the blade in her hand, tearing downward, *eating* the threads of Elias Stoneridge's soul. The blade had a terrifying *living* quality, which was ironic considering its use.

"It went well," said Billy. "Look."

Anil and Ilma, the two Elementals who'd guided them, appeared suddenly. It was a trick of the air, which they manipulated to make themselves invisible. Suzie didn't understand it, but they'd slipped back to the Ring of Scythes without detection.

"Wow," said Jason. "Frank will be excited."

"Where is he?" asked Billy, looking around the secret library. Suzie glanced around the room as well. This room she'd discovered; it was her safe haven, maybe even her home.

"Luc was making a fuss about you guys being sick for a week," said Jason. "Frank went to take care of it. To shut him down before it became a big deal."

"Are you cold?" asked Billy as Suzie shuddered a second time. Frank had *taken care* of Luc. What had he done to the albino? Why was it always Frank who *took care* of these situations?

"I'm fine," she said. Billy gave her a look, his scarred eye contracting. He turned back to Jason. The more she looked at his disfigured face, the less it bothered her. Billy had stayed by her in the village of the 'Mentals. He'd been the first Death who was nice to her. And the kisses. She wasn't completely sure how she felt about Billy, but she liked the kisses. Billy had warmth, a comfort she didn't sense anywhere else in this world. When she passed her Final Test in a couple of weeks, she'd be sure to come back and take Billy to the Living World with her. Maybe she'd take Jason and Frank too.

"The plan's set," said Billy, "Exactly as Suzie proposed. The 'Mentals will storm the College at noon tomorrow. The campus will erupt into chaos. Suzie, you have to be in Sindril's office when all hell breaks loose. You'll find what you need and get out. If he catches you stealing, or realizes that you took anything…"

"He won't," she said. "I'll find the proof I need, grab it, and leave before he even gets back. The 'Mentals will help us spread the word of what he's done. He's up to something, and once the Council finds out, they'll have to fire him. If I can get rid of Sindril before I leave this world, Athanasius and the other 'Mentals won't have died in vain."

Jason let out a long, deep breath. "It's a long shot," he said. "But we're all in this now."

"All for one and one for all," said Billy. "Like the Musketeers."

"The trick is making sure I'm in his office before noon," said Suzie. "If I go too early, I'll have a hard time staying, but if I go too late it will look suspicious."

"Give yourself fifteen minutes," said Billy. "Any more and he'll get suspicious. But any less and it'll be cutting it too close."

"What exactly are you looking for?" said Jason.

"I don't know," said Suzie, "but I'll find it somehow. Anything about the Dragon Key might be good, or something that shows he's up to something." She frowned. It was still hard to believe that the 'Mentals had no idea what the Key was. Was it only a rumor? If it *had* been a ploy to attack Lovethar a million years ago, why would Frank's friend suffer for mentioning it?

Too many questions remained. Even if everything the 'Mentals had told her was true, and she was descended from 'Mentals and

Lovethar, it didn't explain why Sindril wanted her here. Bridging some gap between Elementals and Deaths sounded noble and grand, but the 'Mentals hadn't brought her, the Deaths had. Somehow, she doubted Sindril cared if 'Mentals and Deaths got along. She'd seen his parade, where 'Mentals were whipped like slaves. No, something else was going on, something darker.

"We attack at noon," said Anil. "Good luck, Suzie."

* * * *

The East Tower loomed in front of her, blocking the sun. She'd pictured this day as dark and stormy, but now that it was here, the sun was shining and a refreshing spring breeze blew wisps of fallen petals across the canyon courtyards of the College. Deaths milled about the campus in short sleeves. A pair of Deaths tossed a boskery ball back and forth. Birdsong lingered in the air, which smelled of strawberries. Would anyone else notice the strong smell?

She glanced at the East Tower again. The massive pillar of writhing stone stretched far into the clouds, covered in tiny windows. Gnarled fingers of stone pointed skyward from every level of the gigantic stalagmite tower. The enormous doors were open, but a white-haired Death she'd never met stood at the entrance.

She turned to Billy. "What time is it?"

"Eleven thirty-five. Still haven't learned how to read an hourglass, even after all this time?"

She looked at the enormous hourglass built into the side of the courtyard. She counted the lines. Yes, it was a little after eleven-thirty. They'd start in five minutes.

"You ready?" asked Billy. No one paid any attention to them.

"Tell me honestly, do you think this will work?"

"It's hard to say," he replied. "A lot depends on luck. You're a smart girl, Suzie. I think it's a good plan, and if anyone can pull it off, it's you. You'll do great." He looked her in the eyes, and she felt that familiar tug as her mouth approached his. At the last moment, she turned and kissed his cheek.

"After this is over, I'm going to miss you," she said. "If other Deaths found a way to sneak to the Living World—"

"Your grandfather was a 'Mental, not a Death. Even if I did find a way out of this world, I'd keep losing weight. I'd become skeletal and die. Besides, nothing's left for me in the Living World."

"I'd be there," she said.

"Yeah."

"It can't be over for you. What if you ripped your contract?"

"Suzie, this isn't the time to worry about that."

"The Final Test is only two weeks away. I still want to go home, but I don't want to leave my friends. I don't want to abandon you and Frank and Jason."

"We'll be fine," said Billy. "Whatever happens, Suzie, I'm glad I had the chance to meet you."

"Me too."

"You should go now," he said. "You have five minutes to get into his office. Then you have fifteen minutes before the 'Mentals come."

"Are we still doing what we planned?"

"With that guy at the entrance, I think we need to." He gave her a wink and counted down from three on his fingers. They'd been standing in a corner, now she screamed and ran into the courtyard.

"Leave me alone," she yelled.

"You're a stupid girl," said Billy in a loud voice. A few heads turned. "You don't belong here."

"Your face looks like someone puked acid. Why don't you go away?"

Billy shoved her. He pushed her lightly, but she fell back as if he'd thrown her with all of his might. She staggered away and ran to the entrance of East Tower.

"Please," she said to the white-haired Death at the entrance. "This guy's been teasing me, like all the other boys. Headmaster Sindril told me I could come to him for help. I'm sick of the taunts." Out of the corner of her eye, she watched Billy turn and run away, pretending to be scared of retribution. She was on her own now.

"You are the female Death," the white-haired Death said. He adjusted a pair of glasses to stare at her. "Yes, yes, who did you want to see?"

"Headmaster Sindril," she said. "He told me to come to him for help."

"The Headmaster, yes? Hmmm, doesn't sound much like the Headmaster. He told you that you—"

"May I go to him?" she asked. This was taking too long; she needed to get to his office now.

"Yes, yes. Fine, go ahead."

"And which office is his?" she asked.

"Didn't you say that he sent for you?"

"He told me to come to his office. This is my first time. Please, which office is it?" Was this Death stupid or senile?

"Hmmm. Yes, yes. Hundredth story, below the Council chamber." The Death adjusted his glasses and continued to stare at her as she walked around him and through the double doors.

She went to the elevator, trying not to sprint. She pressed the button and waited. Glancing back, she noticed the white-haired Death still watching her. He smiled a disturbing, half-toothless grin.

The elevator arrived with a ding, and she got on, pressing 100. It rose for a full five minutes, higher and higher. The doors opened on to a dark hall. White flowers started to glow, and soon an enormous golden chandelier filled with the flowers lit. A solitary pair of doors stood at the end of the hall. They were dark red, bordered by ornate gold carvings. Door knockers in the shape of human skulls stared at her with ruby eyes. Beneath the left skull, a small sign said *Mark L. Sindril, Headmaster of Deaths, Junior College and Senior College.*

She looked back at the elevator. It was now or never. Did she still want to do this? She remembered her first time in the library and pictured Sindril's voice.

"And what of the girl herself?"

She remembered the sentence, and the chill that'd gone through her spine. He is planning something, something about me. He might even want to kill me...

She pictured Athanasius. He'd told her that she was important.

"Susan," said Athanasius, "is far more precious than you realize. She is—" He stopped suddenly and turned his head, but it

was too late. A scythe flew through the air and landed in his neck. Athanasius fell to the stone floor in a pool of blood.

Athanasius had died for her. Sindril had murdered him in front of her. The blood, the golden eyes, and her own scream echoing in her ears. She clenched her fists and reached for the knocker.

Yet she hesitated. The man behind these doors terrified her. He killed Athanasius himself, he could kill her too. He was too powerful. She'd be gone in a couple weeks anyway. She'd never have to worry about Sindril again. Maybe she should leave.

As she paused the gold on the door seemed to melt, and the red paint turned to red flames. A pair of green eyes stared at her; eyes like Giri's.

"You are strong," said the eyes.

She felt their heat, and the comfort of the flames.

"Plamen?" she asked in her mind.

The eyes looked surprised and they vanished. The flames disappeared.

Suzie reached up and grasped the knocker. She knocked a single time and the door opened. Sindril stood on the other side, pulling up his monocle. His angular face frowned and then opened into a smile as he scratched his beard.

"Susan Sarnio," he said, "what a surprise. Come in."

He led her inside a luxuriously decorated suite. Lush oriental carpets covered the floors, and large, intricately-carved sculptures of birds and Dragons surrounded her as she walked forward. A wooden screen separated a smaller room with couches, and doors painted bright colors led away from her in either direction.

Sindril led her to a massive oak desk and sat down. He gestured for her to sit in one of the large leather chairs in front of it. Large bookcases, filled with hundreds of books, and reminiscent of her secret library, stood on either side of the room. Behind the desk, a large circular window looked down on the College like a massive eye. Three golden telescopes pointed to different parts of the window. The top of West Tower rose in the distance, but below them, the ground was a blur beneath the clouds. An eagle flew by.

Sindril leaned back in his chair. The room was dim. The bright window behind him surrounded Sindril in a halo of glaring light. The effect was intimidating. He moved a few sheets of paper on his desk, pulled out a black cloth, and started polishing a crystal ball.

"Well, Suzie, what brings you to my office?"

"I'm sorry to interrupt you, sir." *What time is it?* She'd taken too long to get here; the revolt could start at any minute. Yet, did she have to stall? "I was teased again today, this time by my own housemate."

"Teased?"

"At the beginning of the year you told me you'd help if the Deaths bullied me. I wanted to come sooner, but I've been afraid. I'm sick of it."

"And you come *now*, two weeks before your Final Test?"

Sindril tossed the cloth onto his desk, folded his hands together, and frowned. She looked away and swallowed hard. He wasn't buying it.

"I was nervous," she said. "You're male too." His eyes narrowed, and she hoped she hadn't crossed a boundary. "I didn't know who to trust." She dug her fingers into her leg, hating what she had to say next. "But after you saved me from that terrible 'Mental, I realized you were on my side."

"All right," he said.

"It's probably too late, but I wanted to come here and get away. I doubt I can get through these next two weeks at this rate. And many people fail—"

"Which housemate bullied you?"

She bristled. This was a mistake. She didn't want Billy to suffer.

"He said one thing," she said. "But it wasn't a problem. Punishing him won't matter. It's Luc, one of my classmates. He's been the worst. He even interfered with my last Reaping and had to be sent back early. He's bullied me every day since I arrived. I hate Luc."

Sindril's eyebrow rose. He glanced at some of the papers in front of him. "Luc is the reason you came here? You're tired of him picking on you. He's Francois's brother, isn't he? How has his brother been?"

"Frenchie was rough at first, but he's changed, or so he says. He stopped picking on me after that Reaping. It's Luc who's the bigger problem."

"Interesting," he said. "I will take care of Luc. He won't bother you for the rest of the year."

"Thank you," she said. That phrase again...*take care of*...what exactly did he mean?

Sindril neatened his papers and looked at her, pausing as they studied each other. *What does he see?*

"Anything else?" he asked. Oh no, she hadn't taken long enough. She wanted to go to the window, but couldn't. Where were the 'Mentals?

"I was wondering what will happen at the final exams."

"I can't discuss that with you, Suzie. I can guarantee Luc will leave you alone until then, but it's all I can do."

"What will you do to him?"

"That's not your—" He broke off as a sound like thunder exploded far below them.

"Excuse me for a moment," he said. He stood and walked to one of the telescopes, adjusting the dials. Suzie's heart pounded hard against her ribs, echoing in hears like thunder. Sindril would hear her fear. Someone knocked on the door behind her.

"Come in," said Sindril, peering through his telescope.

"Sir," said a Death Suzie didn't recognize. "It's the 'Mentals. They're attacking the College."

"I see that," said Sindril.

"Only, sir, it seems to be—"

"Yes?"

"It's women, sir. Women 'Mentals."

"Gather the Council," said Sindril. "And ready the defenses, we'll deal with this."

The Death bowed and hurried out of the room.

"You should wait in the Tower," said Sindril, turning to her. "Go to the first floor."

"Are the 'Mentals attacking again?" she said, her voice shaking. "I don't want to go anywhere. I'm scared." She stared ahead, forcing her eyes to tear.

"Don't cry," he said. For a moment, his expression softened. He walked to one of the doors and opened it, pulling out a large scythe.

"I won't touch anything," she said. "I don't want to be near the chaos if it's anything like Styxia." That part at least was true.

"You can go to the lower floors, nothing will happen—"

"You had to rescue me from those awful 'Mentals," she shouted, through her tears. "I can't take that again. I swear I won't even move until someone comes for me, or I'm absolutely sure it's over."

He stared at her as another crash thundered outside.

"Fine," he said. "Stay here until the chaos ends. This shouldn't take long. Keep away from the windows, and don't touch anything. Stay put and I'll deal with this."

He gave her a hard look and then walked out, slamming the doors behind him. A third boom rang out, and the entire Tower shuddered. For a moment she froze, fearing Sindril would come back. After a minute, she eased herself off the leather seat and walked to the window. She tried to peer below, but all she made out was clouds and smoke. She peeked into a telescope without moving it, by standing on her tiptoes.

Deaths ran from roaring balls of fire as 'Mentals strode calmly through the campus. She recognized Kasumir's white hair; the 'Mental raised a hand and two Deaths fell to the ground cowering. A Death ran toward Kasumir with a raised scythe. Another 'Mental raised his hand and a geyser of water burst beneath the Death's feet, knocking him down. Suzie turned back to the room. She didn't have time to watch the melee, though she hoped her friends wouldn't get hurt.

How would she find anything? Where should she even start? The suite was massive, probably taking up most of the entire floor. Six closed doors, not counting the ones leading to the elevator, stood around the room, perhaps leading to other doors. And what if Sindril discovered she'd been spying?

Suzie took a deep breath.

"You are strong," she said aloud, echoing the words she'd heard in her visions.

She walked to the bookcases first, skimming the titles of the books. She didn't recognize any of the names. She slid a thin book down: "MacFarlen's Guide to Growing Flower Lights." No help. She tried a thick volume near the bottom: "Boskery: The Complete Rules." She pushed it back onto the shelf.

Suzie walked to the massive desk where Sindril had been sitting. She tried the bottom drawer, but it was locked. She tried the next drawer up. Inside she found stacks of papers. She leafed through them, but they seemed to be academic reports from teachers. Beneath the reports, she found inventories for food, supplies, mortamant, and scythes. She closed the drawer. The final drawer slid open with a loud creak. Inside she found quills and blank pieces of parchment, probably used for contracts. An array of small knick-knacks, trifles that reminded Suzie of tourist shops back in the Living World, littered the rest of the drawer.

She pulled out a small silver chain with a large, gaudy pendant with a picture of Niagara Falls. Behind it, she found two marbles, a tiny Statue of Liberty figurine, old coins, and a handkerchief with embroidery that said "Mom's Kitchen." She pulled out a worn, wrinkled photograph. It showed a teenage boy holding hands with a young girl. They were sitting on the hood of a car, parked in some woods. She turned the photo over, and on the back, she found the words "Best Date Ever" in cursive. Suzie put the photo back in the drawer.

She was about to close it when she spotted another trinket: a small ceramic dragon. She pulled it out. Like the other trinkets, it looked like something from the Living World. The dragon was painted bright green with red eyes. It sat on a small pile of treasure. Suzie swore she'd seen the same figure at a Renaissance Faire when she was younger. She turned it over again. The top of its head seemed discolored. She ran her finger over the spot where the paint had worn away. *Click.* The dragon's head popped down and a small compartment under the treasure popped open. A silver key fell on the carpet below.

Suzie put the dragon down and picked up the key. This was an unexpected stroke of luck. She guessed what it opened. Reaching down, she unlocked the lower desk drawer. The drawer was large but almost empty. She reached for a shimmer of metal and pulled up a small ring: a silver band of metal with a carved silver dragon's head on the top. She looked at the ring and heard a shudder.

Nothing too special about the ring, but it did have a dragon on it. Did Sindril think this was a Dragon Key? She heard the sound again and glanced up. The 'Mentals must be close to the tower.

The ring shook in her hand and she noticed the crystal ball on Sindril's desk. A cloud of smoke swirled in the center of the crystal and she heard another shudder. No, not a shudder, a growl emanated from the ball. In the smoke, something moved like a great piece of leather. *Or a wing.*

"Not now," growled a low voice, deeper than anything she'd ever heard. The voice thundered with terrible malice, and she shoved the ring into her pocket. As soon as it was out of sight, the cloud of smoke vanished and the rumbling noise stopped.

She froze for a minute, watching the crystal, but nothing stirred. She was right, Sindril communicated with Dragons. This is how he'd talked to them in the house, outside her secret library. He must have brought his crystal and used this ring. It was taboo. If the Deaths had a religion, communicating with Dragons would be their greatest sin. She had the proof. She had Sindril's ring.

Using the key, she locked the drawer again. She was about to put the key back in the dragon, but instead, tucked the key into her pocket as well. If Sindril couldn't open his drawer, he wouldn't know it was missing. A desperate plan, but it would at least buy her a little time. Enough to spread the word of what Sindril had done.

She closed the other drawers and started to leave but hesitated. She had a key and a dragon-ring in her pocket. A Dragon Key? No, she still had no idea what the Key was. Kasumir claimed it didn't exist, but Sindril had mentioned her. *"What of the girl herself?"* he'd asked. He must have been asking the Dragons. He had been talking into the crystal. She had proof, but she needed answers.

She looked around the room again.

"Leave," said a voice. *"Leave now."*

The carpet of the floor grew hotter and the walls melted into flames. The green eyes stared at her.

"I only have a ring," she said. "I need more. I need to find out why he wanted me."

"*This isn't the time*," said the eyes. "*Spread the word, take away his power and then, when he is weakest, confront him. It is the only way. If you stay, he will find you.*"

"Are you Plamen?" she asked the eyes. The green flames narrowed, and the world around her seemed to cool.

"*Yes*," said the eyes. "*I am your friend.*"

"Why have you been doing this to me?" she demanded. "What do you want?"

The flames vanished and the eyes started to fade.

"*We will speak soon, I promise*," said the fading voice.

Suzie checked her pocket, feeling the ring and key. The desk looked as it had before she'd opened it. She took a deep breath and hurried to the double doors. She left and took the elevator down.

"Susan?" asked a voice as the elevator opened. She looked up and stared into Sindril's beard. His monocle was gone, and he had scars on his sweaty face. A streak of blood ran down his cheek.

"I—" she froze, sweat beading on her forehead. "I thought it'd be safe. The battle was dying down."

"I told you to wait," he said.

"I'm sorry."

"The situation is still dangerous. Stay inside the tower until I can find an—"

"Suzie," shouted a voice from outside. Frank ran through the open doors of the tower. Sweat dripped from his face, but he looked unhurt.

"Headmaster," he said. "I've been looking for my friend here. Everything seems safe. I'd like to escort her home."

"I don't have time for this," muttered Sindril. "Fine, but avoid Eastmoor Corridor or anything near the Ring. Those areas are still unsafe. I have to get more scythes. Bring her directly home."

"Yes, sir."

"Susan," said Sindril as she turned away. She tried not to clutch her pocket.

"Yes?" she asked.

"I will remember our talk. He won't bother you anymore."

"Thank you," she said. She turned and walked away, with Frank behind her. They left the tower but she didn't stop walking. She couldn't stop or she'd break down in tears.

"Did you get it?" whispered Frank.

She nodded and kept walking. "What's in the corridor?" she asked.

"The 'Mentals attacked hard but fled quickly. Some went to the corridor, others to the Ring. They were holding many of the guys from Styxia as prisoners beneath Eastmoor Corridor. We're not supposed to meet everyone until tomorrow."

Suzie glanced around. The campus was mostly deserted but Deaths still ran through some of the courtyards with scythes raised.

"Quiet," she whispered.

"I didn't speak aloud," said Frank. She turned to face him. His mouth didn't move, yet somehow she heard him say. "I am your friend."

"It was you," she whispered.

Frank opened the door to Eagle Hall and ushered her inside. He stood outside their door and looked back at her.

As she watched, Frank's dark eyes brightened to a furious green, like green fame.

"My given name is Plamen," said Frank. His mouth hadn't moved, yet the voice sounded clearly in her head. "I am your cousin."

"No," she said. She needed to sit down.

"I'm sorry the visions were frightening," he said. "I'm not a seer, like my mother. One day I will be, but I'm still learning, and it's difficult to control."

"No." It was all she could think to say.

"I've been in disguise to infiltrate the College. I wanted equal rights and helped organize the Styxia movement. It was you, Suzie, who did it. You have Sindril's ring, and we can prove he was a traitor. You did it."

She slapped Frank in the face. "You lied to me," she said. The door to Eagle Two opened.

"What's going on?" asked Billy.

"We'll talk inside," said Suzie.

Jason sat at the kitchen table. He looked up as she came in.

"Well?" asked Jason. "How'd it go?"

"I found something," said Suzie. "I was right."

"What'd you find?" he asked.

"I'll tell you in a second, first Frank has something he'd like to share."

She turned to Frank, who stood near the door. "I'm sorry," he said, lowering his head.

"What happened?" asked Billy.

"He's been causing my visions."

"The 'Mentals said it was someone named Plamen," said Billy.

"My name is Plamen," said Frank. "I am an Elemental in disguise." He raised his head and his eyes glowed with green fire. "I only wanted to help."

"How does giving Suzie weird visions help anything?" demanded Billy. "What do you want?"

"I'm still your friend," said Frank. "I'm still Frank." He sighed. "But I'm also Plamen. I recognized Suzie when she first came to the In-Between. I worked for Athanasius, and she was a relative. I had both my mother's visions and my own. Suzie returned to the World of the Dead to help bridge the gap between 'Mentals and Deaths. She's inspired change already, two revolts in the past few months alone. And now she has proof that we can use to overthrow Sindril."

"Why speak to me in visions? Why not tell me who you were the first day you came here?"

"Elementals are not allowed on campus, except as servants. How would I become your friend if you didn't trust me and spend time with me? I like you, Suzie. I like you a lot. As for the visions, at first I wanted to nudge you. I tried to show you visions of Lovethar, hoping you'd learn about your own heritage. I thought if you became curious enough, you'd discover the truth, and you did."

"Were you ever going to tell me who you actually were?"

"I wasn't sure how you'd take it," he said, reaching up to the cheek she'd slapped. "But time's up for me. We're going to the library today, and a few of the Elementals have already recognized me. My parents told you my name when you went to their village. It's not a secret anymore." Frank spread his hands and his eyes faded back to dark brown.

"No one caught you before this?" asked Billy.

"One did," said Frank. He put a hand on Billy's shoulder. "And I am sorry. The truth is that they were attacking me when your face was hit."

"Why would they attack their own kind?" asked Suzie. "Didn't you help to organize the Styxia revolt?"

"I was one of the chief organizers," he said, "but Paryas was never that bright. I grew up with him. He saw me and believed I was helping the Deaths. I guess no one told him otherwise. He threw fire at me. When I dodged the flames they hit Billy, who was already out cold. Paryas died a moment later with a scythe in his back. Billy, I'm sorry, and sorry to everyone for lying."

Billy stood and frowned. His disfigured face contorted as he looked at Suzie.

"You're still our friend," he said. "And I think I understand why you did it. This also explains a lot, like why Suzie kept having visions and how you 'took care' of the albino."

"I sent him home," said Frank. "He never meant Suzie any harm. Luc had found one of the albino's brothers and threatened to kill him if the albino didn't use his skills on Suzie. Even in my village, we looked down on Fearmongers. He's probably here now as part of the revolt."

"He's here?" asked Suzie.

"Susie, everything I told you in visions is true. You are strong, and I am your friend. You have more support here than you realize. The albino was looking out for his family. That's done now. You have nothing to worry about. I promise."

"No more lies," she said.

"No more lies."

She gave Frank a hug. "I forgive you," she said. She wasn't angry. In a way, it made sense. He *had* helped her. Besides, she did need Frank. She needed all of her friends.

"Tell me one thing," said Billy.

"What?" asked Frank.

"Did the Gray Knights win because of you? Was it some 'Mental ability?"

"No," said Frank. "We won without any help in that way." He smiled. "But let's face it, 'Mental or not, I'm still a better player than you."

Billy smiled. "What do we call you?" he asked.

"I'd prefer Frank. Think of it as my new nickname. Besides, I don't want the Deaths to find out. Not until Sindril's gone, at least."

"We won't tell anyone," said Suzie.

"What proof did you find?" asked Jason. "Will it work?"

"It will," said Frank as Suzie pulled out the ring. "I don't know how, but it will."

Suzie looked at the tiny ring.

The Dragon's mouth stood open as if ready to breathe fire. Had she glimpsed an actual Dragon in the crystal? Would this tiny ring be enough to overthrow Sindril?

Answers had started to come. Lovethar, her visions, the way Sindril had communicated that day. Who would have guessed that Frank and Plamen were the same?

Only one problem remained: Sindril. She thought of his lies, of his words outside the library, and of the scythe-like grin he wore after he murdered Athanasius.

"We'll bring him down," she said. "He'll pay."

CHAPTER TWENTY-ONE

The Ring

They walked out of the Ring of Scythes toward the library. The campus was quiet. Most of the 'Mentals had fled, but the Deaths remained wary, wondering where they'd went. Suzie smiled, she was about to visit them.

"Frank," asked Jason. "How are you a second year? If you went into disguise when you met Suzie—"

"My abilities allow me to enter minds. I did a little…persuading. Nothing damaging, but enough to convince the Deaths that I'd been here for a while."

Suzie didn't like that. She didn't like to think of Frank as a liar. He was her friend, or at least she hoped he was.

"What will you do when they find out?" asked Jason.

"Hopefully Sindril will be gone, and Deaths will be more accepting of us. Elementals built this campus, I don't understand why we can't study here, or at least be respected."

"You're an idealist," said Billy. "That's why you go to such lengths."

"It's true," said Frank. "I'm an idealist, but I'm practical enough to keep myself out of trouble."

They turned from the path and started down the winding trail to the house. A crowd stood outside the building.

"Son," said Kasumir as they approached.

"Mother," said Frank. The two embraced.

"Son, may I?" asked Kasumir.

Frank nodded and the white-haired 'Mental touched his forehead. She smiled.

"Yes, it's clear now," she said. "You've helped us a great deal, Plamen."

"Frank. I go by Frank now."

"I named you Plamen, and I will call you Plamen. Suzie, you have the ring with you?"

"Yes."

"Then let us go inside. Giri and the others are waiting in the library. It is a clever space. Built by Elementals, of course, and rediscovered by you, Susan. Fitting, don't you think?" Kasumir smiled.

Suzie followed them inside, glancing at the side room. Frank patted her on the shoulder.

"You were right about Sindril," he said.

"And wrong about you."

"Come on, they're waiting." He led her past the bookcase and down the stairway. The library was crowded, even with many 'Mentals waiting outside. As she entered, the room quieted and everyone turned to watch her.

"Hello," she said meekly.

"Susan Sarnio is a hero," said Kasumir. "She braved Sindril's lair to retrieve the proof we need." The 'Mentals cheered.

"I found this in a desk drawer," she said, pulling out the ring. She'd opened a drawer and stolen a ring. Did that make her a hero? She doubted it, but also doubted they'd listen.

Kasumir took the ring from Suzie.

"Suzie, this ring alone will not suffice. However, you beheld a Dragon, in the crystal. You learned the way he communicates."

"Yes, the ring made a cloud appear in the crystal."

"I observed it in Frank's mind," said the seer. Her dark eye sockets stared at Suzie like two empty holes. "He was watching you, Suzie. This is the proof we needed, and is what I'll show the Deaths."

"How can you show them something from my mind?"

"You've had visions all year," replied Kasumir. "One of the Elemental abilities is to influence the mind. If Plamen, Giri, and the others with a similar ability join with me, we can broadcast a brief vision to the entire College. We will show them what you witnessed."

"But he'll know I was in his desk. He'll realize I stole his ring." Even as she said the words, she realized how foolish they sounded.

"Suzie, he'll find out soon," said Billy. "Once he realizes the ring is gone—"

"But what if no one believes it?" asked Suzie. "You're talking about visions, like what I had? I didn't believe my visions for a long time."

"A strong, concentrated vision will be enough to raise doubts," said Giri. "Sindril isn't in charge. He's only one of the Council. If the other eleven find out, he's likely to be sacked. And if we broadcast our vision twice, he'll have everyone doubting him. Dealing with Dragons is the worst possible thing a Death can do, Suzie. The Council always feared they'd return and start a second war."

"Sindril hated us," said Kasumir. "His anti-Elemental policies are worse than any before him. Many on the Council feel sympathetic to us. Sindril never has. If we can remove him from power, we would shake the very foundations of the College. Deaths would have no choice but to listen to us."

"He killed my friend," said Suzie. "I want him to suffer. What do I do?"

"I must enter your mind, however, I need your permission," said Kasumir. Frank turned away.

"I'll do it," said Suzie. "Let's do it now."

"We will," said Giri, "but not here. We need a way to amplify our own powers so we reach the entire campus."

"The towers?" asked Billy. "They're massive. What if you signal from them?"

"I doubt we'll be able to get back on campus," said Kasumir. "The guard is up, and the College is on alert. One attack is all we'll get, though it was a huge success. We rescued twenty prisoners, and only lost two."

"We should take a moment for the two who died today, and the many who died on Styxia," said Frank.

Suzie lowered her head. Who had died? Was it Anil and Ilma, who'd helped her sneak back and appear invisible? Maybe Lucina, the strange bush woman who she'd met in the village, had died. Was it the albino? Perhaps two total strangers lay dead. Had they died for her, or had they given their lives for some ideal of equal rights? What could she do to make it up to them?

"The Ring," said Suzie, raising her head. "The Ring of Scythes. It surrounds the entire campus, and you said scythe blades have special powers."

"It's true," said Hinara. "The scythes are powerful. Combining Elemental power with scythes could be risky."

"The Scythe Ring is programmed by Elementals," said Kasumir. "That's how both 'Mentals and Deaths pass through. Besides, combining our powers is what Lovethar would have done." She smiled. "In all my years, I've never encountered a Death like you Suzie. The plan is settled. We head for the Ring of Scythes."

The crowd shifted. Suzie walked behind Frank. He hadn't changed. He was the same, only more complicated now.

"Mother," said Frank as they left the house.

"Yes?"

"Before we do this, I'd like to help Billy. Can someone here help his face? It was my fault."

"No, it wasn't," said Billy.

"Say no more," said Kasumir. "Dwyna. Melpoma."

Two young girls with glowing blue eyes and blue hair stepped up. They curtsied to Suzie.

"Can you heal his face?" asked Kasumir, pointing to Billy.

"It will take time," said one of the girls.

"The three of you stay here," said Kasumir. "The rest of the 'Mentals as well. Only those able to broadcast thoughts need come with us. And perhaps Anil and Ilma, to help mask our presence at the Ring."

Anil and Ilma were alive. She surveyed the massive group of Elementals. She smiled when she spotted a green-skinned nude woman walking from the side of the building. Lucina smiled back at her.

"You ready?" asked Frank.

"Do I go with you guys or stay here?" asked Jason.

"It'd be best if you and Frank headed to the Ring before the rest of us," said Kasumir. "If all is clear, we won't be far behind."

"Stay safe," said Jason.

Frank gave her a look. She smiled at him and he nodded.

Frank and Jason walked away as a group of 'Mentals crowded around Kasumir. Giri stepped up to Suzie.

"You're a strong person, Suzie. You're the only female Death, and now you're taking on the headmaster himself. Plamen told me that you have a test to determine if you return to the Living World."

"Our Final Test," said Suzie. "It's in two weeks."

"Well, if you don't pass, by any chance, come to us at any time. The Elementals will always be your friends."

"I'll pass the test," she said. "I will go home."

"Of course." Giri nodded.

After a few minutes, they started down the road. Suzie didn't speak. The 'Mentals seemed to respect and admire her, but the only 'Mental she knew well was Frank, and before yesterday she'd never dreamed he was anything other than a Death.

If you don't pass the test. What would she do if she failed? She'd been away for a year; surely her parents thought she was dead. What about her brother Joe? Did he miss her, or was he relieved to have her out of the house? No, he'd miss having someone to pick on.

It seemed far away, like a distant world. It felt...off for some reason. A nurse who smelled like strawberries, or was it gingerbread? And her friend with the funny voice. Crystal. Like the ball Sindril looked through to speak to Dragons.

As she reminisced, she remembered Billy telling her about his dog, Comet. Her dog had been Bumper. She remembered how strange it had been to meet him in the In-Between. Cronk had shown him to her to prove that she was a Death. And here she was, the first female Death in a million years. Now she was going to attack Sindril. She wondered if history would remember her as betraying the Deaths, as Lovethar had a million years ago. No wonder Deaths hated women.

"Stop here," said Kasumir, raising a hand. The 'Mentals stepped to the side of the road, waiting beneath some trees. Suzie counted nine 'Mentals total. She was the tenth of the group, and, as always, alone.

But she wasn't alone. She had many friends. An entire group of 'Mentals were risking their lives for her. Even Frenchie had apologized when Luc bullied her during the Reaping.

She paused. She had a life here. As much as she denied it, she was happy. What did she have in the Living World? Who did she honestly have? Crystal was a friend, and of course, Joe and her parents. So many other faces. A doctor, her teachers. What would they say if she suddenly turned up after being missing for an entire year? What would Mom say? *Mom*. What would Mom say if she told her grandpa didn't come from Italy, he came from the World of the Dead? Would Mom believe she'd held their dead dog? She'd probably send Suzie to a lot more doctors.

"They're ready," said Kasumir. "Frank sent the signal."

Had he? Suzie wondered if he sent flames and talking green eyes to his mother.

They walked the rest of the way to the Ring of Scythes. Anil and Ilma moved their hands in circular motions, shaping the air around them.

"Suzie," said Kasumir, "I need to enter your mind now. I need to witness what you observed in Sindril's office."

Suzie nodded and closed her eyes. She remembered Sindril's ornate desk, and the drawer filled with trinkets. She pictured the smoke swirling in the crystal and the terrible voice.

"That's perfect," said Kasumir.

Kasumir, Giri, Frank, and Hinara joined hands with three other 'Mentals. They stood in a semi-circle around Suzie. Jason watched from the other side of the Ring.

The handles of enormous oversized scythes formed a tiny ridge in the ground, as the mammoth-sized scythe blades pointed upward, joining to form an arch. Thousands of the arches made up the Ring of Scythes. She'd been through this arch, the exit toward the library, more than any other. "Concentrate," said Kasumir. The 'Mentals closed their eyes but nothing happened.

"Will we see it too?" asked Jason.

"I'm trying to reach the Ring, but the scythes are too strong." Kasumir grimaced.

"Suzie," said Frank. "Help us."

"How? What do I do?"

"Bridge the gap," said Frank. For a moment, she thought he was referring to lofty ideals again, but then she realized what he meant.

She stepped onto the ridge and reached out a hand, touching Frank, at the edge of the semi-circle. Reaching with her other hand, she grasped one of the blades.

"Suzie," said Jason. "What are you—"

She never heard his last words.

She touched the mortamant, the strange metal of the scythe. A shot of pure electricity jolted through her body like lightning. Every part of her body throbbed with sudden pain. In her mind, she pictured Sindril's desk, the dragon ring, and the clouds in the crystal. At the same time, she saw thousands of Deaths. The entire campus opened in front of her. She looked at each of them, and she knew they could see her. They could see *through* her to the vision pouring out of the 'Mentals, the vision of her in Sindril's office.

One by one, Deaths flashed in front of her face. Jason had the vision, and now Hann. It passed to Luc and Frenchie, to Cronk, even to Lord Coran and the Council. She saw them all; she could feel them all. The towers of the College, and the canyon-like stone mounds beneath it. The thousands of men taken from the Living World, taken to be Deaths.

Then she saw Sindril. The pain left her and the vision started to fade. Yet his face remained.

"Susan," he said. Then he was gone. She released the blade and a stream of blood ran down her palm.

"It's done," said Kasumir. "You did it. The vision will replay itself two more times to every Death before it fades."

"It's over," said Suzie. "Did it work?"

"Did the Deaths witness it?" said Kasumir. "If that's your question, the answer is yes. You made sure that they did. Grabbing the scythe like that was brilliant."

"I bridged the gap," she said.

"I knew you would," said Frank.

They walked down to the library. Her hand hurt and her head spun. It was over, the plan was done.

"Suzie," shouted Billy, breaking her from her thoughts. She looked up and was glad to find him smiling.

"Your face," she said.

"Yeah." He embraced her, kissing her on the mouth. She blushed but kissed him back. As he pulled away, she admired the new face. A small scar lingered under Billy's eye, and the top of his ear looked red, but otherwise he looked like he'd never been attacked.

"Thanks Frank," said Billy.

"I got you hurt in the first place," said Frank.

"You made up for it," said Billy. "How'd it go?"

"It was a success," said Kasumir. "The vision was delivered. We have nothing else to do but wait. It's time we said goodbye."

"You're leaving?" asked Suzie.

"Things may improve, but even with Sindril gone it will take a long time before Deaths and 'Mentals truly get along. I only hope the new Headmaster is more understanding. Plamen, let's go. We have to circle halfway around the campus before we can head home."

"Mother, I'm staying here."

"They're bound to discover that you're a 'Mental eventually," said Kasumir.

"Right now only Suzie, Jason, and Billy know. And if things are going to change, I want to be on the other side of the Ring, making sure things go smoothly."

Kasumir smiled. "I'm proud of you," she said.

"As am I," said Giri.

The three hugged for a time, until the 'Mentals took to the road, heading back to their village. Lucina turned and gave Suzie one last smile.

"I'll miss them," said Frank, "but we'll meet again."

"Let's go home," said Billy. "It's been a long day."

* * * *

Sindril resigned as Headmaster the next day. At first, Suzie didn't believe the rumors, but Lord Coran himself announced the news. While eating dinner in the hall, the Council walked in, minus Sindril. Coran claimed that Sindril had chosen to pass on the responsibility to a new Death, following certain important questions. Then the Council marched out.

"We did it," said Suzie.

"I can't believe it," said Billy.

"The one thing I wanted to do before I went home," said Suzie. "I don't even care about what game he was playing, I'm glad he's gone. After what he did to Athanasius."

"Do you believe things will change?" asked Jason. "Will the 'Mentals and the Deaths ever get along?"

"Maybe," said Suzie, "but that's a good sign." She pointed to two Deaths who hurried to bring gorgers to the tables. A male Elemental pointed to where they had to go.

"Deaths work fast, don't they?" said Billy.

"I guess they do," said Suzie.

The 'Mental noticed them looking and walked to their table. He had bright yellow eyes, a yellow beard, and a long tail.

"Thank you, Susan Sarnio," said the 'Mental. "For what you've done."

"You're welcome," she replied.

"My father," he continued, "my father was Athanasius."

"Susan," interrupted a voice behind her.

She turned to face a Death in a purple robe. It was one of the Councilmen, a Death she didn't recognize. The yellow-eyed 'Mental bowed and hurried away.

"Susan," said the councilman. "Lord Coran would like to speak to you."

"Now?" she asked.

"Yes, he'd like some words alone. I will escort you."

She nodded and followed the councilman away from the lower hall. He led her outside and across an open space. They entered one of the larger stone mounds and headed up a flight of stairs. He knocked on a large oak door and opened it.

"He'll see you in here," said the councilman.

She stepped into a classroom she'd never entered. Numbers and equations covered a blackboard at the front of the room. She'd almost forgotten about math, her least favorite subject.

"Susan Sarnio," said a voice. Seated behind the teacher's desk was a man who looked over ninety. The thin wisps of hair around his head were as white as Kasumir's hair. Lord Coran wore a white robe, and of all the Deaths she'd encountered in this world, he looked the part better than any other did.

"Lord Coran," she said.

"I don't know how you did it," he said, "and frankly, I don't want to. It was a risk that you took. Some will be unhappy, and you won't make any friends from this."

"I'll be gone in less than two weeks," she said. Besides, he was wrong. It *had* made her more friends than she'd ever had before.

"Sindril hasn't resigned," said Coran. "The truth is the Council confronted him about the visions. He admitted to contacting Dragons. It is a grievous offense, as I'm sure you are aware."

"Yes, sir."

"Please relax, Susan. I'm not angry with you. In fact, I want to thank you."

"Sir?"

"I've been wary of Sindril for some time, but never dreamed he'd be involved in something like this. We've started investigating others to discover if he had friends here at the College. You helped to avert a war."

She nodded.

"At any rate, what's done is done. However, I will tell you something else."

"Sir?"

"Sindril is missing. He's fled the College and might be dangerous. I don't want anyone else to know at this point, but be careful Susan. He might come to you."

"To take revenge?"

"He was headmaster for twelve years. You took that away from him in a day. Wherever he is, be careful."

"Thank you, sir. I will."

"You may go, Susan. And one more thing. Good luck on your Final Test. After everything you've done here, it might be better if you did return to the Living World."

She nodded and left the room. The councilman was gone, and she walked alone to the courtyard. She glanced at an hourglass then decided to go to Eagle Two. She paused outside, looking at the drawing of an eagle clutching scythes. It felt like home.

With the others gone, she grabbed an apple and headed outside again. Where was everyone? She spent fifteen minutes walking the College, but didn't see Billy, Frank, or Jason. Maybe they were at the library. She walked away from the campus, through the Ring of Scythes, and entered the small house. The dusty room was comforting.

She walked toward the bookcase when a hand grabbed her shoulder and spun her around. Someone shoved her backward, slamming her back into the books. They clamped a hand over her mouth as she tried to scream.

"Hello Susan," said Sindril.

Pure panic coursed through her. He wouldn't kill her, would he? She was a Death, even if only a student. If she died now she'd cease to exist. Her parents, Billy, Frank...no one would remember that she'd ever been born. Tears started to fall from her face.

"I'm not going to hurt you, if you keep quiet," he said.

She tried to nod against his hand, and he relaxed his grip, letting her breathe. He stepped away and picked up a scythe. Why hadn't she seen him? Had he been waiting for her?

"You've watched me kill," he said. "I'd do it again, but I'm not allowed. They told me to bring you alive. Give me the ring. The one you stole."

She fumbled in her pocket and handed it to him. He laughed as he looked at it. Her eyes darted around the room. Sindril closed the front door and glared at her. No way out. He stepped forward, still holding his scythe.

"You probably believe I stole this," he said, waving the ring. "I didn't. It was a gift from the previous headmaster, who received it from the headmaster before him." He smiled. "The Headmaster's Secret, they called it. A Dragoncall. Leftover from when the College was first

234 | CHRISTOPHER MANNINO

built. Used by souls to talk to Dragons, in the days when Dragons brought souls from the College to the Hereafter. The Dark Days, as some call them." He looked at the ring again. "I wonder how many other headmasters used it," he said. "Perhaps none, or maybe all of them."

He put the ring in his pocket and stepped even closer. For a moment the scythe wavered, but he put both hands on the handle and lifted. The blade hung right above her head. She felt the power dripping from its blade, the *hunger* of the metal, ready to devour her soul. Sindril's eyes narrowed in anger.

"Twelve years," he said. "Twelve years gone. Did it ever occur to you, Suzie, that I'm not your enemy? That you and I want the same thing?"

"And what is that?" she said.

"To go home," he said. "To return to the Living World." He changed his grip on the scythe, still held above her. "They took me when I was eighteen. *Eighteen*. A fluke, they told me later. Like you, I was one of a kind, and I didn't belong. Too old to be a first year; they decided to forgo my Final Test. I was never even given a chance. I'm afraid I don't even remember the headmaster who was responsible for that." He laughed. "No one remembers him. He's been *erased*." Sindril's lips spread into a wide grin. Suzie's heat raced even faster with his threat. The scythe pulsed with anger and excitement.

He pulled up the scythe, took a step back, and placed it against the wall beside her. "I tried everything, but of course, no one returns."

Suzie thought of the picture with the two teenagers. Had that been Sindril?

"And then I overheard some 'Mentals talking about a Dragon Key," he continued. "I questioned one, but he hadn't heard of it. I remembered the Dragoncall, the ring you found. What could I lose? Of course I used it." For the first time since attacking her, Sindril relaxed. He leaned against the wall and turned away. Suzie glanced at the door, but she'd never make it fast enough.

"It doesn't exist," he said. "But the Dragons promised to bring me back to the Living World themselves, if I brought them a living female Death."

"What do they want with me?"

Sindril laughed. "I didn't ask, and don't care. They needed a female Death. I spent years planning to kidnap one, but that idiot Cronk did the job for me. He was half-asleep and wrote your name on his list. All I had to do was approve it, which I did."

"Cronk?" she asked. "My teacher?"

"It's because of him that you came here, not me. Although once you arrived, I needed to keep you here. That's why I wrote your Final Test myself." He grinned at her again. "You will fail."

"And if I do?" she said, trying to sound brave. "You'll bring me to the Dragons?"

"You'll come yourself," he said, "and I'll be waiting. I want to go home, Susan. Surely, you can understand that. If you come to the Dragons, they will help both of us return."

"I'll never believe anything you say," she said. "I'd never help you. You're a murderer, a liar, and a traitor."

"You're a stupid little girl," he snarled, spinning to face her again. "How long have you been coming here? I closed the Ring hoping no one would follow me. How *did* you find yourself locked outside the Ring that day?" He stepped right up to her. She smelled wine on his breath.

Suzie closed her eyes and called out inside her mind. Would Frank hear her? Was he close enough?

Sindril looked at the scythe. "I won't kill you," he said. "They'll never help me if I do. Nevertheless, I doubt they need *all* of you. I could take a hand, perhaps. As a souvenir."

Suzie moved against the bookcase. Her hand reached what she hoped was the red book. She pulled and the books shuddered. It was the right one! She leaped forward as the bookcase swung open. The scythe fell to the ground with a loud clang. Sindril stumbled backward with a stunned expression. Suzie ran toward him with her arms outstretched and knocked him to the floor. He grunted as the two hit the floor hard; Sindril slammed his head and his eyes closed. For a moment, Suzie lost her breath. Her head and arms stung but this was her chance. She pulled herself off Sindril and staggered to her feet. His body was slumped against the front door. Could she move him?

Sindril groaned and moved an arm. He must be knocked out. No time to move him. Suzie spun and darted through the open bookcase. She ran down the stairs and into the library.

Sindril groaned in pain behind her; then she heard footsteps on the stairs.

"Help is coming," said a voice in her head. She glimpsed Frank's green eyes as she ran into the library. Hundreds of bookcases filled with books, tablets, and clutter surrounded her. At least she could hide.

She ducked behind a bookcase and edged away from the stairs, desperate to stay silent. Sindril yelled. She could hide here for a few minutes, but not forever.

"Come out, little girl," he said. He grunted and she heard sliding wood. *Crash.* A bookcase fell. He must have pushed it over. *Crash.* A second bookcase slammed to the floor sending a massive cloud of dust into the air. It was hard to breathe, but she had to stay quiet. Sindril tossed books around, and a third bookcase fell with a crash. This time, Suzie couldn't control herself. A tiny cough escaped her mouth. It seemed to echo, like footsteps.

"Gotcha now," said Sindril. "I just want a hand, or maybe a finger. A little souvenir to take to the Dragons. Come on, Susan." The bookcase behind her rocked as he rounded it, and she ran to the side of the room. There were no more bookcases, just piles of stone slabs. She jumped onto one of the slabs, backing into the wall. Sindril emerged, covered in sweat. The scythe in his hands glowed with a fierce light.

"Come down, Suzie. The game's over. No one's coming to save you now."

He paused, and a confused expression crept over his face.

Sindril dropped the scythe. He screamed, staring at his robe. Suzie couldn't see anything on it. Sindril turned and ran away from her, yelling in complete horror. He stopped at a tall shape.

The albino grabbed Sindril and stared into his eyes. The Death shuddered, whimpering. He started to cry.

"Please, please no," bawled Sindril.

The albino dropped him to the ground, and Sindril ran away. She heard footsteps on the stairs, and the sound of sobs growing softer. The albino turned to her and held up his hand. Then he followed Sindril up the stairs and out of the library. Suzie sank to the floor, ready to burst into tears herself. Frank and Billy arrived a few minutes later.

"Are you all right?" asked Frank.

"He's gone?" she asked.

"That was the same Fearmonger Luc used on you," said Frank. "He's been living in the forest, not too far from here. I figure he owed you an apology. You remember what he can do. He followed you two into the library when he came to the open bookcase. Sindril won't bother you anymore."

"Suzie," said Billy, wrapping her in his arms.

"I'm okay," she said, wiping away the tears. She'd never been more frightened, not even when the albino had attacked her. "Thank you, Frank."

"Is everyone safe?" asked Jason, stepping over a fallen bookcase.

"It's over," said Suzie. "Sindril's gone. He told me he's going to live with the Dragons."

She didn't tell them the Dragons wanted her alive, or that Sindril claimed he'd written her Final Test and she was guaranteed to fail. She didn't believe anything he said, but he was gone now. She'd never have to see him again.

"We were helping Jason with his scythe work," said Frank. "In case it's on the Final Test."

"The albino," she said. She remembered the terror she'd felt back when he'd attacked her. "I almost feel sorry for Sindril."

Billy raised an eyebrow.

"Almost," she added, smiling. "Let's go home. Right now, that's all I want."

CHAPTER TWENTY-TWO

Home

The party was Billy's idea.

The night before the Final Tests, no one slept. The test meant everything. If she passed, she'd go back to Mom and Dad. Back to the Living World. She'd go home. Rain splattered outside the windows of Eagle Two. Suzie watched the water falling, picturing the tears her mother must have shed after Cronk vanished. Had they given up all hope? On the other hand, were they still waiting for her, hoping she'd knock on the door?

Thunder rumbled in the distance. If she passed, she'd never have to lift a scythe again. She'd leave this world and eventually it'd be nothing but a long, bad dream. A long dream, at any rate. Had it honestly been bad?

If she passed, she'd never see Jason, Frank, or Cronk. She'd never watch a 'Mental turn into a bush, or create visions with their mind. She'd leave the most amazing place she'd ever been to. She'd never see Billy. She blushed at the idea. Billy was more than a friend. He was... more.

"C'mon Suzie," he said. "You defeated Sindril, and tomorrow you'll go home. It's time to celebrate."

Celebrate. But is going home worth celebrating? In two days, it'd be her fourteenth birthday. Where would she celebrate that? With her family, who assumed she was dead, or with her new friends, who made her feel alive?

Billy poured sodas. Frank passed out stolen gorgers, while Jason strung up balloons and streamers.

"I'm going to miss you guys," said Jason. "Don't get me wrong, I want to go home more than anything, but you guys are my friends."

"We made a good team," said Frank. "And look at what we accomplished. The headmaster's fled, we uncovered a plot with Dragons, and the 'Mentals finally have a shot at being treated fairly. I'd say this has been a great year."

"I'll drink to that," said Billy, raising his soda.

They played games and talked for hours. Billy and Frank re-enacted their boskery victory, breaking a lamp in the process. At one point, Frank streamed music directly to their minds, although Suzie found she didn't like that much, and he stopped.

After a while, Billy and Suzie stepped outside.

The air still smelled of rain, but the clouds had passed. A thousand tiny spots twinkled above.

"The stars are beautiful," she said.

"You are too," he replied. He took her hand. "Suzie, I want you to pass the test. I do. But when you do, I'll miss you." He turned away. As hard as this was for her, she'd forgotten that it must be hard for him too. Billy had chosen to fail his test, but she had a family back home.

"I'll miss you too," she said. They hugged for what felt like hours.

* * * *

The sun shone brightly as she walked toward the black cube in the center of the campus. Its walls seemed to suck in sunlight, and it reminded Suzie of Kasumir's dark eyes. Nearly every Death failed.

"Good luck," said Frank.

"Good luck," echoed Billy.

She nodded and walked to the open door. Hann stood in the center of a hallway, holding a clipboard. Jason, who'd entered half an hour earlier, was somewhere inside.

"Suzie," said Hann, clapping her on the shoulder. "We had some rough times, but good luck. You're in room five." He pointed, and she walked down the hall.

She stepped into room five. The room was entirely black, yet strangely light on the inside. Cronk stood in the center of the room, holding a piece of paper.

"Cronk, are you crying?"

"Your t-t-t-test," he said, handing her the paper.

She read the single sentence, written in ornate handwriting:

Kill the one responsible for your presence in this world.

"Sindril said he wrote this," she murmured.

"To g-g-go home," he said, handing her a knife. Tears fell down his face.

"Sindril is responsible," she said.

Cronk shook his head.

"It w-w-was me. I wr-wr-wrote your n-n-name. I'm s-s-s-sorry."

"If I kill you, then you cease to have ever existed," she said.

Cronk nodded.

"You're my friend," she said. "I'm not going to kill you."

"You m-m-m-must. If n-n-not, you don't g-g-go home."

She looked at the knife. If she left this world, she'd never get a chance to kill Sindril. There must be another way home.

Home. Suddenly she understood what the word meant, and what she had to do.

She'd known for some time now.

She turned the knife around, and handed it back to Cronk hilt first.

Sindril was right, she couldn't pass this test. Yet, somehow a part of her had suspected she didn't want to.

"I am home," she said, opening the door.

* * * *

Billy and Frank stood talking outside the Examination Room. Frank frowned as Billy tried to hide a smile.

"I failed the test," she said.

"What?" asked Frank.

"Sindril wanted me to kill Cronk. The exam said to kill the one responsible. They may think it was Cronk, but Sindril's the real reason I'm in this world."

"You didn't do it?" asked Billy. "You wanted to go home."

She sighed. "I do. I want to go home, but not that way." She thought of Sindril's words. He'd told her to come find the Dragons.

"There isn't another way," said Frank. "Suzie, you're a true Death now."

They waited by the Examination room for another hour, but Jason didn't emerge. The door closed after the final first year.

Suzie pounded on the door and Hann emerged.

"Suzie?" he said.

"My housemate Jason. He hasn't emerged yet. I wanted to make sure he's okay…"

"Jason passed his Final Test," said Hann. "One of only two to pass this year."

"Who was the other?"

"Luc," said Hann. "Both of the boys have gone back to their families in the Living World. The rest of you have three months of vacation before training begins again. I look forward to teaching you in class next year."

Suzie walked away, dumbfounded.

"Only two passed the Final Test," she told Frank and Billy. "Jason and Luc have gone back to the Living World."

"Wow," said Frank.

"You don't believe they had to kill someone?" asked Suzie. "I can imagine Luc doing something horrid like that, but Jason?"

"Every test is different," said Billy.

Jason had passed. Her friend. He'd been with her as they took on Sindril, and had defended her against some of her bullies. They'd spent a year together in art class and now she'd never see him again… He had passed. And Luc had passed, too, of all people…

They walked back to Eagle Two. Suzie was too deep in thought to notice the College around her.

What had she done? She hadn't considered. She just handed the knife back to Cronk. He had kidnapped her. Why hadn't she ended it and gone back to her parents?

"Suzie?" asked Billy.

She paused, staring at the ground.

It wasn't fair. Why was Jason going home and not her? Why weren't they going home together? Why had she been weak? She'd failed. Her one chance at going back to her parents. How could she do this to them?

Billy put his arms around her and pressed his face to hers. He kissed her lightly on the cheek.

"I betrayed my parents," she said. "I'll never even get to say goodbye to them."

"Suzie, you had no choice," he said.

"I did have a choice." She paused. "A part of me *wanted* to stay." It felt terrible to admit, but was still a relief.

"Suzie, that's okay. I chose to fail my test," he said. "I'm glad you're still here. Who knows, maybe one day we'll figure out a way to sneak you home. Your grandfather did it."

She nodded and reached up, touching his face. Even when it had been scarred, it was a comforting face to look at. She didn't feel sad anymore.

"This world needs you, Suzie," said Frank. "Elementals and Deaths face a new era. An era you helped forge. The Living World can wait. This is your home now."

Billy looked into her eyes.

"Suzie, I can't tell you about 'Mentals or new eras, about ways home or the choice you made. But I do know we need you here." He swallowed and his eye glistened with moisture. "I need you, Suzie."

"Thank you," she whispered.

Frank started walking toward Eagle Two. Billy and Suzie followed him, holding hands.

She had something now, something she hadn't had in a long time. Hope.

This world didn't frighten her anymore. Even if she never saw her parents again, at least she was where she belonged.

"I have a confession," said Billy. "I'm not upset that you're staying."

She kissed him on the cheek.

"I have a confession of my own," she said.

"What?"

"I'm not upset either."

She laughed as they opened the door to Eagle Two.

"This is home now."

MEET THE AUTHOR

Christopher Mannino

Christopher Mannino's life is best described as an unending creative outlet. He teaches high school theatre in Greenbelt, Maryland. In addition to his daily drama classes, he runs several after-school performance/production drama groups. He spends his summers writing and singing. Mannino holds a Master of Arts in Theatre Education from Catholic University, and has studied mythology and literature both in America and at Oxford University. His work with young people helped inspire him to write young adult fantasy, although it was his love of reading that truly brought his writing to life. Learn more, and enjoy exclusive free content related to the World of Deaths, at www.ChristopherMannino.com

* * * *

Did you enjoy School of Deaths? If so, please help us spread the word about Christopher Mannino and MuseItUp Publishing. It's as easy as:

•Recommend the book to your family and friends
•Post a review
•Tweet and Facebook about it

Thank you
MuseItUp Publishing

MuseItUp Publishing
Where Muse authors entertain readers!
https://museituppublishing.com
Visit our website for more books for your reading pleasure.

You can also find us on Facebook:
http://www.facebook.com/MuseItUp
and on Twitter:
http://twitter.com/MusePublishing

CPSIA information can be obtained
at www.ICGtesting.com
Printed in the USA
FFOW05n0647031215